TO HANG A REBEL

D. Harold Turner

Illustrations
Merle Smith

Gage Publishing
Agincourt

Canadian Cataloguing in Publication Data

Turner, D. Harold, 1912-
   To hang a rebel

   ISBN 0-7715-9368-6

   I. Title.

PS8589.U76T6   jC813'.5'4   C77-001284-1
PR9199.3.T87T6

Printed and bound in Canada
1 2 3 4 5   GP   81   80   79   78   77

Acknowledgements

The author wishes to acknowledge his debt to those scholarly works dealing with this critical period in the history of Canada. William Kilbourn's fascinating work, *The Firebrand: William Lyon Mackenzie and the Rebellion in Upper Canada* (Clarke, Irwin, 1956), was a treasure trove of information. Other useful sources of information included Charles Lindsey's *The Life and Times of William Lyon Mackenzie* (P. R. Randall, 1862 — Coles Canadiana Reprint edition, 1971); David Flint's *William Lyon Mackenzie: Rebel Against Authority* (Oxford University Press, 1971); and William Lyon Mackenzie's own writings.

Much help was gained from *The Town of York*, edited by Edith G. Firth and published by the University of Toronto Press (Champlain Society, Ontario Series, 1966). Una Abrahamson's book, *God Bless Our Home* (Burns and MacEachern, 1966), was a real fountain of knowledge regarding the social customs, house furnishings, and costumes of the period.

A special word of thanks must go to Miss Gladys Harvey of Ottawa, for her untiring and exact search of the archives in Ottawa for so many necessary details. Special thanks, too, are due to Miss Florence Harris for her literary criticism and loving support. Without the secretarial expertise of Mrs. Elsa Aikenhead of Winnipeg, I doubt if this story could ever have been completed.

Above all, the author acknowledges his debt to his sister, Mrs. Norma Walker of Winnipeg, for all the tedious writing of letters and arranging of affairs — and for her unfailing belief in TO HANG A REBEL.

To my wife Bessie,
who listened always with love and sympathy and faith.

Chapter 1
A Lonely Road Ahead

Doug Lachlan stood on the door-sill of the log house where he had been born. He watched Da' hoist a heavy pack on to his back. Da's stocky figure stooped under the load as he strode down the path to the rail fence. The fence separated the Lachlan farm from the Toronto-Niagara road — the road to the United States border, where Da' was heading. Beyond that Doug could not imagine the trails that would lead far, far west to the Red River settlement that was Da's final goal.

Doug was scared. He wanted to run after his father — perhaps he should help with the pack of food and supplies Da' was toting. "Foolishness!" Doug told himself. There was only enough for one in that pack, just enough to help feed Da' on the long way. The urge had not been strong enough even to move Doug's feet from the sill. There would be no use. Da' wasn't taking him with him, that was sure, no matter how he might coax.

And Doug hadn't coaxed. He had known all along there was no use in wheedling. Doug was proud of himself that he hadn't teased to go. That pride kept him now from being a whining bairn, grabbing at Da's coattails, blubbering.

"Douglas," Da had said. "I must go to Selkirk's settlement on the Red River. We've not heard from your brother, Graham, these past ten months and more. I've a feeling inside me he needs me." Doug knew "the feeling." Many Scots, like his father, possessed the "second sight" that let them know when loved ones were in trouble. Last night he had not disputed it. He did not ask, "Am I to go, too?" He only looked. Da' shook his head.

Often they did not need words between them.

Da' knew the hurt that would be in Doug. He knew the silly tears that threatened Doug's eyes. "I must travel fast and light, and one can go faster and lighter than two." Da's voice was kind. "I've made plans for ye, boy. We'll eat supper the now, and then we'll talk of what ye are to do while I'm awa'."

Doug turned away without a word more. His father sat down in the big walnut chair that he had made for himself many years ago. Before Doug was born. When Graham had been a small baby and the mother was still alive. Before the bad cholera had come to the Canadas, the dreadful disease that had taken her and many another from the settlements up and down the lakes.

The chair was solid and comfortable. Big, to fit his father's thick body. Almost black in the back and the arms. Smooth and softly shining from the rubbing of rough homespun and from the long polishing Da's hard hands had given it over the years. Many a time Doug had fallen asleep in it, waiting for Da' to come home from political meetings in St. Catharines village. There was a soft cushion filled with lamb's wool and covered with the same grey homespun of their clothes. The mother had made the cushion herself, a surprise for Da'. Doug remembered the time. How she had laughed! Doug heard her merry laugh in his head and caught himself turning quickly to see her. He turned back shamefaced. It did not do to be thinking thoughts of the dead. But the stubborn thoughts went on. Da', not noticing, had sat in his chair. His mouth had fallen open and his eyes had sprung wide at the comfort suddenly under him. Yes, how she had laughed. Doug would never forget that time. He was nine then. The next summer the mother was gone. That was all of five years ago. Now, at nearly fifteen, he could smile over the cushion.

He busied himself serving up the supper oatmeal. Since the mother had died he had taken the cooking and cleaning on himself. Da' worked hard on their scanty, stump-bedevilled fields. He needed to come home to a hot meal at nights. Doug always had it ready for him when he entered the door.

He did his share in the fields, too. Why, just the other day Da' had said, "Douggie, I couldna' have done a cleaner job of stumping myself." Da' had kicked the root as if he knew just how Doug hated it — had fought it the way he had fought Gordie McNee at Mr. Vicars's school in the village. Gordie had laid the black insult on him — called him Vicars's pet because Doug had read — without a mistake, mind you — from a long piece called "Childe Harold" that Mr. Vicars had received from a friend in England. That didn't make him Vicars's pet, though. He just found reading easier than most folks did, he guessed. But farm work had its place as well, and he knew what it was to harden muscles in the fields right enough. Gordie McNee knew it, too.

And so Doug thought about anything and everything to keep back that one bad thought: Da' was going away. Going away . . . without him.

Da' waited till Doug had finished washing up the bowls and spoons. Then he said, so quietly Doug almost didn't hear him, busy and all as he was with his roundabout thoughts, "Bring up a stool, laddie, and we'll talk, man to man." Doug set the stool close to Da's knee. "I've thought on this lang and lang, Douggie, and I see no way out of it." It was Da's way always to think everything out in his mind before speaking. Everyone in the whole of the St. Catharines district listened when Da' spoke.

"Your brother, Graham, is a good, steady lad. He'd no' have gone ten months without a word to us. It's not as if he'd gone off into the wilderness. The Red River is a settled place now. And the last word we had of him, by yon travelling preacher man from up Hamilton way, told us he had a good job in Fort Garry. He was well satisfied with the work and pay. He's adventurous, but not over-foolish. He'd no' have gone off on any expedition without letting us know. Na', na', it's what I said. I have the feeling. Graham sair needs me and I must go."

"But what of me, Da'?" Doug asked then. The thought of staying alone on the small farm — for perhaps better than half a year — frightened him. "What of me?"

"I've not forgotten ye, laddie," Da' chided gently. "I want ye to go to York — Toronto they call it now, though the name doesna' come easy to me yet. I want ye to go to Mr. William Lyon Mackenzie and stay with him till I come for ye. Ye recall me telling of Mr. Mackenzie, Douggie?" Da' cocked a questioning bushy eyebrow at Doug. Doug nodded miserably. He did not want to go to Mr. Mackenzie. He wanted to go with Da'. "Ye've often heard me say how we were lads together in Dundee in the auld land before we all came out to the Canadas. Many's the fight I had as a boy on wee Willie's behalf. Not but what he was a tiger in a fight himself, but he was aye ower small for his age, and a bit strange. The big boys would have made porridge of him had I not helped him a bit. We were guid friends or as much as his stubborn pride would let him be. He will take ye in, I know. I've written a letter and ye'll carry it to him. He's a gey important man. He was elected first Mayor of Toronto and now he's owner and editor of *The Constitution*."

Doug knew that Da' had read every copy of *The Constitution*. Da' had been a subscriber to it and to Mr. Mackenzie's earlier paper, *The Colonial Advocate*, for as long as he could remember. There were many people, he knew, who thought Mr. Mackenzie was a dangerous man because of his ideas on Reform that he published in his paper.

"He's still wee Willie Mackenzie and my friend. Ye must do his bidding in all he asks of ye. Help him in every way to pay for your keep. I've little cash to give you — not above ten shillings — for I'll need every bit I've saved to get me to the Red River. I'll put out a ham from the smokehouse for ye to take with ye. I wish ye could take the bacon, too. We've three sides left from last autumn's curing, an' ye'll not find its like this side of the capital. But, there, a ham will be all ye can carry besides the old carpetbag with your clothes in it."

"You won't be going with me, Da'?" Doug knew the answer, but he could not keep the question back.

"No, Douggie, I dare not. I'd lose days going and coming. I hope to find a wagon train in Buffalo heading west to the Dakotas. 'Twill make travel the faster can I find me one that needs a driver. It's now, in April, that they'll be making up the trains and I must be there as soon as can be. Ye must catch the stage in St. Catharines tomorrow afternoon and ride to Toronto by your lone. It will cost four of your shillings, but it can't be helped. The other six ye must give to Mr. Mackenzie to spend for ye as he sees the need. I'm trusting ye to be the man I've seen growing in ye this last year. You're a boy no longer, Douglas." Da' looked at him sternly, but with a pride in his blue eyes that made Doug feel warm and brave.

"I'll not fail you, Da'."

"Tomorrow ye must take Flora to Mr. McNee. She's freshening, and I've told McNee he may keep her calf for his trouble. He has the oxen, Billy and Mac, already. He borrowed them this

morning. Mrs. McNee will come over to fetch the poultry.

"I should be back before the snow flies again. And you may be sure, laddie, I'll waste no time on the way."

Doug had slept but fitfully that night. Even so, the dreaded morning came faster than he expected. Now, standing here alone at the door of the little log house, he wondered just how much of a man he had in him.

Da' had stopped now, where the road bent to the east at the edge of the farm. He raised his hand in the strong way he had when he met men he knew and respected in the streets of St. Catharines. It was Da's way of saying again, "You're a man now, Douggie." Doug tried hard to make his own lifted hand seem confident. Then his father turned, stepped 'round the bend, and the trees cut him off from view.

What if, like eighteen-year-old Graham, Da' simply went and was never heard of again? With that thought, Doug wanted to run down the path after Da'. Then he thought of Da' stopping at the bend to salute him. He kept himself still for a moment till the sickening beat of his heart slowed a bit. He turned and went into the house to do the last chores before he locked the door behind him. Then, with his clothes in the carpetbag in one hand, and the ham, tied up in a muslin cloth, in the other, he went to the barn to fetch Flora to drive her to the McNees, their neighbors on the side toward St. Catharines.

He drove Flora out of the barn and started her across the yard toward the path that Lachlans and McNees had made between the two places in the twenty years since the two families had settled there. Then, after closing the barn door carefully, he picked up his satchel and started after the cow. A good thing Flora was a kind, obedient beast. He could carry his bundles with him. He had no wish to come back to the house again until he came with Da'. Already, somehow, it had a deserted look that made him shiver a bit and turn his eyes steadily forward toward his goal.

Mr. McNee and Gordie were standing watching as Doug drove Flora into the yard. McNee was a tall, stooping man with hair the color of bleached straw and sparse side whiskers like last year's fox-tail grass.

"Weel, weel." Mr. McNee's voice was a slow, high-pitched whine. "So yer feyther's awa' tae the west, is he? And you're left a lorn orphan. Weel, it's not likely ye'll ever see him again. It's heathen country he's going to, and that's the truth of it. Juist bear in mind, Douglas, that if the wairst comes tae the wairst, ye may come back and live wi' us. I could use a laddie like you to help me. It would free Gordie to study his lessons. I'm detairmined tae make a lawyer out of him. I'm sure ye could earn yer board and keep.''

''Thank you, Mr. McNee.'' Doug kept his voice low, though anger burned every inch of his body so that his back fair itched with the heat of it. ''I'll remember your offer. But Da' will be back before the snow flies. He has promised.''

Gordie, beside his father, said nothing. He only looked his hate. Doug knew that he had not forgotten or forgiven the beating in the schoolyard. Was it only two weeks ago? It seemed as long as that since last night's talk with Da'. Gordie had no reason for resentment. Doug had received a thorough birching from old Vicars for starting the fight. Gordie had been let off with a scolding.

Only when Doug said his good-byes and turned out of Mr. McNee's yard toward the road, did Gordie run after him and shout, ''Aye, come back, Doug Lachlan. We'll let ye sleep wi' the pigs. 'Tis all ye're fitted for.''

Doug did not turn. He would not let Gordie know how frightened that jibe made him feel. What if Da' did not come back? What if Mr. Mackenzie would not have him? He stiffened his back and marched on. Come what might, he would never ask the McNees for help. He struck out at his best speed, his carpetbag slapping his leg and the big ham jouncing on his shoulder. First stop: St. Catharines.

Chapter 2
A Long Walk Begins

St. Catharines was but a village, six miles north of the Lachlan farm. Most of its houses, like the houses in the other villages and towns on the shores of Lake Ontario, were made of logs. In the last few years some buildings made of brick had begun to appear along the tree-shaded, muddy streets.

Doug had to pass the school on his way to the stage in the centre of town. Mr. Vicars must have been looking out the school window. He often did. He would stand there, his back to the class. His voice, like the drone of a giant bee, would go on conjugating a Latin verb or humming out the exploits of Julius Caesar in Britain. He would seem unaware of his pupils. But let a girl or boy pass a note or make a move to throw pepper on the hot stove, and Mr. Vicars would whirl and lay about the heads of the culprits with the hardwood pointer he always carried in his hand. How did he know? Doug had heard some of the boys whisper fearfully among themselves that the devil himself stood at Vicars's elbow those times. Da' had laughed, and Doug knew it was nonsense. But with the schoolmaster's eye on him he could almost believe the tale.

As Doug drew near, Mr. Vicars appeared in the doorway of the small log building. His knobby shoulders in shiny black broadcloth were hunched up to his ears as always. He crooked a commanding finger at the boy. His dark brows were drawn down in a forbidding frown. Doug's breath came a little faster. The thin face had a power to dry up the most innocent boy's spit in his mouth. Doug licked his lips nervously as he approached the teacher.

"Ah, Lachlan. I understand you are going away to the flesh-pots of our colonial capital," Mr. Vicars bleated in that light English voice that could make you cringe even before he brought the birch down across the tight cloth of your pants-seat. "Beware that you do not fall into sin, Lachlan, for you are going, so your father tells me, to dwell in the house of that godless and rebellious man, William Lyon Mackenzie. Your father will return in time, we trust, so that your sojourn in the house of Baal may not harm your immortal soul, Lachlan. But I have misgivings. Indeed, I have sad misgivings. I thought your father was too loyal a subject of His Majesty, King William, to trust his son to a republican. But then, he did not consult me when he made his plans.

"What I wanted to say, Lachlan, was this: You have a good mind, one of the best of all the boys I have taught in this Godforsaken wilderness. . . . " Doug felt himself redden at the unexpected praise. He drew his shoulders back as tightly as he could. In spite of his own hunched shoulders, Mr. Vicars always insisted on a soldierly posture in the boys he taught. "Use your mind. Remember that God appointed some to rule — an aristocracy, and some to obey — the lower orders. Mr. Mackenzie trifles with the ways of Providence when he talks of a government controlled by the people of this province. He is a son of Satan, and you must beware of him."

"Yes, Sir," Doug promised. It was all he could say.

"I trust no ill will befall your father, whom I respect as a loyal servant of the King. I trust he will return." The teacher shook his head. "But I wonder. Yes, I wonder . . . " he murmured. Then he turned back into the schoolhouse.

"Why was it," Doug thought rebelliously, "that all the grown-ups were determined that Da' would never come back?" Doug would not believe it. Da' would return! He would! He had promised! The ghosties of doubt ran about in his mind. What if they were right? The Red River was far away, fifteen hundred miles or maybe more to the west as Da' must go. There were many dangers on the way. Indians, floods, a broken neck in a fall from steep cliffs, perhaps. Dozens of horrible possibilities ran cold fingers through the front of his mind as his fears opened the doors to them. Old black crows they were, every one of them. He turned off the main road, and, by cutting through bush lots, circled the town. He would wait here, outside the village, for the stage and flag it down.

Suddenly he thought of the reluctant way his father had said, "It will take four of your ten shillings to ride the stage." His father had worked hard for those shillings. It was like spending Da' himself to give them up to the stage driver. "Na, na, Douglas Lachlan," he whispered to himself. Ye'll not do that. "How far is it to this York-Toronto? Fifty miles? A hundred?" He did not know. "I'll walk it. That I will. And if I have my way, Da' will have his ten shillings in his hand again. I wish I had thought of it before I left. He could have taken the money with him. He might need it. There was but four pounds, eight shillings, and sixpence last time we counted it together. 'Tis not much to carry him more than a thousand miles."

Doug picked up his bag and the ham he had put down. He turned his face in the direction of Toronto and trudged smartly off down the potholed road.

Chapter 3
A Whisper In The Dark

An early April wind had blown in a heavy cloud-cover during the night. When Doug had left his bed at dawn it seemed to him that the grey sky matched the greyness within him. He had almost welcomed it. Fitting it was that the heavens should lower on Da's departure and his own loneliness.

On the way to St. Catharines he had been glad of his homespun overcoat. His doeskin waistcoat under it with the double row of polished horn buttons down the front was comforting under the push of the icy north wind. Da' had killed the doe himself, skinned it, cured the hide. Mr. McPherson, the tailor in St. Catharines, had made it up for Doug.

"As good as a brick wall for keeping out the wind," Doug had thought as he swung along the road. "Better!" For it had shaped itself to him and hugged him close. His brown muffler was a comfort, too. His wool mitts were in his pocket if his hands grew too cold. He had pulled the stiff-crowned, peaked cap well on his head against the sharp gusts. Walking had helped to keep him warm, too.

But now, in the afternoon, the sun had come out and the wind had died down. He was much too warm. He unwound his muffler and took off his coat. After a moment's thought he tied his scarf around his folded coat, knotted the ends, and slipped his arm through the loop. Hung over his shoulder, resting on his left hip, the coat was out of the way. His hands were free to pick up his bundles. He was proud of his ingenuity. And he no longer sweated under the heavy homespun.

His heavy jackboots over thick woollen stockings were still

hot. He considered taking them off and going barefoot. Cool mud between his toes would be nice. Da' would roll his Scottish burr at that idea: "Ne'er cast a clout till May be out!" Better not. April, however warm, was too early for bare feet. To arrive at the Mackenzies' with the grippe would not warm his welcome.

He shouldered the ham, picked up his satchel, and, with freer stride, set off down the road again. Sticky clay was thick on the logs that formed the roadbed. One careless step and down he would go. "What a filthy mess you would be in then, Douglas Lachlan. The Mackenzies would set the dog on you. So step easy, laddie."

It helped to talk aloud. The road seemed less lonely. Not a soul the whole of the way from St. Catharines. The mail coach from Niagara was late. Small wonder. The roads were bad this time of year. Places there were in plenty where the men passengers would have to get down and put shoulders to the wheels if they hoped to get to Toronto. He was just as glad to be afoot.

Before too long he would have to seek a place for the night. "What should I do?" he wondered. "Ask for lodgings at one of the farms hereabouts? No! I will not. I would have a clack in my ears would deafen a donkey what with, 'Where are ye off tae by yer lone?' And, 'Why are ye travelling to Toronto?' And, 'Ye'll no' see yer Da' again.' I couldna' bide it. I'll camp in the woods. I've oatcakes in my satchel. There's water in the streams. I've flint and tinder for a fire. I've a knife and my wee axe to cut fir boughs for a shelter and bed. 'Twould be fun, surely." He dared to dance a few steps of a reel at the thought. Then he sobered. "I must put as many miles as I may under my two feet while daylight lasts." He stepped out briskly.

He waited until April gloaming darkened the blue of the sky. Without his coat, he began to feel the chill of the evening on his back. He looked for a spot to camp. He knew the place he wanted: not too far from the road, open to the skies for a good fire, with a running stream or a spring for water, and with enough young growth to cut down easily for a lean-to. Water was the first need. He listened. Before long he smiled in satisfaction. There it was, to his left: the sweet gurgling of water running from the higher land, among the tree roots, and down toward the road. The shallow ditch beside the road shone black where the stream spread out. He jumped the ditch, landed with a great squelch in the thick mud on the other side, and passed in under the trees that walled the side of the road.

Under the trees the bed of pine needles was firm and dry. He bent down to feel with his hand. Warm it was, too. No dampness would come up through his bed of fir branches to chill him. He pushed on a bit, tracing the sound of the water. He had not far to go. Stepping out beside a shallow stream, he had no more than to skip across. He knelt and scooped a handful of the bubbling water up to his mouth. It was sweet and cold. He looked about. Here in the open the pine-needle bed was thin. Grey rock pushed its way through in more than one place. A safe bottom for his fire. Back among the trees there was plenty of good fallen birch. Plenty of firewood to keep him warm the night through.

Before the last light had faded on the clearing, Doug had a satisfying pile of fuel on hand. No stumbling about in the night for wood. Da' had taught him that. Da' had taught him, too, how to lash poles together with wild grapevine to make a windbreak for himself, and how to lay a carpet of fir tips to make a bed. With the happy dance of flames in front of him, he sat cross-legged in the opening of his three-sided shelter and drew his satchel to him. From it he took out a bundle of oatcakes that were wrapped in a cloth. Da' had taken a similar great pile with him. Each cake was as round as a saucer and as thick as his hand. A filling and tasty supper.

"One I will allow myself tonight," he said. It was hard to resist eating them all. "I do not know how long it will take to get to Toronto. I must make them last out." He ate slowly, enjoying each nutty mouthful, making the cake last as long as possible. After he had picked every crumb from his front, he went down to the water and scooped some up in his cupped hands. When he had a good full feeling in his stomach he returned to the fire. He put on his warm coat, wrapped his muffler about his neck, piled up the fire with fresh wood, and crawled into his shelter. A turn or two made a place in the fir needles for his elbow, his hip, his shoulder. Warmth flowed in on him. He yawned once, turned his cheek sideways on his satchel-pillow, and was asleep.

Suddenly Doug was sitting up wide awake. He stared into the dark. Some sound had wakened him. His fire was almost dead. Only a few live embers still winked at him. A cold wind had started the tree-tops slashing at each other. But it was not the

noise of the wind, nor the cold, that had wakened him. He knew that. An animal? Coon? Skunk? He listened. If only the wind would stop so he could hear! He waited. Nothing! He forced himself to get up to renew the fire. He tiptoed to his woodpile and slipped out a couple of logs. The scraping of wood on wood seemed too loud; the wind in the trees breathed heavily. His feet wanted to run.

"Steady, lad," he told himself. "What's in the woods to fright you? You've camped before with Da'." "Aye, but Da' was with me," he reminded his bolder self. "And Da' would be ashamed of you this minute." He deliberately thumped a piece of firewood on the ground. He felt better. He felt better still when the birch bark flared and lit up the clearing. He sat and put his hands to the warmth.

Then he heard it — a high-pitched sound. Doug's legs gathered themselves under him almost of their own accord. He stood and listened. The sound again — the high voices of angry men stabbing the night. Why *here*? Miles from anywhere? In the middle of the night? He was on his toes, ready to run. The voices came nearer. The glow of his fire might be seen from the road. He sprinted to the creek, scooped up a capful of water for dousing the flames. He froze as he bent at the sound of crashing among the trees that bordered the road. There was a moment of silence. Even the wind held its breath. Suddenly the silence was shattered by a whisper. "What have we here?" The low-pitched, husky voice kept Doug frozen where he knelt.

Chapter 4
Doug Learns About Robber Barons

"A boy is it?" The speaker gasped for air. " 'Tis Rafferty's luck for sure, and me needing a heavy fist on my side. Douse the fire, boy. Hurry! Maybe they've not seen it yet."

Doug obeyed without thinking. As he flung water from his dripping cap on the flames, there was a swoosh — then smoke and ashes blowing about where the flames had been. He turned and stumbled to the creek once more. A second capful flattened out the last sparks. Darkness came down like a wall about him. Wet smoke drifted past his head north on the cold night wind.

There was more crashing over near the road. The voice of the whisperer came again, this time from the other side of the camp. "Too late! Don't give me away, boy. For the love of God, don't give me away!" That was all. A desperate cry. The fright in it made Doug's stomach drop suddenly and fearfully. There was no time to answer. There were lights moving quickly in time to the crashing among the trees, but before they got to him hands grabbed Doug roughly. A harsh voice cried out, "I've got the rebel! I've got the rebel! Bring up the lanterns."

"Let me go," Doug shrilled, and was angry at himself for the childish sound of his voice. "Let me go!" He said it again and hoped it sounded more manly as Da' would have him.

There were three lanterns held by three shadowy men, and three or four other men stood nearby. The best lighted was the man who held Doug — a craggy-faced man with grey side-whiskers and a thin, high-arched nose. Because of the shadows thrown up by the horn lanterns, his frightening eyes seemed skull-like. He was a gentleman by his clothes. His tight, high

boots looked expensive in spite of the mud splashed up on them, and his green coat and the white shirt above his satin waistcoat must have cost pounds and pounds. His dark cravat was still neat about his neck despite his running about in the night. All this Doug saw in a flash before he kicked out at the man's ankles. "Let me go!" he cried again. The fact that it was a gentleman who held him so roughly increased his fears. Everyone knew there was no reasoning with gentlemen.

"Why, it's a boy. 'Tisn't Rafferty, Squire," one of the men exclaimed. They all crowded closer.

"A boy?" There was hard disbelief in this man, called the Squire, as he leaned closer to look. There was violence in the shove he gave Doug as he released his grip. Doug staggered but kept his feet. "What are you doing here, boy?"

"I'm on my way to York — Toronto, I mean," Doug stammered. "To stay with friends," he rushed on. Doug knew better than to use Mr. Mackenzie's name. Rich men were not likely to be friendly toward the editor and owner of *The Constitution* even though he had been Toronto's first Mayor and an important man in the province.

"Why are you out here by yourself?" the Squire demanded. "A runaway apprentice, most like," he said knowingly to his companions. "Why did you put out the fire when you heard us?"

"I thought you might be thieves. I don't know. I was scared."

" 'Tis not the action of an honest boy. What is your name? Where are you from?" The questions came in harsh bursts.

"I'm Douglas Lachlan, Sir. My Da' has a farm near St. Catharines." He told his story about Graham and Da'. "I'm walking to Toronto, Sir, to save money. We're poor folk," he finished. The Squire was silent for a long moment, as though he were weighing the story.

"So!" It was all he said, but Doug felt relieved. Then came the question that Doug had been dreading. "Did you hear a man run by on the road a few minutes back?"

"No!" Doug felt he should say more, but not another word would come. He hoped his unflinching eyes would satisfy his questioner. At the same time he wondered why he should defend that unknown man who had whispered in the dark. Still, he had told no lie. He had not heard the man "run by" on the road.

The shadowed eyes glowered down on him a moment. It

seemed as if the man would question him further. Doug braced himself. He did not want to lie.

"He's got clean away, Squire," a voice from outside the circle spoke up. "We'll not find him tonight. He'll have holed up somewhere while we've been wasting time here. Come on, 'tis way past midnight. I want my bed."

"Downing's right, Squire," another voice chimed in. "We might as well all go home.

"All right," the Squire agreed. His eyes left Doug's face at last. He took a step away, then he turned again. "Do you want to come with us, boy?" He did not sound quite so frightening. "You can have a bed in my stable if you wish. 'Tis five or six miles back the way you've come."

"Thank you, Sir, but I'll stay here," Doug refused firmly. He was not drawn to the man in spite of the offer. There was too much of the rich tyrant about him. Scots did not take kindly, Da' always said, to prideful lairds. "I'll light my fire again. I'll be all right. I would just have to make up those six miles again in the morning. I'll manage, Sir."

" 'Tis your choice." In the light of the lantern, Doug saw the green-coated shoulders shrug with indifference. The party moved off — the others, as if by habit, making way for the Squire as he led them back toward the road.

It did not take long to scrape away the wet ashes and logs and get a new fire started with dry branches. As he worked, Doug wondered about the whole incident, above all about the whispering unknown — "the rebel," as the Squire had called him. The upper classes — the Family Compact was what Da' had called them — labelled all the men of the Reform Party, "rebels." Da' was a Reformer, but he was no rebel. No one was prouder of his British background than Da'. No one. Had the rebel stolen away as his pursuers thought and hidden while the Squire asked his questions? It would have been a good chance. Doug felt a little disappointed. He would have liked to see the face that went with the voice. Was it as Irish as the whisper had been?

The flames sprang up, throwing a giant shadow of the lean-to against the wall of trees behind. Doug looked uneasily around. His feeling of security was gone. The fire did not help. It only made the darkness under the trees blacker. Dozens of eyes could be peering at him. He turned his head from side to side, staring into the blackness. The crackling of the burning logs seemed loud, for the wind had died down. Had the Squire and his men really gone? Had they just pretended? Perhaps they had circled about and were waiting to pounce out again if the Irishman came back. What would they do if they found that Doug had not told the whole truth, had defended a rebel? He shivered and bent close to the fire. Its warmth was comforting.

He felt eyes on him. He was sure of it. He straightened and pivoted on his toes, ready to run. As his face came about in the direction of the stream, he jumped; his legs took him half a dozen steps before the figure by the creek stopped him with a word.

"No," the man said. "Don't run. Sure, I wouldn't harm your littlest finger. Not the boy who stood up so bravely to the fine gentlemen visitors. Come, sit down with me by the fire and tell me about yourself." The man was moving slowly toward the lean-to as he spoke. It was as if he did not want to startle Doug. "Of course, I heard what you told Squire Collins. Aye, that's his name. But come and tell me more. They'll not be back this night."

The voice was light, gay. Doug looked at him, some of the uncertainty already fading under the charm he felt in this man. He realized why the Squire could have thought he had the stranger in his grip. He was a little man, not much taller than Doug himself. He had no hat and his jet-black hair fell over his forehead like the bangs of a colt. Under the bangs the black eyes looked enormous. They seemed to shine in the firelight like the eyes of a forest deer. That was the quality you felt in this man — wildness. Untamable, but gentle. In that moment, when they faced each other, Doug found himself giving his whole trust to the little Irishman. Without another word Doug moved around the fire and the two sat down in the opening of the lean-to.

Doug was surprised at himself. He felt no shyness sitting this close to a man whom he'd never seen before. He turned to have a closer look at his companion. Almost at once he saw that the black curls were matted and stiff, and that dark stains had run down under the hair on the left temple. Blood! He was hurt, this new friend. He realized, too, that the stranger was cradling his left elbow in his right palm and that the left hand clutched tightly the cloth of his right shoulder. Even as Doug watched, the fingers of the hand curled into a fist in pain. The dark eyes closed. Beads of sweat rolled down under the bangs.

"You're hurt!" Doug exclaimed. "They've hurt you." The man opened his eyes and smiled.

"A bit of a blow on the head and a crack on the arm. I'll mend. No bones broken."

"It's a cut on your head. It's been bleeding. Wait, I'll bathe it." Doug picked up his cap and ran to the creek to fill it again with water. When he returned he dumped the oatcakes out of their cloth and into his satchel. Ripping off the end, he dipped the cloth into the water. "It's really clean," he offered apologetically.

"I'm sure it is." The smile was a bit crooked.

Doug bathed the cut. It still oozed blood, but it looked cleaner and healthier when he had finished. A strip from the same cloth, wound on an angle over the cut, made a bandage and, at the same time, made the little man look like a kindly little pirate. Doug had to laugh at him. The patient laughed with Doug. "A pirate, is it? Aye, a sadly battered pirate I'm feeling this minute. I'd not want to run my guns out on any ship of the line, you'll understand." One last service Doug did. He took off his muffler and made a sling of it to support the injured arm.

"There," said Doug, "does that feel better?"

"Bedad, it's a new man I am entirely. And now let us have the introductions. My name is Patrick Rafferty, as perhaps you remember the Squire's henchman named me." Doug nodded. "And yours, I know from my eavesdropping, is Douglas Lachlan. Would Andrew Lachlan be your father?" Doug nodded again but Rafferty gave him no chance to speak. "I know your father from travelling to St. Catharines to political meetings, though I've never had much private conversation with him, you'll understand. He's a staunch Reformer like myself, that I do know."

"Is that why yon Squire called you 'rebel'?" Doug put in quickly while Rafferty was drawing a breath.

"To be sure it is. All the high-stomached boyos of the Family Compact, the aristocrats of our little colony, think anyone who wants to change one letter of the Act that set them over us is an unholy traitor, fit only for the hangman's rope." Rafferty laughed. "Indeed, I'm a rebel for the saying of just that, and so are you for listening to me, Douggie."

"Then Da' is, too." Doug laughed in turn. Da' a rebel was a funny idea. "Da' says the men of the Family Compact have all the important positions in the country — judges, bankers, sheriffs, justices of the peace. They control the money — "

"Your Da' is right," Rafferty broke in. "With the money they control the law itself and the very seat of justice. Like the robber barons of the old lands, they are. They sat on their hills above the highways and sent out their private soldiery to rob the merchants of their goods, and common men like you and me had to pay dear for the little that the robbers would sell them."

"But why didn't the common folk join together and fight the barons?" Doug demanded.

"A good question, Douggie, my boy. A simple answer is hard to give. For one thing, the barons had the money and the goods. The common folk might pass laws, but they had to eat. The barons could refuse the very food for their mouths if the folk ventured to rebel. And the barons had their soldiers to hang anyone who dared rebel. What could the people do?" Rafferty frowned. Doug shook his head. He had no answer.

"The Family Compact — most of them are related to one another — are very like those robber barons," Rafferty went on. "The Executive Assembly is like the castle on the hill, and it stands square on the road of progress. They control the public money — money that belongs by right to people like you and me. They dole it out as they see fit.

"The Legislative Assembly — that's you and me and your Da' and Mr. William Lyon Mackenzie — can pass all the laws we like. But if the laws don't please their Lordships in the Compact, sure, they just toss them out."

"I know 'tis bad," Doug agreed. "Da' says so often. But do you know Mr. Mackenzie? I'm going to stay with him while Da' is away in the West."

"Do I know Mr. William Lyon Mackenzie!" Rafferty laughed joyously. "Tell me," he asked, brushing his brown fist under eyes that brimmed with laughter, "is he the friend you mentioned to Squire Collins that you are to visit in Toronto? Glory be! You *were* a wise lad, or the saints were with you, that you did not mention his name to that little robber baron of these parts. Sure, he'd have had a stroke. It's because I work with Mr. Mackenzie that I was running for my life, which you saved, no less, and I'm grateful to you indeed."

"What did you do, Mr. Rafferty?" Doug set himself to hear what had brought the Irishman to his camp.

"Call me Pat. A man who saves another's life can't be going about mistering the man he rescued. So Pat it is."

Doug nodded shyly.

Chapter 5
How Rafferty Fought The Squire

The story Pat told was an exciting one. The Reform Party expected Sir Francis Bond Head, the Lieutenant-Governor of Upper Canada, to call an election soon. Pat's job for the Reform Party was to go from place to place to set up Reform clubs and to help choose leaders to stand for election when voting time came. But choosing leaders alone would not help.

"The Family Compact — bad 'cess to them — control the polls where people come to vote," Pat explained. "They're not above putting their bullies, armed with cudgels, at the polls. If a man dares to try to vote for a Reformer instead of a Tory, these bullies beat the living tar out of him. Any man will vote as he's told with a stick beating a tattoo on his head. We have to see that we have our boys there, too, to protect those who would vote our way. That's the why of the Reform clubs."

Late that afternoon Pat had gathered the people of the district to encourage them to stand up to Squire Collins's bullies at election time. He knew the Squire would object but the meeting, he had thought, was secret. He had expected no trouble. "The people turned out, some twenty men and almost as many women. Tired they were, from fighting stumps on their bits of farms, but they came." Pat's eyes glowed with his pride in those men and women. "I had begun my talk, coaxing the people to stand up against Squire Collins's men. Ah, I was a magnificent persuader, Doug, believe me. I got them to the point of forming a Reform club. But no further. But before we could even take a count of those willing to defy the Squire, I saw the lordling himself, with half a dozen of his little private army, heading my way. Each

man carried a stick that looked big enough to be one of the famous Cedars of Lebanon. I did not stay my going. I'm hardly of the size to face those arms and me with nothing to fight with but my two fists. I ran.''

"How did they catch you?" Doug felt all the excitement of the tale.

"I was misfortunate, so I was. My farmer friends closed ranks just as I ran toward them. I think they meant to protect me, but before I could break through them, I got these." He pointed at his arm and head. "The arm first. Then my head burst open. And then there was nothing but darkness before my eyes.''

When he had got his wits back, he found himself locked in Squire Collins's cellar — with a stout door between him and escape. "I knew I faced a trial in the morning and a long jail sentence at the end of it at the best. Or hanging for treason at the worst. That cellar was as black as the Squire's black soul, but above my head I could just make out the glimmer of a window. I could not reach it, but by feeling my way about I found a barrel, a big one. 'Twas heavy, as my poor arm soon told me, but I dragged and rolled it beneath the window.

"I could hear voices and loud laughter above me. No doubt Squire and his cronies were celebrating the capture of a dangerous traitor. In the barrel was a spigot. I worked at it to loosen it. It came out finally, and after it a stream of molasses. I clambered upon the barrel fast. I'd give a pretty to have seen Collin's face when he came for me and found himself ankle deep in blackstrap!" Rafferty and Doug chuckled.

"As quietly as I could, I broke out the glass. For once I was happy to be a small man, for, truth to say, 'twas a mighty small window. For all that, I wriggled up and through and made off down the long drive to the road.''

"How did they find you were gone?" Doug questioned.

"Perhaps I wasn't as quiet with the spigot as I thought," Pat admitted. At any rate, the race was on that ended by Doug's lean-to.

"Now," said Rafferty, his story done, "the night is far gone. We must be away from here at the crack of dawn. 'Twould not do for our friends to come back and find the two of us together. If we squeeze hard, we can both find room inside your windbreak for a couple of hours of sleep.''

"All right," Doug agreed. He was surprised that in spite of all the excitement, he was sick for sleep. He yawned mightily and crawled into the bed of fir tips.

"Mr. Mackenzie must be proud to have you help him," he murmured.

"Och! I'm but one of many who would give his life for William the Lion," he heard Rafferty reply. Then he was asleep.

When Doug awakened, the sun was well up. His muffler, neatly folded, lay beside him. Rafferty was gone.

Chapter 6
The Road To Toronto

By the end of that day Doug began to wonder if his legs would hold out to Toronto. Walking the corduroy was exhausting. You could get no rhythm to your step. The rounded logs that made the road were slippery, and no two logs were the same thickness. You were forced to change stride at every step, and you had to keep your feet tensed like a mountain climber to feel for a good foothold as you set them down. At times Doug could walk beside the road, but in most places, this time of year, the path beside the road was deep in water.

It was too lonely, too quiet. The loneliness was worse than the aching feet. He whistled. He sang. He talked to himself. Any sound was good that broke the stillness. He was glad whenever a squirrel sat on a pine branch and scolded him. He would stop and scold back until, with a flirt of its tail, the squirrel went about its business. Then he would take up the leg-cramping walk again, his spirit a bit lightened for the moment.

He saw no one until about ten miles east of Hamilton, when a farmer's cart caught him up. The farmer, a big, red-faced man, with the sleeves of his homespun shirt rolled up above massive muscles, scowled at Doug. He did not speak, merely jerked a huge thumb at the seat beside him. Before the thumb completed its movement, Doug's foot was on the axle and he was sitting down on the plank that served as a seat. "I'm that grateful to you," Doug started. The farmer said nothing, not even his name, but Doug did not care. Someone to talk to was what mattered. "My name is Douglas Lachlan." The farmer grunted. Doug ran on. About Da'. About Graham and all. Grunts were all he received in reply. "I'm going to Toronto," Doug tried once more. The man did not even grunt at that. Doug waited. "Are you going to market in Hamilton?" The farmer turned on him. The scowl grew ferocious.

"Stow the gab, boy." His low voice was a snarl. "I'm sorry about your brother, but I've troubles enough of my own. I can't meet the taxes the government has put on me. I have to go and beg some weaselling Family Compacter for more time. Fat lot of good begging will do. If you're tired, climb back in the wagon and go to sleep. I'll take you to Hamilton. Now shut up!" Doug had opened his mouth to sympathize. He shut it quickly and clambered over the seat into the box of the wagon. The box was empty except for a tarpaulin. Doug lay down on it. In spite of his hurt feelings, weariness swept over him.

The hum of voices and the shouts of stallkeepers wakened him. As he sat up and looked about him, he realized that the wagon had stopped on the edge of the market place. The owner of the wagon was gone. Doug climbed slowly out of the cart, gaping about him as he did so. The market place, indeed the whole town, was bustling with people. He wanted to see everything, and he wandered about the stalls in front of which crates of fowl squawked and gabbled, or a pig or two squealed and rooted in the trough. But he soon tired of the market's noise. The wharves attracted him, and he made his way down toward the forest of masts and yards of the two-masted schooners. Like the branches of trees, the bowsprits shadowed the docks. There was bustle and shouting here, too. But it was more ordered noise, little of the confusion of the market place. Men loaded and unloaded with quick efficiency. Their practised movements were exciting. Never had he seen so many lake boats in one place. Never had he heard such swearing, such banging of crates, such clap of lumber thrown down, such clanging of ironmongery. He lost himself in watching and listening.

Suddenly he came to himself. He felt lonelier than ever with all these unknown people about him. Either he had grown smaller or the people had grown bigger. The feeling of not mattering to anyone urged him off the capstan where he had perched to watch the hustle-bustle. He hurried away, breathless. Through crowded streets, along the lakeshore, and out into the countryside beyond

he hastened. Soon he was back on the highway with the comforting walls of trees on either side of him

Only a few miles from the city he turned a bend in the road and
saw another farm wagon and another farmer. This farmer had his
stormy face turned on the rear left wheel of the wagon. The wheel
had slipped off the logs and buried itself almost to the axle in the
clay that formed the shoulder of the road. As Doug clattered on
the logs toward the young farmer, the man turned a long, thin
face to him.

"Bad luck," Doug sympathized.

"It's the only kind of luck I've had in this beastly country."
Doug was aware that this was a gentleman's voice, but there was
a blob of mud on the end of his thin nose, and streaks of mud on
each cheek. A clown's face. Doug almost laughed out loud. "A
year of bad luck!" the man cursed. "Devil take everything! I was
never cut out to be a farmer. Not in this forsaken country, anyway. I must have been a lunatic to come here." He was so in
earnest that he took an unwary step toward Doug. His feet flew
up, and down he went on his backside. Doug couldn't hold the
laughter in.

The man grinned a little and stood up carefully. "See what I
mean? Disaster under my two clumsy feet. And no way out. All
the money I have is tied up in a piece of ground, full of trees and
stumps I will never get rid of in my lifetime. Right now, if I had
two pounds in my pocket, I'd walk away from the lot. Land,
horse, wagon, and all."

The horse, an ancient sway-backed, bony-ribbed creature,
whose best hauling days were over, turned a thin face to Doug.
The poor creature's face was so like the young man's that Doug
laughed again.

The young fellow followed Doug's glance. "Stupid beast! I'm
the laughing stock of my neighbors because I was tricked into
buying him. Not that I could afford a better. But you'd think he
was too old for shenanigans. The fool shied at a weasel that ran
across the road under his nose. He reared and then ran. And this
is the result." He waved a rueful hand at the wheel deep in the
mud. "Well, a clerk in a counting house, as I was back home in
England, should never try farming, I guess. Though I always
dreamed of owning my own land one day. I wasn't even a very

good clerk. But why do I pour out all my troubles on you, a boy? Sorry. Go along. But if you come across someone with a team, would you mind telling him of the fix I'm in and ask him to help me?''

"Och, I don't think we need a team," Doug responded cheerfully. "Have you an axe in your wagon? If not, I have my small axe." He patted the haft of his hatchet confidently.

"As a matter of fact, I have. I almost used it on the wagon a few minutes ago, I felt so desperate."

"Give it to me, and go sit in the wagon till I'm ready for you," Doug instructed. He did not want a foolish immigrant getting in the way of what he had to do. It was strange how feckless the new Englishmen were, most of them.

He took the axe from the man's hand, a hand, he noticed, that had long, shapely, helpless-looking fingers. Not a farmer's hand. Doug felt lonely for a sight of Da's strong, broad hand. He floundered through the clay into the forest. He found what he was looking for — a straight fir, young, but heavy enough for what he had in mind. It did not take him long to fell it and strip the branches. He took up the butt end under one arm, and with the axe in hand returned to the edge of the forest near the wagon. He dropped his pole on the ground and vigorously attacked a dozen or so saplings. He stopped a minute and looked about, then he called to the man sitting hunched up on the wagon seat, waiting and watching with lacklustre eyes.

"Come and help me now!"

The man climbed down with some speed. Doug felt ashamed of his impatience. The young immigrant was so eager to be of use.

"What do you want me to do?"

Doug had surveyed the situation. He had seen an oak stump, still sound and hard, lying under the trees nearby — a leftover from making the road. He pointed it out.

"We must get yon stump up on the corduroy. I can't do it alone."

"Well, I've a strong back. It's the only asset I have." The man was laughing at himself now, bitterly, but with humor, too. "I think I can manage that." Together they wrestled the awkward, heavy old remnant of a tree to the low end of Doug's ramp.

"You've not a rope, I suppose, in your wagon?" Doug asked.

"As a matter of fact, I have," the young farmer shot back at him. "I bought a new one in town this morning."

"Good," Doug applauded. "Fetch it and throw me an end."

The man obeyed. Doug looped the end of the rope about the roots of the stump. He knotted it expertly. "Now," he ordered, "do you be pulling while I shove." The young man threw his back into the task. Little by little, the knobby, cantankerous load moved up the ramp on to the corduroy. Doug wrestled it, with the man's help, into position near the sunken wheel. The broad roots gave it a firm footing. Doug picked up the axe again and cut a notch in the top edge of the stump nearest the wagon. As he chopped, he could not help casting a sour look at the man beside him. That axe blade was none too sharp to cut into this seasoned old piece of hard oak. If the young fellow was aware of Doug's dark looks, he did not let on.

Doug fetched his pole and, using the stump as a fulcrum, slipped the butt end under the axle. Fortunately it was not a heavy wagon. Like all else about this Englishman, it was not really adequate. Doug would have had a much better, bigger, stronger wagon himself. Still, it was not beyond their handling.

"Do you go to the horse's head, and when I shout, lead him into the centre of the road," Doug ordered. When the man was in place with his hand on the horse's bridle, Doug reached for the upper end of the pole and began to pull down on the lever. For a minute or two he thought he was going to have to call on the farmer for help. "Oh, he'd only get in the way," Doug told himself, and put his young muscles to straining harder. The wet clay had a tight grip on the wheel and was reluctant to yield. Doug swung himself up on the pole and came down with all the weight he could muster. There was a loud sucking noise. The wheel came out of the mire. Doug grinned to himself with pride. He swung the wagon sideways on the lever and shouted, "Now!" The horse moved forward and the hind wheels banged safely down on the firm road bed.

The Englishman stopped the horse and came back with out-stretched hand. "By Jove," he chuckled, "you're a wonder. You'd not be interested in a half-share of my poor little farm, would you? We'd make a regular team."

"No thank you," Doug replied. He was not sure if the man was joking or not. It was hard to tell with Englishmen.

"I'm sorry." The young man sounded as if he meant it. "Of course you must have a family who'd not part with you. By the way, my name is Bell, Herbert Bell. All my friends call me Bert, and you've been a real friend today."

Doug told his name and as much as he cared to of his circumstances.

"Now," said Bert, "can I give you a lift on the way? My farm is not far off the main road, but I'm in no hurry. I'll take you farther along your way."

"Thank you." Doug grinned to soften the Scots pride he suspected was in his voice. "I'll not trouble you to go out of your way, but if your farm is not too far off the road, I'll come with you and show you how to sharpen an axe. You'll not cut down many trees in a day with yon dull thing."

Bert laughed. He still had his clown face, but it was no longer hopeless. Doug's success with the wagon seemed to have wiped out all Bert's doubts and woes.

"It's a bargain," he agreed. "But you must stay and eat with me. Spend the night, if you will. I'll guarantee to fill your stomach with better than inn fare. I can cook not badly if I can't do much else, and I've a pair of woodcock hanging. We'll have a feast."

"I'll not stay the night, thank you," Doug answered. "I must get on to Toronto and to my friends. But a hot meal will be a welcome change from my oatcakes."

Bert Bell's log cabin was only one small room with a fireplace in the wall opposite the door. Doug eyed the room critically. Bert was no better housekeeper than he was farmer. The table in the centre of the room was a clutter of books and a pile of newspapers. One cleared space, where Bert evidently ate all his meals, held two pewter plates, both with the dried up remains of a meal on them. Bert grabbed up the plates and some cutlery at once.

"Sit down," he invited, and pushed some books to the floor from the bench drawn up to the table. "I'll just wash these up." Doug did as he was told. He was timid about offering to help in another man's house. He was surprised to see Bert scrape the plates out on the doorstep. And he was horrified when Bert pulled out of a big iron pot some socks he had put to soak, dumped the water out, filled up the pot with water from a pail without even rinsing the pot, and proceeded to wash the plates. Still, the woodcock was grand when, at last, Bert set it before him. His house might be a piggery but he was as good a cook as he had boasted.

Bert never stopped talking. Doug learned of his home in England — lost by his father's gambling — and the wearying job of clerk in a banking house when he had quit school because there was no money for fees.

After the meal Bert got on to politics. Poor as he was, he was still an ardent Tory. "I'm appalled," he declared, "at the terrible ignorance of my neighbors. They can scarcely read and probably can't write their names. Yet many of them are Reformers. They want to run the country, if you please. It would be laughable were it not so frightening to think they might some day take over the government."

Doug made noncommittal noises and then was ashamed that he did not argue with Bert. Da' would have. "There are two sides to every tale," he managed to get out. And then to prevent Bert's going on, he changed the subject. "Come along and let me show you how to grind an axe properly. 'Twill at least pay for my eating you out of better than a week's supply of food."

"Nonsense!" Bert objected. "I am still in your debt." Doug would have none of that. He rose from the table and led the way outside. He had seen a grindstone by the door. Bert turned it while Doug showed him how to hold the axe so just to whet the edge. He made Bert try so that he could be sure his teaching had some good effect.

It was with little reluctance that he left Bert at last and started on his way again. Bert was pleasant, but they could never really be friends — not with Bert's Tory leanings. Squire Collins, Rafferty, the farmer who could not pay his taxes, and now Bert. He had learned from Da', of course, but 'twas not the same. This way he was getting into men's minds and hearts himself. Men like Collins and Bert could not help but be Tories. It made him feel much older to have grasped this fact for himself.

Doug's next lift came the following day. He was travelling down the road, shouting verses to the trees that marched like giant grenadiers in brown uniforms, and green shakos. The verses came from the "Childe Harold" poem that Mr. Vicars had made him read to the school. Funny how the lines stuck in his memory when he so often forgot the things he was supposed to remember. The verses were all about the Battle of Waterloo, and Brunswick's chieftain who got himself killed in the battle:

> "There was a sound of revelry by night,
> And Belgium's capital had gathered then
> Her beauty and her chivalry, and bright
> The lamps shone o'er fair women and brave men."

They were wonderful lines to shout. He got to the part he liked best: "Arm! Arm! It is — it is — the cannon's opening roar." Suddenly he knew he was not alone. In fact, he realized now that for some time there had been the clip-clop, clip-clop of a walking horse behind him. He had been so lost in the poem that he hadn't noticed. He turned quickly, his face red with confusion. There on a tall white horse was a man in black clothes with a large, shallow black hat that people called a "shovel" hat. The man's neckcloth was gleaming white as were the cuffs that showed at his wrists. His legs were encased in long black gaiters. Doug knew that the man and horse had been pacing him. His face grew even redder when he thought of the poetry he had been reciting.

"Good morning, boy," the man greeted him, in a voice as big as his body. A rich, preacher's voice. Even if he had not seen the clothes and hat, Doug felt he would have known that the man was a preacher, one of the itinerant Methodist preachers whose parish was the whole colony and beyond. "Is this the way you have been taught to keep the Sabbath, shouting the secular verses of a lecher instead of walking properly to church with prayers on your lips?" The tone was stern and accusing. Doug dropped his eyes and scuffed his toe against a log. He had forgotten completely that this was Sunday. He put down his ham and his satchel to ease his tired arms before he answered.

"I am sorry, Sir, but this is my third day on the road, I guess, and the days slipped by without my reckoning of them. I did not realize it was Sunday."

"Three days alone on the road? Strange. What is your name, boy?" Doug told him, and told his reason for travelling as well. "Then you will be of the Presbyterian persuasion." The big, black-browed man seemed disappointed. "This, no doubt, explains your forgetting the Holy Day. I am Reverend Alfredo

Barnes.'' The preacher pulled black, bushy brows down on his nose in a frown. "You've heard of me, Lachlan?"

"No, Sir," Doug admitted. Reverend Barnes seemed indignant for a moment, then the black brows relaxed.

"Folk call me Batty Barnes." Barnes's sudden deep bark of laughter startled Doug. "Well, Lachlan, since you won't be attending service in your own church this day, we will stop right here and have one of our own. You shall sit on that stump yonder." Barnes pointed to the side of the road. "I will stay here. My saddle shall be my pulpit, by God's blessing." Doug did not dare disobey. He plowed through the mire and perched on the stump the preacher had indicated.

The sun marched noticeably across the sky while Doug sat unmoving, as he had been taught to do on the backless benches of his own church, and listened to the thunder of Reverend Batty Barnes.

"I take as my text, this day, the commandment, 'Remember the Sabbath Day to keep it holy,' " Barnes boomed. A jay that had set up a squawking now sat silently on a branch of a birch across the road and seemed to listen to the words. "My sermon I will divide under three headings. First, sins of commission; second, sins of omission; and, third, sins of heedlessness. And that is your sin, my young traveller. For you should have counted the days and known today was the Sabbath. Oh, you shall feel the flames of wrath for your heedlessness. You shall remember the days you have lost and count them to your sorrow in the deepest fires of Hell." Barnes's voice dropped to a threatening whisper and Doug, although he really did not feel sinful, felt a chill slide up his backbone. Oh, Barnes was a powerful preacher, no doubt of that. He developed his headings cleverly with stories from the Bible, then used stories of people he knew as a way to drive points home. Some of the stories were amusing though Doug knew Barnes would say it was sinful to be amused on the Sabbath. One of them was about a man with whom the Reverend Barnes had worked to bring him to repent his evil ways.

"Oh, this man was a man of substance, very wealthy. But he had sinned and on a Sabbath, and I learned of it." Barnes's head was thrown back, his eyes were closed, and his voice trembled as he began his tale. Now he opened one eye and cocked it at Doug. "No matter how I learned, I knew of the blackness of his soul.

And then just as I brought him to the point of confession, didn't he up and die of a heart failure, robbing *me* of the reward of bringing him to the throne of mercy. Talk of sins of commission! The sinful root-pulling old rascal! How dared he?''

He was silent a moment, apparently remembering the man's impudence. He opened one eye again on Doug. "But he was punished. I saw to that. I informed his wife of his sin. She did not even appear at his funeral. She told the neighbors. They did not attend his funeral. Believe me, it is a fearful thing to go to Hell unmourned, alone. God's will was done." Barnes's trembling tones tugged at the heartstrings and it seemed a fearful thing indeed to be buried alone like that. At last, after a long prayer for Doug's soul and safety on the road from all the temptations Barnes felt a boy might face, the preacher uttered a sonorous "Amen" and opened his fierce black eyes on Doug. "Now, boy, come along. I'll take you up behind me and help you along your road. You're a good boy for attending me so well, and a fortunate boy, indeed, for you've heard the best sermon I ever preached in all my fifteen years of the Lord's service in this colony."

Doug lost no time scrambling up behind the preacher. He was glad of the ride but still a little afraid of the companion. It was an unhurried ride. The big horse ambled slowly along, twitching a big ear constantly back to the sound of Barnes's voice. Barnes never stopped talking. Mostly his talk was of the rebels of the colony and the fate in both this world and the next that awaited those desperate men who dared to question God's chosen governor and the assembly.

The fourth ride came on the last morning. A farmer going to market in Toronto picked him up. Then, within a mile or two of the city's boundary, he stopped. "I'm dropping you here, lad," he announced shortly. "There's a tollgate a mile up the road. I'll be forever condemned if I'll pay toll to travel on such a bone-cracking contraption of a road. A road the Compacters have promised a dozen times to repair. I turn off hereabouts. I've a way through the swamps that no one knows but me, and I'll have no witness to my going. Down you get, and quickly. I've no mind for someone to pass and see the way I go." Doug leaped on to the road. The old fellow whipped up his horses and pulled ahead around a bend. When Doug reached the turn, farmer, cart, and horses had all disappeared. Try as he would, he could not find, even on the rocky sides of the road, the place where the rig had turned off.

And so it was that on this fourth day, about noon, Doug found himself leaving the forest road and making his way past houses that came thicker and thicker as he went into the city of Toronto, his new home. For how long? Doug wished he knew.

Chapter 7
Doug Makes A Friend

Toronto frightened Doug. He had scarcely moved in from the
outskirts when he realized he was afraid. The stink hit him first.
Coal gas, mostly, he decided, but also the foul odors of slops
thrown out in the street and the sour smell of the swamps at the
lake edge. The wind off the water carried the odors into the city.
Partly, too, the people stank. There were so many of them. They
rushed past him both ways. They bumped his shoulders front and
back. And they never saw him, never knew he was there.

St. Catharines was so small that everyone knew everyone.
Here in Toronto, the capital of the colony, you could live a
lifetime and not know half the people. Hamilton, small as it was,
had frightened him. In Toronto even the houses seemed to crowd
him. They closed in on either side as he walked, until he felt that
they were leaning in on him. His heart beat fast from fear.

Suddenly, Doug turned and began to run the way he had come.
His bag banged his knee and the ham bounced on his shoulder.
Immediately people looked at him. They swore at him as he
bumped into them; they tittered and they laughed. He stopped.
His face felt red and burning. He had made a fool of himself.
"Are ye a coward, Doug Lachlan?" he scolded himself. "Da'
wants you here and here you shall stay. Unless you want to go
back and feed the pigs for the McNees."

He felt a bit better. His short run had brought him back to a
crossroads. He did not want to go back through the people who
had laughed at him. He turned toward the lake. "I'm more likely
to find Mr. Mackenzie down where the important businesses

are.'' He was only guessing that the business district would be near the lake.

He found himself presently on a broad street that ran east and west. Here the houses seemed to open out, as if they were making way for more important buildings. It became obvious that this was one of the important business sections. There were more people, that was certain. Doug found himself dodging hurrying businessmen. How was he to find Mr. Mackenzie's print shop? Pat Rafferty had warned him that rich people hated Mr. Mackenzie. All the men bustling along the street seemed like rich men. No one besides himself seemed to wear homespun clothes. How would he know if they were the editor's enemies? If he stopped the wrong man, he would be in for a long jawing, at the least. He might even be prevented from going to Mr. Mackenzie.

Doug stopped. He looked for anyone who might be a Scot and a farmer. Someone like himself. There was no one.

Kitty-corner across the intersection was a large church. There, lounging against the wall that surrounded the church, were four boys. They weren't talking. They watched the crowds. Doug looked them over. Their clothes were not homespun, certainly. But they weren't richly dressed. And there were boys in St. Catharines who never wore homespun.

He looked at them individually. One was taller and older than the rest. He might be seventeen or even eighteen. He spoke suddenly and Doug noticed that two of the three others gathered about him and listened. They never took their eyes off him. He was good-looking. Square jaw, thin straight nose, fair hair that waved away from the centre of a broad, high forehead.

The dark, curly-haired boy on his left was a big fellow, too. Not so tall, but broad-shouldered and heavy. His mouth was sulky and drooped at the corners. His eyes were dark. Doug did not like his face.

The boy on the right of the tall one was a nondescript sort. About Doug's height and age, but narrow in the shoulders. His face was narrow, too. His hair was mousy brown and straight, his complexion unhealthily white. His only call to notice was his eyes. They were so close together that they were startling in an otherwise ordinary face. Doug didn't like his looks either.

The fourth boy Doug liked on sight. He hadn't bothered to

shift his position when the tall one spoke. He was about Doug's height, but slight, not stocky like Doug. His broad face narrowed to a firm, pointed chin. His longish black hair had a highland man's sheen to it. But what Doug saw most vividly were the boy's blue eyes. They were alive, and they looked kind. "I'll ask him where to find Mr. Mackenzie," he decided.

He was across the street before his shyness hit him. He stopped dead for a moment, then shrugged off his embarrassment and moved toward the group. Four pairs of eyes fixed themselves on him. Three pairs turned cold.

"Would you please tell me where I can find the shop of Mr. Mackenzie . . . Mr. William Lyon Mackenzie?" Doug asked in a small voice.

The tall lad eased himself away from the wall and sauntered across the grass toward Doug.

"Mr. William Lyon Mackenzie," he repeated softly, as if thinking who that might be. His voice sharpened like the crack of a kindling stick. "Did you never learn to say 'sir' to your betters?"

Doug stiffened with the anger in him. "Da' says . . ." he began. Then, without finishing, he turned on his heel. Instantly the big fellow circled him.

"And what does your Da' say, yokel?" he mocked Doug's tone. There was an ugly twist to his mouth and a hard glint in his hazel eyes.

Doug's heart lurched sickeningly. He was going to have a fight. He knew he wasn't going to get away without one. The tall boy's two cronies had closed in behind him. Doug looked around at them. Curly-top's nasty smile was close to his left ear. He turned to the right. Pasty-face's scared grin was not so close, but he was ready to jump at a nod from Hazel-eyes.

The black-haired boy moved out from the wall. His blue eyes looked gravely at Doug and Doug's courage flowed back into his shaky knees. "Leave him alone, Peter," he commanded. His eyes remained on Doug.

"Are you telling me what to do, young Todd?" The tall boy hooted with laughter. "I'm giving a country bumpkin a lesson in manners. Since he's asking for that dirty republican, Mackenzie, he's probably rebel as well. You interfere and you'll get the same lesson."

"The great Peter Robinson," Black-hair laughed. "Upper Canada's noblest aristocrat. Well, *Todds* are no bumpkins, and I tell you if you fight this lad you'll fight me, too." Doug winced at the "bumpkins" bit of Todd's speech. Maybe he was a country boy, but he'd not give betters to any of these Toronto louts.

"You needn't fight for me," he growled. "I've fought bully boys before." He turned to his tormentor. "What I was about to say to your Lordship," he started — and a good feeling went through him when he saw the blaze of anger in tall Peter's face — "my Da' says there is not a man born who is the better of a Lachlan, and not many to equal us either."

"Jamie! Rob!" Hazel-eyes Robinson snapped first at Pasty-face and then at Curly-top. "Grab him. We'll take him behind the church here. If Todd interferes, I'll handle him."

The two boys caught Doug's arms. He refused to fight them. He could not beat all three. He kept his head up and his mouth held tight as he let them lead him toward the gate.

"If you go through with this, Peter," he heard young Todd behind him, "I'll tell your father. Your father and mine were talking just last Sunday, right here outside St. James's Church. Your father agreed with mine that the only way to stop rebellion in this colony is to treat all the people with the respect due to them."

Young Robinson snickered. "My father is a politician. He agrees with everybody. Respect? That's exactly what I'm giving this rebel, you ass."

"Then you must fight me first." Todd's voice was quiet but firm. "I know you can beat me. But I'll mark you first and give Lachlan a sporting chance with you. Believe me."

They had reached the yard at the back of the church. It was screened from the street by the wall and by tall maples almost in full leaf.

"You don't think I'm going to fight him?" There was real amazement in Robinson's voice. "I don't fight with people of his sort. He's not a gentleman." That was harder to take than "bumpkin." Gentle folk at home did not talk that way. They were all farm folk together.

Robinson had been looking around sharply as he spoke. Now he strode across the yard and picked up a stick some boy had cut and left lying. It was green still and whipped the air with a nasty

swish as Robinson swung it. "Now Rob," he shouted, "hold him!"

Doug had dropped his satchel and the ham to be ready for this moment. It gave him some satisfaction that the heavy ham had landed on Rob's foot, causing the stout one to grunt angrily. But ready or not, it was no use. Quick as a flash Rob's arm whipped about Doug's neck, cutting off his wind and pulling him down. He fell on his knees, then kicked out. There was a shriek from Pasty-face Jamie as Doug's hob-nailed boot caught him on the shinbone.

"Hold his legs, Jamie," Peter ordered. Doug felt Jamie fall across him. He thrashed out. Rob's hold tightened on Doug's throat. Wisely, he lay still. He felt the hot sting of the stick across the seat of his pants and braced himself for the next one. It did not come.

Above the roaring of the blood in his ears he heard Todd's voice, cold as a knife-blade in December. "Let him go, you two, or I'll give you the same."

The arm around Doug's neck loosened, then withdrew slowly. The weight came off his legs. Doug scrambled to his feet. Rob lay back, leaning on his elbows, frightened face to the sky. Doug turned 'round. Jamie was twisted up into a ball of fear. He whimpered. Doug lifted his eyes. Peter Robinson was hopping about, his left arm clasping his right shoulder. His face was dead white. There was sweat on his forehead. The stick he had used on Doug lay on the ground. Over it stood Todd. In his hand he held a second stick — a club.

"You've broken my collarbone," Peter Robinson screamed. "My father will sue your father for this. He let forth a howl as some unfortunate movement caused him more pain. "You've broken it, I tell you."

"I doubt it," Todd retorted. "And more's the pity. I warned you I wouldn't let you do it." He turned to Doug. "Are you all right, Lachlan? I'm sorry I couldn't save you from that one crack." He smiled and his blue eyes shone with fun. "It took me a deuce of a time, you know, to find a weapon."

"I'm gey fine," Doug smiled back. "Mr. Vicars, our schoolmaster back home, has given me worse. I'm grateful to you."

While they talked, Rob and Jamie scrambled to their feet. They led the groaning Peter out of the churchyard.

Todd dropped his club. "I think I want to sit down. I've never hit anyone like that before," he confessed. "Not with a stick." He led the way to the back steps of the church. The two boys sank down on them, Doug as gratefully as his champion. He felt drained.

"I'm Laurence Todd," his companion began after they had sat a moment. "What's your name? Besides Lachlan, that is?" Doug told him. "I shall call you Douglas the Black," Laurence grinned. "Like the Douglas in Sir Walter Scott's books."

Doug wished he could think of a name like that for Laurence, something that would show what a real hero he was. He just grinned at Laurence. "I'm black enough, I'll wager," he agreed. "I've been eating dirt." He took out his handkerchief and rubbed his face. "Mr. Mackenzie will wonder have I been rooting with the pigs."

"Oh yes, Mr. Mackenzie," Laurence put in. "If he's expecting you, I'd better show you the way."

"Oh, he's not. That is, he doesn't know I'm coming." Douglas explained about Graham and Da'. "I'd like to sit here awhile and talk. But perhaps you're in a hurry?"

"Not a bit. We've got holidays right now. Some of the resident boys came down with measles, and they won't let us go back until the outbreak is over. Upper Canada College, you know. Lucky us."

"Then we can talk awhile? I want to find out how people act in Toronto. I don't relish being called a bumpkin."

"I'm sorry about that," Laurence apologized. "It must have sounded to you as if I were siding with Peter. I wasn't really. Peter is a great snob. He only listens to people whose families have as much money as his people do. I was just reminding him that my father is a banker and that his father is very glad of my father's advice about money. I don't think you're a bumpkin. Peter is the bumpkin, actually. He's only interested in hunting and fighting. When he's sure he can win. Not but what I like hunting, too," Laurence hastened to add. "But I like to know things, too. I read a lot."

"So do I, when I can get the books. Old Vicars is good at letting me read his. He has a whole roomful. I've read most of them. I've done lots of hunting, too. With Da'. This waistcoat is made from a doe Da' killed.'' Doug opened his coat to show the soft leather vest.

"That's beautiful,'' Laurence admired warmly. "I wish I had one like it.''

"Come autumn, maybe you and I could go out together and get us one,'' Doug suggested eagerly.

"That wouldn't be half grand,'' Laurence agreed.

Doug's face clouded. "Will Peter's father really sue your father? I wouldn't want to cause trouble.'' Doug's proud Scottish soul cringed at causing anyone to spend their bawbees over him.

"No, no,'' Laurence asured him. "His father will twig him properly for fighting again. Peter knew that. He was just trying to scare me. Peter's all right, I guess, when you get to know him. We get on, but he knows I won't jump for him the way Rob and Jamie do. He hasn't had much chance to be anything but a snob and a bully. His people are important. Maybe you've heard of them?'' Doug shook his head. "People jump to obey when a Robinson speaks. Imagine your telling Peter that a Lachlan had no betters — not even the Robinsons!'' Laurence lay back and laughed until the tears ran down. Doug found himself annoyed at the laughter, but suddenly it was catching. He began to laugh, too. The two boys rolled with the fun of it.

At last the laughter died and they sat up. A new thought came to Doug. His face sobered. "People loathe Mr. Mackenzie. Why? What's he done so bad?''

Laurence looked grave in turn. "Not everybody. My father doesn't. We talk a lot together since my mother died.''

Doug nodded. "Like Da' and me.''

"I must admit most of our friends are Mackenzie-haters. Father says that if Mr. Mackenzie stuck to politics in his paper, more people would be for him. He says many of Mr. Mackenzie's ideas are right. Like the people not controlling the country's money. Things like that lost England the States.''

Doug nodded again. Da' had said much the same thing.

"But you see . . . '' Laurence broke off. He looked doubtful a moment, then he rushed on. "Mr. Mackenzie's a bit of a muckraker, you know. He digs up ugly stories about people. Only about his enemies in the government. He doesn't always tell the truth quite. Father says so, anyway. Take the Robinsons, for instance. From Virginia. Robinsons were big plantation owners for donkeys' years. They gave up a lot to live under English rule. Well, not long ago, Mr. Mackenzie printed a horrible story about them. That their grandmothers or great-grandmothers, something like that, were low types from the London streets. Shipped to the colonies to get rid of them. Bought by the Robinson men at the auction block like cattle. I don't remember the exact words. You can see why the Robinsons hate him. Even if it were true. And nobody but the Robinsons know that." Laurence grinned. "There have been other stories, too. About other important people. He hates so many. He even attacked my father. He doesn't like bankers."

Doug looked troubled. "I'm sure Da' doesn't know about those stories, though we do take *The Constitution* and took *The Colonial Advocate* when Mr. Mackenzie owned it. I think Da' believes what Mr. Mackenzie says. He would never send me to live with a liar."

"Father says newspaper men call it 'reporting.' Anyway, Father has said many a time that if so many people look on Mr. Mackenzie as their champion, he must have right on his side. I expect you will have to think of him that way. I don't suppose he lies to his family and friends. Just in his newspaper. Maybe he believes what he prints."

Doug's face brightened. "I expect you're right. I know Da' believes in Mr. Mackenzie's politics. And I must think as Da' does about that. I suppose we're enemies really, you and I. You're Family Compact and I'm Reformer."

Laurence grinned mischievously. "I'll hear plenty about that when we visit the Robinsons. They'll tell my father. . . . " Laurence sat up primly and pursed his lips. He turned his eyebrows up in a clownish imitation of Mr. Robinson. "George, you can't let Laurence associate with a Reformer's son, a low rebel. You really can't, you know." He grinned again. Doug answered with an uncertain smile.

"And what will your father say?"

"Oh, he'll say what he always says. 'Laurence must choose his own friends. I trust him to choose only worthy ones.' You'll like Father. Besides, he's a Whig, not a Tory like the Robinsons. And that's next door to a Reformer."

"I hope he'll like me. That's more important." Both boys

knew now that they were going to be fast friends.

"You'd better wonder if Mr. Mackenzie will let you be friends with *me*. If Family Compacters hate Mr. Mackenzie, he returns their hate a hundred times. As I said, he's the best hater in the colony."

"He can't stop me being friends with whom I like," Doug asserted stoutly. "Da' never questions my friends. I'll make that clear."

"Wait and see," Laurence counselled. "You haven't met the Mackenzie family yet. You'd better be getting along to them now." He looked up at the sky. The sun was more than directly overhead. "The Mackenzies will be sitting down to a meal soon. Most folk in Toronto have dinner about two. You had better get there before it's all eaten up. Come on." Laurence rose and picked up Doug's satchel which he had carried to the foot of the steps. Doug hefted the ham on his shoulder.

"Where do I go?"

"I'll go with you. You came too far down King Street. We'll have to go back to York Street. That's where he lives. It's not far. I don't think there is any use going to his shop. It'll be closed until after dinner. Most shops close at this time."

The two boys left the churchyard and Laurence turned his steps toward York Street. It was only a few minutes' walk to the corner of the street on which Mr. Mackenzie's house stood. Doug felt his heart beating faster and a growing panic seized him. What if Mr. Mackenzie did not want him? He scarcely heard Laurence at his side chattering about the fine building that could be partly seen ahead of them, ". . . Osgoode Hall . . . Law Society." Doug could not take it in. Indeed, he found it hard to make his eyes focus on the building at all. "Here we are," Laurence announced cheerfully, and then becoming aware of Doug's misery, he put a hand on his friend's shoulder. "Got the collywobbles, eh? Don't worry. Your father wouldn't have sent you here if he didn't think everything would be all right. Now, you must go to the door."

Only then did Doug raise his eyes to view the house. It seemed enormous to him. It was square, made of stone, with a centre door of dark wood. It rose two storeys and a half; over the window that was set into the wall over the door, there was a cornice. On either side of this central section, both downstairs and up, there were two sets of windows. "How many rooms are there?" Doug wondered. The structure seemed to stretch well back. How could he, coming from a three-room log cabin, ever fit into this enormous mansion?

"It's verra grand, is it not?" he whispered to Laurence. The anxiety made his Scottish speech very plain.

"Not really." Laurence smiled encouragingly. "There are many bigger, more elegant homes in Toronto."

"Aye, perhaps," Doug retorted, "but I'm not expected to live in them for, goodness knows, how long. I'm scared, Laurie."

"A fellow who can stand up to Peter Robinson isn't going to be scared of a house. Come, cheer up. They won't roast you for dinner."

Slowly Doug stepped away from his friend and advanced lagging step by step until he stood at the top of the steps under the porch. He turned. Laurence still waited on the street. Doug raised a hand. "I'll see you again soon?"

"Tomorrow, if you like," Laurence called cheerfully. "I'll wait in St. James's Churchyard for you." He turned then and marched away down the street. He was whistling. Doug felt deserted. How could Laurie leave him standing at the door? And whistling? What if they slammed the same door in his face? Aye, Laurie could be cheerful well enough. He didn't have to face a bunch of strangers.

"Och! What's wrang wi' ye?" he chided himself. "Laurie knew you'd never get your courage back till he left. Ye're on your own, lad, as ye have been from the first. Get on with the job as Da' would want ye to."

He turned, raised the round brass knocker of the door and slapped it down hard, once, twice, three times. The door vibrated like a bass drum. He dropped his hand at his side and stood stiffly, waiting for the door to open.

Chapter 8
Doug Meets The Mackenzies

The big door opened just as Doug raised his knuckles to rap again. In the opening stood a young man, short, wide-shouldered, auburn-haired. His rosy cheeks looked fatter than they were because of his fluffy red side-whiskers. He looked worried at first; then, as he became aware of Doug, his thin lips curled up in a kind smile.

"What can I do for you?" The voice was low and pleasant.

"I'm looking for Mr. Mackenzie, Sir. I'm Douglas Lachlan, and I've come to stay with Mr. Mackenzie."

"Indeed? I'm James Mackenzie. Mr. Mackenzie's son and his right hand man. I travel about the colony selling space for advertisements in my father's paper. I'm his printer, too, when he needs one. I'm his bill collector. I do them all!" James Mackenzie's laugh was free and friendly and Douglas found it easy to laugh with him, though he was not sure just what was funny. "I didn't know Father was seeking a new apprentice."

Oh, I'm not, Sir. An apprentice, I mean. My father is a friend of Mr. Mackenzie. He had to go away to look for my brother . . . in the Red River Colony. . . . Doug was trying to get his whole story into one sentence. He was embarrassed. He wanted to run away. He could have managed on the place at home himself until Da' got back from the Red River. His feet would not obey. Those eyes, sombre again, were on him.

"We should have waited for Da' to write and get word back," he thought. "Ah, but that would have taken days," that stronger Doug answered. "And when Da' got the feeling about Graham, he had to go." That's the way it was with Highland second sight.

The people who had it were its servants and must obey when the sight was on them.

"It will be pleasant for my father to have a young visitor." James Mackenzie smiled again. "I have to be out of town much of the time. You can be very useful to my father in my place."

Doug let his held-in breath out in a rush. This son of Mr. Mackenzie evidently did not think it strange that Doug should be here asking for a place to stay.

"Do come in." Young Mr. Mackenzie put out a hand and took Doug's satchel from him. At the same time he drew him into the dim hall. There was a settle just inside, at the left of the door. Doug set the ham thankfully down on it. Time later to speak of it. He waggled his shoulder to ease away the last strain of it. He was aware of stairs running up straight ahead of him and of reaches of the house opening out behind the stairs. "My father is just sitting down to dinner. Come and eat with the family. You'll find it a very large and noisy family, I'm afraid. Five sisters — can you stand so many girls at once? — two apprentices who have their noon meal with us, the present printer, and my stepmother and my grandmother. And we all talk at once. Except when father has some important announcement to make. Then we are all very still and attentive, I assure you. Listen to them." There was a great hubble-bubble of voices coming from the room at the left behind the stairs.

"But come, we've not shaken hands yet." James put out a hand to Doug — strong though small, like all of him. Doug warmed to James Mackenzie. He stepped forward and took the hand. It was comforting, and somehow it was like Da's. It did not let go either when the handshake was done, but drew him down the hall past the stairs to the closed door behind which voices gabbled and clacked. One voice dominated the rest. Its piercing tone and intensity gave Doug an excited feeling. It scared him though to realize that in one moment he would be facing the owners of all those voices.

"You'll get used to it." The young man seemed to know Doug's fear. "In a week you'll be making as much of a row as any of them." He gave the door a push.

Doug had time to catch a glimpse of a sunny big room with a table full of people running the length of it. Then, out of no-where, something orange-colored flew through the air and struck him full in the face. It covered his eyes and nose and mouth. Doug reached up to claw it away. It felt like hair. There was a burst of laughter — not unkind, just happy laughter. And above it that exciting voice Doug had heard said, "Listen to this!" The laughter stopped. The voice stopped, too, then went on in a lower, less excitable key. "Oh, it's you, James."

"Yes, father, I. . . . " James got no further.

"Who's that you have wi' you?" The voice rose in pitch, not waiting for an answer. "Oho! Oho! Don't tell me. 'Tis Andrew Lachlan's boy, the young Reformer champion. 'Tis he! 'Tis he! I know. I've been reading a letter about his brave deeds this very minute."

By that time Doug had cleared the orange missile from his face. He held it in his hands and stared stupidly at it. It was just what it felt like — hair. Bright, orange-colored hair. He was terrified. What had he done?

"Bring him here, James. Bring him here." Doug learned very soon that Mr. Mackenzie never waited for anything. "Come along, boy, and let me shake the hand of a reforming hero. And bring my wig with you. My head is getting cold."

Doug looked up then. At the far end of the table, like an old-faced little boy, was a man, smaller even than James. Doug's eyes involuntarily went to the man's head. A wisp of grey fuzz all over a big, shiny dome of a head. A wicked smile on an elfin face beneath the dome. A thin hand stained with printer's ink reaching high above thin shoulders that barely showed above the table level. This was Doug's first picture of William Lyon Mackenzie.

Doug moved at last. He could not get rid of the thing in his hands fast enough. He trotted the length of the table that was silent now, as everyone sat and observed the newcomer. The table seemed crowded. Two young lads with ink-blotched faces. An older man. Some little girls. A woman. Doug could not sort out all the people in the room.

Doug put the wig in the outstretched hand. With a single gesture Mr. Mackenzie shook the hairpiece and clapped it over his dome. A pat here, a pat there, and the wig was in place. Quite accurately so. Mr. Mackenzie must have had a great deal of practice hurling, then replacing that wig. The last pat was like a signal to the others at the table; they fell to eating and talking to each other in the same excited way. Doug and James and Mr.

Mackenzie were washed into a quiet corner of their own by the flood of sound.

The hand, free of its job of hair-straightening, reached out once more for Doug's hand. Like James's, it was warm and friendly. There was a difference though, and for a while Doug could not determine where the difference lay. Then it struck him suddenly as Mr. Mackenzie's hands shot out in a wide gesture. James knew always what his hands were about. But Mr. Mackenzie's hands moved, darted, jerked, and waved constantly — as if they had a life of their own.

Right now they were darting at a brown-haired woman at the door end of the table. "Isabel, a place here beside me, if you please, for young Lachlan." "Och," Mr. Mackenzie turned to Doug, "I know all about you. Did you not save the life of my friend and helper, Patrick Rafferty? It's all here in his letter to me. I was just about to read it to our little assemblage. It came by this morning's post, though I'd no time to read it then. I'll read it now. Listen, all of you, to this. It's like an adventure in a story book."

Doug put out a protesting hand. "Please, Sir," he begged.

In the silence that had fallen on Mr. Mackenzie's trumpeted order for attention, Doug felt himself grow hot with embarrassment. Then those shining blue eyes of Mr. Mackenzie's turned on him and for a long moment searched into him. "Very well, young Lachlan. I shall respect your wishes. You are as modest as you are brave."

Doug knew in that instant that he had come home.

Chapter 9
Doug Hears Of Spies

"You must meet my family and my employees!" Mr. Mackenzie diverted attention from Doug's red face. "James you have met already." James had taken his seat at the table two places down from Doug. "My wife, Isabel." Mr. Mackenzie's hand darted toward a sweet-faced woman whom Doug had already identified as Mrs. Mackenzie. She was fetching a plate and silverware to set before Doug. She smiled warmly and put a hand on his shoulder as she leaned over him to arrange the silver. "I am pleased to have you," she said softly. Doug knew she meant it. He felt himself smiling for no particular reason. He just felt happy.

"My mother," Mr. Mackenzie continued, "Mrs. Mackenzie." For the first time Doug became aware of a still figure, wrapped in a plaid shawl, sitting in the place of honor at Mr. Mackenzie's right. He became aware of two lively blue eyes observing him, all the more alive because they were set in that immovable, wrinkled face. The face was narrow and the thin lips invisible so that you could not tell if she were smiling. But those lively eyes almost spoke! Doug felt they were bidding him welcome. He dropped his eyes, abashed a little by the long stare. He remembered what Da' had once said of his own father. "A tower of strength, he was, Douglas lad. A veritable tower of strength!" Mrs. Mackenzie, he felt, was such a tower. He stole another glance at her, but the eyes were turned away from him to Mr. Mackenzie and there was such a blaze of love and pride in them that Doug quickly looked away again

Mr. Mackenzie was going on. "Halfway down the table is Mr. Robert Rutledge, my printer, and the three rogues at the foot are Alan, Ian and Lovell, my apprentices. Don't play at taws with them. They'll rob you blind.'' Doug did not know if Mr. Mackenzie was joking. He did not smile. But the boys did — wide, engaging grins that were at once mischievous and friendly. ''And finally,'' Mr. Mackenzie concluded, ''my daughters. Barbara at your left. . . .'' Doug turned and looked into a ten-year-old face that was a young reflection of Mrs. Mackenzie's.

''Tell me why Father says you are a hero?'' Barbara, smiling, questioned Doug. ''If you don't I shall tease Father until he tells me. He never says no to us.''

''Witch, be silent!'' Mr. Mackenzie reprimanded her indulgently. ''Beyond James is Janet.'' A brown head was pushed out across the table. A freckled face puckered at Douglas and then broke into a captivating smile. ''As you can see,'' Mr. Mackenzie teased gravely, ''Janet will never be a great lady. Her mother cannot keep a bonnet on her when she goes out in the sun. She never learns that the sun tells tales on her with new freckles every day. Across from Janet is her sister, Margaret. She, to my sorrow, is another wild Scot like myself.'' Indeed there was a strong resemblance, Doug noted, even to the red hair. She seemed not one whit abashed by her father's criticism. She opened her mouth in a grin revealing her missing front teeth. ''Helen, my second youngest, seems to have left us.'' Mr. Mackenzie's hand pointed out a three-year-old who had fallen against her grandmother's arm in a sound sleep. ''And my youngest, Elizabeth, is a babe in a cradle beside my wife's place. She is the greedy one. You may have heard her screaming for her dinner just as you came in. I expect she's asleep now.'' Mrs. Mackenzie nodded happily from her place. ''Douglas will meet her at a later time when she is awake. And last, I must not forget Jock,'' Mr. Mackenzie wound up. A little black bundle of Highland terrier barked and leaped up into his master's lap at the sound of his name. He looked at Doug and barked again, then jealously turned to lick Mr. Mackenzie's face.

''What a houseful!'' Doug thought. ''Da' could not have known. Where will there be room for me in all this?'' His eye caught Mrs. Mackenzie's and she smiled encouragingly at him as if she had caught his thought.

By this time Doug was wolfing the mealy puddins that Mrs. Mackenzie had set before him: sausage skins stuffed with

oatmeal and onions and flavored with herbs from the garden. To Doug this was the finest meal he had eaten since the mother died. He ate enormously. Mrs. Mackenzie, seeing his plate empty, rose and refilled it. Doug looked his thanks and shame for his appetite.

"Now Douglas, my boy, let us talk about you," Mr. Mackenzie began as Doug started on his second helping. Doug suspended his chewing and looked expectantly at Mr. Mackenzie. The little man was eyeing the room as if he suspected a lurker behind the dresser or the side table. Doug, still chewing steadily, followed his host's eyes around. He realized that James, Mr. Rutledge, and the apprentices had gone.

Mr. Mackenzie's left hand caught Douglas's right wrist in a grip that froze his fork to the plate. His voice dropped to a hoarse whisper. "Your friend, Pat Rafferty, has plans for you, if you are agreeable. He wants you with him. Only, I repeat, *only* if such an idea meets with your approval. This is your home for as long as you wish it. Your father was aye my friend and champion, and I would do nothing that you feel is against his wishes. But the truth is you could be of great help to the cause of Reform in this colony."

"I, Mr. Mackenzie, Sir?" Doug managed to swallow the mouthful he had been chewing. His eyes rounded in amazement. "Why, I know only what I have heard Da' say. He admires you very much, Sir, and I feel sure he would wish me to help you in any way I could, but I don't see. . . ."

"You will, my boy, you will. Let me explain." Mackenzie released Doug's wrist, but Doug could not go on eating. He put his knife and fork down and turned his chair to face the little man squarely. Mr. Mackenzie in turn pushed his chair away from the table and brought it around to the corner to be nearer Doug. Doug could hardly take his eyes from the seat of the chair, for he saw that Mr. Mackenzie was sitting on a thick book. His toes barely touched the floor.

At that moment Barbara stirred beside Doug. "Papa?" she started uncertainly. Mr. Mackenzie switched his attention to his daughter. "I am sorry, Papa, but if Mamma is going to take lessons with Janet and Margaret and me this afternoon, we shall need the dictionary."

"So you will, my pet," Mr. Mackenzie agreed. He stood up.

Margaret climbed down from her chair, circled behind Doug and, clasping the heavy book to her thin chest, trotted out of the room. Mrs. Mackenzie rose to pick up the sleeping Helen. Old Mrs. Mackenzie, for all her years, stood up as lightly as a cat and moved to the door. As she went, she held out hands to Margaret and Janet who accompanied her out of the room. Only Mr. Mackenzie and Doug and Elizabeth asleep in her cradle were left. Mr. Mackenzie crossed to a window beside the dresser. He stood a moment, looking out, those willful hands knotting themselves nervously behind his back.

"No wonder he sat on a book," Doug thought. Standing, he was even shorter than Pat Rafferty, and Pat had seemed only boy's height.

"So few to trust. So very few," Mr. Mackenzie murmured as if he had forgotten Doug's presence. There was a little silence. Doug did not know what to say and Mackenzie seemed to be lost in disturbing thoughts. Suddenly he wheeled on Doug. Doug jumped a little. "Even my own household!" The bewigged little man showed a tragic face. "Oh, not my wife and mother. Not my son, James. They are eternally loyal, and they put up with much for their love of me. Not even Rutledge. He sometimes drinks more than is good for him, but he would not betray me. My apprentices? I do not know. Not many months ago, I was forced to get rid of one who was paid by my enemies to spy on me and report meetings and conversations that took place here and at the shop. Fortunately for me, he was true only to the money he could make out of the scheme. He offered to lie to his employers if I would pay him more than they offered. A bold rogue. I dismissed him in a hurry, you may be sure. But the others? Have they been got at? This was part of the reason for not reading Rafferty's letter aloud. I thought better of it, and, of course, I saw that it would have troubled you. But I could not be sure that Alan, or Ian, or Lovell — good Scottish stock, all of them — would not pass on the contents to my foes."

"I'm sorry, Sir," Doug whispered.

What had Da' got him into? A house where apprentices spied on the master? And what could the master be doing that anyone would pay a spy to watch him?

Chapter 10
Doug Gets A Job

Doug's mind was still in a turmoil of spies and plots. He could hardly keep his mind on what Mr. Mackenzie was saying. He forced himself to listen. "We must organize the friends of Reform." Mr. Mackenzie's voice rose from whispering to full voice, as if he were speaking to a large audience. "It is not easy to persuade men to defy the Family Compact — the landlords who own them like slaves. Believe me, such men *are* slaves, for they are in debt to the rich for the farms they work, for the very seeds they put in the ground. How can they dare to vote as they think? They would be put off their hard-earned land. Their wives, their children would suffer hunger. They would have no roof over their heads.

"Sometimes, Douglas, I feel that we must tear down the whole government and build anew as the Americans did in seventeen seventy-six. They are freer, less bound by wealthy tyrants. Our Family Compact would set up estates and titles and lord it over us, if they could, as in the old country. I wonder often if what we need is a republic like the United States."

Doug was startled. Such talk was treason. "Da' says our English system cannot be beat, Sir," he put in stoutly. "If it can but be made to work, Sir. That's what Da' says."

"And your Da' is right." Mr. Mackenzie's voice came back to normal again, and he smiled. "I would always trust the wisdom of Andrew Lachlan."

Doug could feel his pride straining his waistcoat buttons.

"But now, let us get back to plans for you." Mr. Mackenzie was whispering again and Doug felt uncomfortable. "It is

Rafferty's idea that he could use a bold, brave lad like you. This would be your home, as I said. But from time to time, you would go out of it to join Rafferty in his work of organizing Reform clubs. Did I say join? That is scarcely the word. You see, Rafferty has become well known to our enemies as an organizer working for me. When he calls at a house to bid a man to a meeting of the friends of Reform, that man is marked by the magistrates and sheriffs and squires of the district. He is watched, and does he start off for the meeting, even though it be held privately in someone's home, the hoodlums intercept him on the way and turn him back. With violence, if he persists.''

"Does not the law protect them?" Doug was outraged.

"Our good members of the Compact have seen to it that only their friends are appointed officers of the law. The law, my boy, here in the Canadas, is not impartial as English law is supposed to be. Look at what you saved Rafferty from."

Doug gave his mind to this. He could not deny that Pat had received no protection from the law. Yet, ever since he could remember, Da' had declared that English law was the fairest there ever had been. Was this not English law, after all, in Canada?

"What would I do to help Pat?" Doug put the question doubtfully. He suspected that if he joined Pat, he would be taking on a fight with the law. Just the same, he could feel a tingle in his spine. It would be fun to be with Pat. Perhaps he might rescue the little Irishman again. Fighting men like Squire Collins. Da' would approve of that.

Mr. Mackenzie's whisper became even softer. He moved close and leaned on the table so that he was almost breathing in Doug's ear. "You would go to stay with someone Rafferty picked out for you. He would provide you with a list of names of those he wished to meet with. You would pretend to be a boy out with a gun for shooting. Or just a lad wandering about the roads looking for birds' nests. If any asked, that would be your answer. You would contact these men, tell them the place of meeting, and return, by the next stage, here to my home. There would be no danger to you. Trust me."

Doug felt the sense of adventure go as flat as a burst pig's bladder football. Just to go about and tell folk about a meeting? Not to run for it, Pat and he, with the enemy at his heels? Not even to stay for the meeting? To return tamely to Toronto? No, he would stay and fight the Compact with Pat.

"How will I know where to find Pat?"

"You will not find him, lad. The people with whom you are to lodge will meet the stage. You will only see Rafferty when he feels it safe for him to come. You may never see him. He will get directions to you which you will memorize. Are you good at memory work, Lachlan?"

"Yes, Sir." Doug was glad he could honestly say he was. All those verses he had learned for Mr. Vicars were good training, he guessed.

"Very good. You will memorize whatever instructions Rafferty gives you and then destroy the paper. If the leaders of the Family Compact get to know of your work, you will be of no more use to Rafferty and me. But I say all this as if you had agreed to do this service. I have no right to such a presumption."

"Oh, no, Sir," Doug protested. "I have no doubts about the work. I just hope I can do it properly."

"Very well, young Lachlan." Mr. Mackenzie held out his hand and Doug grasped it eagerly. All the adventure had come back again. "This is Tuesday. You will take the Thursday stage to Boltontown, north of Toronto. Meanwhile, rest and see the city. You know no one here, I take it?"

"Just a boy I met this morning, Sir." Doug thought a minute. Should he withhold Laurie's name? Laurie had warned that Mr. Mackenzie would not approve their friendship. Doug's chin lifted. Laurie had dared the disapproval of his friends to defend Doug; he must dare the wrath of Mr. Mackenzie in his turn. "His name is Laurence Todd." Doug tried to keep the defiance out of his voice.

"Todd?" There was an angry glitter in Mr. Mackenzie's eyes. "The banker's son?"

"Yes, Sir. He saved me from a beating at the hands of a Peter Robinson and some other boys."

"Young Peter Robinson, eh? Hmm. You have begun early to quarrel with the family of the biggest Compacter of them all. What was your quarrel with him?" Mr. Mackenzie seemed to have forgotten Laurence in his anger that the Robinson name aroused.

" 'Twas my mentioning your name to ask my way that began it," Doug explained.

"Aye, that would do it. The rogues hate me. And young Todd saved you. Tell me the whole story." Mr. Mackenzie sat down in his chair again to listen.

Doug told the tale well. When he had finished Mackenzie was silent a moment. He stared at Doug as if he were searching out truth from exaggeration. "I cannot forbid you to see this Todd. It is not my right. I am not your father. I only ask that you remember that his kind and ours are enemies, and must be until this political cesspool in the colony is cleared up. Do not tell your friend too much. Even if he did not mean to betray you, he might let something fall in the wrong quarter. I do not think, whatever the boys of those families might do, that the men themselves would harm you. It is best, however, to be careful."

"Yes, Sir," Doug agreed. He was glad he had told everything.

"Now, run along." Mr. Mackenzie's hand wafted a way to the door. "You will find my wife and mother in the parlor at the right as you approach the front door. My wife takes the girls for their lessons at this time of the day. Isabel will show you to your room. I must go back to the shop. We are putting out an edition of *The Constitution* tonight. Perhaps you would care to watch us. It is exciting no matter how many times you have seen it."

"Oh, yes, Sir. I would."

"Very well. I shall see you again at supper. You may accompany me afterward to the shop." Doug turned to leave the room. "And Douglas. . . ." the serious tone in Mr. Mackenzie's voice stopped him. "If you think better of what we have agreed on, I shall not blame you." His hand waved a dismissal forbidding Doug to speak.

Chapter 11
Doug Goes To Boltontown

On Thursday the spring weather turned to icy rain blown in on a cold north wind. Mr. Mackenzie had to hold hard to his top hat and bend into the downpour as he led Doug, ears huddled into the collar of his homespun coat, to Betts's Inn to board the stage wagon for Boltontown. As they neared the inn, they could see the wagon standing ready at the inn doors. A couple of passengers scurried out of the hostel through the rain to clamber aboard.

Mr. Mackenzie stopped and grasped Doug's elbow. He drew him hastily into the lee of a harnessmaker's doorway. "I'd best not to go any farther with you lest some passenger to Boltontown see us together. 'Twould not do for any in that place to connect you wi' me."

He thrust his fist into an inner pocket and brought out some coins which he tucked into Doug's hand. "For your fare," he explained. "Pay the driver. 'Tis a slow journey you'll have, Douglas." He was only saying what Doug was already thinking as he looked about at the muddy pools of water, dinted like bullet moulds by the leaden drops. "The roads have been fairly dry, but they'll turn to quagmires in this drenching. Now, off with you, laddie. I'll watch to see you get aboard."

Doug stared at the wagon and the passengers boarding it. He had never ridden on a stage, but this was not like the coaches that passed his home farm on the Niagara road. Those were real coaches with doors and padded seats and good springs. This stage wagon was very different. Passengers got into it by way of the window.

Doug climbed the steps and wiggled his way inside. All the

seats but two with their backs to the horses were taken by heavy-shouldered farmers. Doug chose the middle of the empty seats and put his carpetbag under his feet. The window was darkened as the last passenger began his entry. Doug glanced up and the glance turned into a stare. He found himself looking into an enormous purple face in which two pale blue eyes popped on either side of a fat nose. The man, obviously being pushed from outside, strove to force his tremendous belly across the window sill. At the moment he seemed to be stuck. "Pull, boy, pull!" The pouty mouth opened on a gasping breath, but there was no mistaking the authority in the voice. "Pull!"

Doug held back his desire to laugh. He knelt up on the seat and put his hands under the fat arms and tried to help. It was hard to get any leverage. "Pull, dad blast you! Pull!"

All the farmers in the stage wagon had stopped their talk and turned to watch. The strong hands of the man beyond Doug reached over his head and Doug crouched down, giving up his hold to this stronger helper.

"Now, Sir, try again," the farmer suggested. "Porker," as Doug had named the tubby man, strained again. For a moment nothing happened; then, like a huge cork, he suddenly exploded into the wagon and down on top of Doug. There was a flurry of great arms and legs like pickle barrels. Doug had had the wind knocked out of him and he was beginning to think he would be smothered. But in a moment or two Porker was sitting upright in the last seat and was staring nastily down at Doug. He did not say thank you. Not to the man who had helped, either. All the laughter went out of Doug as his eyes met those of Porker. He shrank back against the farmer on his left.

The wagon lurched, and all the weight of the fat man settled back on Doug as the wheels began a steady roll forward. Doug was almost smothered in fleshy bulges. At least, he consoled himself, he should not suffer from the cold with that hot body squeezing him back in his seat.

The road grew worse the farther they travelled from Toronto. Over and over they were forced to climb out of the stage — even Porker a couple of times — and wade through sticky clay so that the horses could climb the hill. Porker said nothing at these times. Indeed, he spoke to no one the whole way. His bulging eyes were full of disdain for everyone in the stage wagon. The farmers had taken one look at his pale violet broadcloth coat, touched their hats to him, and carefully avoided his eyes from that moment on. They didn't look at Doug either for that matter. He did not expect attention. A boy was not important to grown men. He did feel lonely and scared, just the same.

He felt his stomach tumble at the thought that he might not be met. Indeed, he was having second thoughts about the whole venture. It had been exciting to think of fighting side by side with Pat against the enemies of Mr. Mackenzie. Now, he was not so ready for the fight. There was just the least doubt about how lawful the whole business might be. Could such work as he was going to do for Pat and Mr. Mackenzie be treason? Could he be hanged, drawn, and quartered for it? He knew about the hanging. He was not sure of what drawing and quartering might be, but it sounded very frightening.

And it would not be fighting beside Pat. He had almost forgotten that he was not even to see the Irishman. What if nobody met him? He was back to that fear again. Perhaps Pat was not expecting him so soon. He did wish Mr. Mackenzie had waited for a confirming message from Pat. He had hinted that such a wait could do no harm to Mr. Mackenzie's plans. Mr. Mackenzie had pooh-poohed the suggestion. Mr. Mackenzie must know. If no one met him. . . .

When at last the stage wagon rolled into Boltontown in the afternoon of the second day, Doug was tired and body-battered. One of the men grumped, "Boltontown!" Instead of slowing down, the horses picked up speed. Doug craned forward. He glimpsed the last house in the village disappearing behind him. Where was the stage going? How would he get back to Pat? The stage lurched once more as the horses swung to the left. In a minute they rolled into near darkness and stopped. Passengers began to shuffle, gathering bags and parcels and preparing to leave.

"Out you come, Fatty," a bright voice called happily to Porker as the mud-blackened window came down. Then there was a gasp and the brightness went out of the voice. "Beg pardon, Colonel. I didn't expect to see you on the stage." Doug was heaved violently against his neighbor as Porker thrust himself at the opening. Doug scrambled after. He found himself inside a

great barn making a triangle with a frightened young hostler and the glaring fat man.

"Tell Ridley to give you your wages and be out of Boltontown by daybreak." The Colonel did not raise his voice but the young hostler trembled.

"Yes, Sir, Colonel," he mumbled. "I meant no harm."

"And tell Ridley," the icy voice continued, "that I wish to see him. As a landowner and proprietor of the stage he should stir the Assembly up to improve the road from Toronto. Tell him I hold him responsible for the discomfort I have suffered." He swung on a ponderous heel and made for the open double doors.

The hostler turned away, too. "Bleeding old tyrant! Tell him yerself," he muttered as he made his way to help unharness the horses.

Doug felt sorry for him. Where would he go? Where could he get another job? To be blacklisted by the gentry, he knew, could mean no work within a radius of twenty miles or more.

Chapter 12
Doug Meets His "Cousins"

Doug almost forgot the unhappy horse tender. He was too concerned with his own worries. He hurried to the door of the barn and looked out. No one to meet him? Standing in the middle of the great doors, he felt very alone. The other travellers were disappearing already. Suddenly, a strange figure rounded the corner of the barn and strode toward him.

The man was so tall you had to look twice to see the top of him. He was as thin as a potato sprout in a dark cellar. His white face was sprout-colored. He waved a hand like a hay-rake at Doug and called out in a voice that made Doug jump — a harsh cry like the caw of an oversized crow. "Doug! Doug Lachlan! Is it really you, Cousin Douglas? I've not seen you since you were no bigger than a newborn rat. I'm your cousin, Jim Grissler."

By that time the heron legs had brought him to a halt in front of Doug. The two enormous hands caught Doug's two shoulders in a grip that threatened to collapse him like a doll with the sawdust pushed out. Doug struggled painfully to escape. A bright eye in the narrow face winked down at Doug clownishly. The tall frame bent over. Doug thought for an awful moment that the man was going to kiss him.

"We're cousins," Grissler breathed in his ear. "Greet me as a cousin who's been expecting you." The hands pressed a little harder, enforcing the order.

"How . . . how do you do, Sir . . . Cousin Jim," Doug managed, and breathed deeply and thankfully as the iron fingers released him.

Doug trotted to keep up with Grissler's giant steps as they

moved away from the barn toward the road to the village. Grissler had taken Doug's satchell, but even with nothing to carry Doug's trot increased to a run as they turned into the road to the town. Grissler seemed suddenly aware of the pace he was setting and slowed down to let Doug trot beside him.

"Our friend, Pat, decided that we were to be kin," Grissler explained. "There aren't so many folk in Boltontown that you could pass unnoticed." He grinned down at Doug. "Somebody's going to wonder about a young visitor stopping with Minnie and me. Minnie's my wife. We've been married just a year. It's a year since I got my smith's papers and came to Boltontown to set up my forge."

So this great, gangling man was a blacksmith. Doug thought he had never seen a more unlikely ironworker. Surely that white face had never felt the searing heat of a fire.

"If anyone asks you who you are, just tell them you're Jim Grissler's cousin visiting for a few days."

Doug's brow furrowed with worry. His eyes took on a misty look that his father would recognize as a sign that he was going to be reluctantly uncooperative.

"I couldn't do that, Sir," Doug protested. "It's not that I wouldn't. But I'm no good at it. People would know I was lying."

"Well, now, that's awkward," Jim returned agreeably. "Pat doesn't know you as well as he thought he did. He said you had lied to save him back on the Niagara road."

"No!" Doug retorted. "The Squire asked if I had seen him and I had not. It was too dark. It was no lie."

"You're right and Pat was wrong. We'll have to think of something else."

Doug was silent as they moved along, Jim with his smooth glide and Doug jouncing to keep up. He thought hard. Suddenly his face brightened. "I could say I was connected with you, for it's true. I am connected through Pat and Mr. Mackenzie. I could say that and make people believe me."

Jim laughed. "You'll be a politician for sure when you grow to man size. Well, here we are. Minnie will have a bite ready for you. You must be hungry. I must get back to my anvil. I promised Sim Druitt I'd finish putting a tire on his wagon today and I still have one to forge."

They had reached the edge of the village, and on the right-hand side of the road was a big square building of squared logs with open double doors on the end facing the highway. It was dark inside the place. A wagon with one wheel off was propped up, just inside the door. Farther back in the darkness, Doug could see the glow of a fire. Next to the smithy was a small unpainted frame house. Beside the door was a neat flower bed in which green things had already begun to grow.

As they turned off the road on the path to the house, the door opened and a small, dark woman appeared in the doorway. She was dressed in deep red homespun that made her red cheeks, dark eyes, and full-lipped mouth glow with an extra warmth.

"Welcome, Cousin Douglas," she called.

"Hush, woman. Doug says we're not cousins, but just connections. Through Pat, that is."

"I don't care a snap for that." Minnie tossed her head. "We can't choose our near kin, but we should be able to choose cousins. I like the look of Douglas; and if he'll have me, I'll be his cousin to the end of time. Will you have me, Douglas?"

"You're very kind, Ma'am." Doug would have said more, but Mrs. Grissler never gave him time to finish. She was off on a running talk that stopped only when she slept.

"Good. Then you'll drop the Ma'am and call me Minnie or Cousin Minnie. Good gracious! I had an Aunt Symantha Webb who hadn't a drop of our blood in her, but all of us — ten children we were — called her aunt. So that ends that."

"Get away in with the two of you," Jim croaked to cut her off. "Doug is starving, Minnie. Feed him. And I might say it has not escaped me that you've put on your Sunday dress for our male visitor." Minnie laughed at him and led Doug through the door from which flowed the rich aroma of a rabbit stew. Doug's mouth watered.

He felt at home at once with the Grisslers. Their cottage was small, just one room with a fireplace where Minnie did her cooking and one room off at the side. But the ceilings were made extra high for Jim's long length, and that height gave an air of spaciousness to the room. Doug had a place up under the roof which he reached by ladder steps. Up there under the friendly eaves was a pallet bed where he could sleep comfortably under a feather quilt.

Jim and Minnie and Doug sat around the fire after supper. It was pleasant to sit where the warmth of the wood fire could reach him and to listen to the cold April wind crooning in the eaves. The stream of Minnie's rambling flowed over him. He soon was utterly confused by what she was saying. "Now Doug," he heard her begin, "you are the son of Jim's sister, Sarah Grissler. She married young and moved south in the colony. We've not seen her or heard from her for twenty years; she was some older than Jim. Nobody 'round here will doubt it. She married a Scotsman, too, as it happened, though his name wasn't Lachlan. At least, I'm sure it wasn't; I've clean forgot what it was to tell you the truth and Jim don't remember either. He was a travelling man; a real romance it was. Jim's parents were dead set against the marriage. I guess that's why we lost touch. . . . " The light voice went on and on. Doug's eyes began to close.

"Can he not go to bed, Jim?" he heard Minnie beg. "The poor boy's worn out with his trip over that frightful road." Doug forced his eyes open quickly.

"I'm all right," he asserted stoutly.

"That's the stuff," Jim praised him. "You must be awake when Pat comes. And he'll not come till the town's asleep. He has all the plans made for you."

It was very late when Pat came. In spite of his resolution, Doug had fallen asleep on the chair. Jim had caught him as he toppled sideways, and had carried him to the settle that stood against the wall beside the fireplace. Minnie had fetched a wool coverlet and had tucked it around him.

At the first tap of Pat's knuckles Doug sat up, instantly awake and alert. As Jim opened the door, the little Irishman flowed through the crack into the room. At first he did not see Doug on the settle.

"Did the lad arrive?" he questioned anxiously. For answer, Jim pointed. Pat turned. "Douglas, me boy! It's a sight for sore eyes you are, and that's God's truth. Ah, but it's good to see you again." He turned to his hosts. "I've told you how he saved me neck, have I not? 'Tis the real hero he is."

Doug's face grew hot under the praise, but his heart jumped happily at Pat's words. "You make too much of what I did," he protested. Pat would not listen. He insisted on telling Jim and Minnie all over again. They listened with flattering attention. The story sounded much more romantic than the actual adventure had been, frightening though it had seemed at the time. In Pat's story, the forest was more threatening, the darkness deeper, his pursuers bigger and more brutal than Doug remembered them. Pat told it well.

"It's a great tale, Doug, and one you can tell to your grandchildren," Jim remarked. "But why are you so late, Pat?" He turned to the little man. "Doug is fair beaten for sleep."

"Aye, I know he must be. The gentry have been having a special gathering up at the big house. There's been a great coming and going. I felt it was not worth risking being seen when I have been at such pains to show not even the tip of my nose on the outside of Limpy Shaw's house, except for the one visit to you to tell you of Doug's coming. The Tories are getting more than a bit troublesome about Reform meetings all over the colony. Limpy tells me they are as itchy here to break open Reformers' heads as anywhere in the province. If we're to organize, it must be done without their knowledge." He hitched his trousers up sailor-fashion.

"But now to plans." Pat seated himself on the settle beside Doug. "Here is a list of thirty-two names of men in the district with good will toward us." He took out a sheet of paper and held it open to catch the light from the fire. He studied it a moment, then looked around the room. "Come, Doug, to the table by the lamp. You must see this well. There must be no mistake. I'll go over the list with you." Doug hurried to a place on the bench before the table. Pat moved the lamp nearer and smoothed the sheet with his hand to make it lie flat.

"What must I say to these men, Pat?" he queried anxiously.

"You must say this and no more. 'They're choosing a Reform candidate to run for the next Assembly at Limpy Shaw's mill on Thursday next at ten o'clock of the night. Pat Rafferty's to be there.' And then you must find out if the man will risk coming or not."

"They'll come, Pat," Jim put in, in his harsh croak. "The people are getting tired of things as they are. Like the road from the capital. It hasn't had a lick of work these two years. Rumor is that money was allocated for it. We'd be interested to discover whose pockets have been lined with it."

"Some will be afraid to come." Pat answered. "The Tories

won't take kindly to their tenants' voting against them. At any rate, we must know who are brave enough to stick with us later if lawful means of correcting our wrongs fail. I always think of that, though Mr. Mackenzie has always turned his face against outright rebellion. 'Tis the Irish in me, I expect. We are a rebellious race.''

"Will it come to rebellion, Pat?" Doug queried worriedly. "Rebellion is treason."

"It hasn't come to that yet, lad. Don't worry your head about it.''

"I won't if you say so, Pat." Doug smiled into the black eyes so near the level of his own.

"Good boy!" Pat looked at him a minute, then he turned back to his paper. "Now, you must memorize these names and then destroy the list. When the gentry do find out about the meeting, they'll scour the whole of the nether regions to find out who attended it. A list like this found in Jim's house would mean the end of his blacksmithing in this region. He'd never get another job of work as long as he lived. The gentry would boycott him. What's more, they'd see to it that everyone else did, too.''

"I know that," Doug returned. "A fat man had an hostler at Ridley's given the sack today. He was called Colonel — the fat man, I mean." He told what had happened.

"Golightly," Jim breathed. "It must have been young Harry Grimes. I've told him he was too free with the passengers. Golightly won't forgive him this side of Hell. Poor devil. He was to have married Alice Simms. Well, that's an end to that marriage.''

"Ah, our good Christian gentry!" Pat mocked. "But now back to the job at hand. Can you learn the names quickly?"

"Aye," Doug assured him. "I memorize easily."

"Good." Pat pushed his unruly bang of hair out of his eyes for the tenth time since they sat down together. "Then here is something else harder to remember. You must do it. 'Tis a map of the district showing where every one of these thirty-two men lives. Limpy Shaw made it and I'll trust him for accuracy. You see, their names are printed by these little squares that mark their farms. 'Tis a big area. About twenty miles, I calculate. You'll have till Tuesday to cover the ground. You must be back at Jim's before sundown. 'Twould seem strange to any who saw you wandering about in the night. They'd question you, a strange boy and all. During the day 'twill not cause comment for Jim's cousin to be exploring as boys do.''

"Connection," Jim murmured.

"What's that?" Pat demanded.

Jim explained. Pat looked at the boy. "You see," he said flatly, "you must not do anything to make people stop and question you since you're not one to whom a lie comes easily. Connection, indeed!"

Doug flushed under what seemed a rebuke. "I'd do it if I could for you, Pat. But I canna'. I've never been able to lie."

"It's all right, Doug. A man cannot go against his nature." Pat put a warm hand over Doug's. "Just see to it that no one puts you to the test."

"Let's get back to business so we can all go to bed. This is Friday. I almost lose count of the days. Jim, you'll be taking Minnie and your new connection to church on Sunday, I've no doubt."

"We planned to go. Yes, Pat," Jim answered.

"Then you must go. Some of these men will be there. Between you and Doug you can cover any that do turn up. You can introduce Doug around to the men in the churchyard before church. Then when they gather after service, he can get in amongst them and deliver his message, using some pretext or other to speak to them. Can you do it?" Pat turned an inquiring eye on Doug.

Doug felt shyness already gathering like a knot under his breastbone, but he faced Pat squarely. "I'll do it," he promised.

"That's my hero," Pat commended him. "Now, I don't suppose there will be a dozen of these men at church," he went on, slapping the list of names with the back of his hand. "The roads are almost impassable right now for a man to bring his family in a wagon. But the men of the village will be out. If you have to get in touch with me, you can come to Limpy's mill. But only in an emergency. I don't want attention drawn to the mill. I think that's all. No. There's one more thing. Limpy has to go to Toronto on Wednesday. He'll pick you up here on his way and take you with him in the wagon. Is there anything you want to ask me?"

Doug thought hard for a minute, then shook his head. "I don't think so. I just hope I can do what you want, Pat," he offered anxiously.

"I have no doubts about you. You're quick in the head and a brave boy. There'll be no trouble. Just memorize the list and the map as fast as you can. It's time you were in bed now. I'll stay awhile and talk to Jim. Away with you."

Doug was thankful to go. He was more than ready for sleep. On his attic pallet, he listened for a few moments to the murmur of voices in the room below him. Almost immediately, they faded out in sleep.

Chapter 13
Doug Meets Some Interesting Reformers

Doug woke with the sun. A glance through the little window at the head of his bed showed that the rain and clouds had gone in the night. He drew his map and list of names from under his pillow. Memory work was in order. From list to map and back to list he went. In his mind he fixed each name to a location on the map. The map was simply drawn, but it was clear. There were some ten farms on the well-used road to Lloydtown. The road to King was marked with six names of men sympathetic to Reform.

"I'll do those first," Doug told himself. "I'll start calling this morning."

When the first whiff of bacon frying reached the attic, Doug was dressed. He let down the ladder and climbed down. Minnie was at the fireplace bending over the frying pan. "Good morning, Douglas," she greeted him. "Jim is outside washing. As soon as you are ready, breakfast will be on the table."

Doug joined Jim at the wash bench before they went in to sit down to Minnie's heaping breakfast plates. "You'll want to settle down to memorizing names and places this morning," Jim suggested as he tucked a rasher of bacon into his mouth.

"I've done that already, Jim." Doug tried to keep the pride out of his voice. "I plan to start out this morning to deliver the message."

Jim chewed thoughtfully a minute, then shook his head. "A big mistake, Doug. You should be seen about first. Minnie will take you shopping with her this morning. This afternoon I'll take you with me when I return Colonel Golightly's horse to him. Everybody will know you are here then. Your wandering about won't cause comment. You can catch some of the men you want at church tomorrow. Plenty of time.''

Doug knew Jim's plan was best. Country folk everywhere would be curious about the stranger. It was better to satisfy their curiosity first. He agreed.

"Good," Jim commended. "You may get a chance at Dawson, the storekeeper. But only if you get him alone."

Doug's outing with Minnie was a trying time. The sun had brought people out and Minnie missed no chance to introduce her new cousin. "My cousin's only son from down Niagara way. Visiting us for a few days." This was the formula, and Doug, red-faced and embarrassed, acknowledged the introductions. Doug protested when Minnie embroidered a bit on the story to a Mrs. McLeod. She only laughed. "Mrs. McLeod is the biggest gossip in Boltontown. Before the day is out, everyone from the Squire to his meanest cowman will know about you."

She was right, too. Mrs. McLeod did her work well. When Jim and Doug returned the Colonel's horse, Porker himself was in the yard. Doug was a little scared. Would the great man remember that Doug had heard him called "Fatty?" The big moon face was expressionless as Jim, leading the horse, conducted Doug up to be introduced. No one would guess that the Colonel had ever seen Doug before.

"Ah, good afternoon, Grissler." The flutiness of the voice was somehow false-sounding. "A man of your word, I see. I like that in a fellow who works for me." He went about the horse, lifting each hoof to examine the shoes. "Good, good," he kept murmuring. He straightened with an effort. "Well done, Grissler." He looked at Doug. "Your wife's young cousin, I believe." He stepped close and one soft-looking, fat hand closed around Doug's biceps. There was nothing soft about the thumb that ground viciously into Doug's muscle. "Lachlan, is it? Going to be a smith like Grissler here, no doubt. See that you are a good one with a respectful tongue in your mouth." There was one last painful jab before he loosed Doug's arm. "Well, go along, Grissler. See Muldrew. He'll pay you." Porker turned and made his way into his stately house. Doug had no doubt that he had been warned to keep still about the "Fatty" story. He massaged his painful biceps and a deep anger went through him. A cruel man, this Golightly. Cruel and stuck-up. In his own mind, he was different from and better than common people like Da' and Jim, and Pat and even Mr. Mackenzie. It would be good, Doug knew, to beat his fat enemy by getting the Reformers in the district together right under that fat, stuck-up nose.

The next morning Doug went over the lists and the map a half-dozen times before church. He knew he should destroy the sheets as Pat had ordered, but each time he said to himself, "Just once more and then I'll be sure." At last he went to Jim. "I know the names and the map backward and forward, but I just can't make myself tear them up. Do it for me, Jim."

Jim laughed. "Give them here." Doug let them go reluctantly. Jim tore the sheets across and across again. Doug winced at every rip. "Don't be frightened," Jim comforted him. "I'll trust your memory. You won't forget."

The little log church was not more than half full when Jim and Minnie and Cousin Douglas sat down in their pew. Only five or six churchgoers arrived after them. Jim whispered the names of the men to whom Doug must speak when the service was over. There were eight. Doug did his best to put names to faces. He felt his heart knock at the thought of going up to speak to these strange men. People would think him very pushing.

At the end of the service Jim and Doug stepped out into the sunshine, leaving Minnie behind to chat with the women. Jim led Doug up to three men who were deep in conversation in one corner of the churchyard.

"Three of your quarry, all of a bunch," Jim murmured. "Come on." His great smith's hand propelled Doug across the yard. "Morning, you three black plotters," Jim greeted the men. "Planning to assassinate the Governor, I'll wager." He grinned down at Doug. One of the men turned turkey-red. He was not one for jokes, Doug could see. The other two grinned cheerfully. One of the two winked wickedly. "Don't tell anybody," he cracked, and laughed loudly.

"My young cousin, Doug Lachlan, has some news for you. I'll let him tell you." Jim pushed Doug forward. His long legs took him into the crowd around the church door before Doug could say a word. The three men listened to his message with intense interest. "Tell Pat we'll be there," the winking one promised, and the others nodded. "Who else here do you have to speak to?" Mr. Drew went on to ask. Doug told them. "Come

on, we'll see you find them." The farmer took Doug by the arm
and started him across the yard. He stopped. "No need of me.
Jim's rounded up four of your men already." And so it was all
quite easy. Except for one — Captain Anderson. Jim pointed him
out just as they were starting for home.

"Isn't Captain Anderson on your list? There he goes down the
road. You'd better chase after him. Minnie and I will wait."

Doug looked after the stiff military figure that marched away
from the church. He ran. Captain Anderson's pace was a fast
one. Doug was panting when he got within calling distance.

"Captain Anderson!" he shouted. The man turned a darkly
tanned face to him, his sharp white moustache gleaming. Then he
turned away and marched on. Doug could not bellow his message
at that distance. He put on a burst of speed. "Captain Anderson,
Captain Anderson. I have a message for you," he panted.
Anderson stopped then and turned as if to face an oncoming foe.
His cold blue eyes sparkled dangerously.

"Don't know you, my lad," he snapped. "Don't like boys.
And I know no one who would send a message by you." He
turned to go.

"Wait, Sir." The man turned back. He reminded Doug of Mr.
Vicars at his coldest and angriest. He felt his Scots stubbornness
begin to heat his own anger. "I don't mean to be rude, Sir," he
spoke carefully, taking the Scots burr off his tongue as he always
did when he was angry. "I have a message from Pat Rafferty. I
could not shout it, Sir."

"Rafferty? Is he here? Why hasn't he been to see me? What
does he mean sending me a jackanapes with messages?"

"Pat has had so many meetings broken up by the Tories that
Mr. Mackenzie sent me from Toronto to help Pat," Doug
explained.

"Mackenzie must be mad. Boys can't keep tongues still. You
will be bragging to all urchins in the neighborhood that you are
secret messenger for Mackenzie."

"No, Sir, I will not," Doug denied stoutly.

A red spot appeared in the Captain's prominent cheekbones.
"Well," he cut in, "you have a message for me. Deliver it, boy.
I'm in a hurry." Doug recited flatly, then turned on his heel and
started back toward Jim and Minnie. "Just a minute, you are not
dismissed," he heard behind him. His feet carried him two steps

on, then he stopped and turned slowly. "Don't you wish to know if I'll be there?" the Captain demanded. His eyes did not look quite so angry.

"I did not think you would want to entrust me with the message," Doug managed stiffly.

"Tell Rafferty I shall be present." Unbelievably the Captain's eyes twinkled a little. "And tell Rafferty that I like the Scottish spirit of his lieutenant." The Captain wheeled as if the road were a parade ground. He marched away, leaving Doug with his mouth open.

When he got back to Jim and Minnie and told them about his trouble with Anderson, Jim explained a bit about the Captain. "He's retired from the army. A real spit-and-polish man, I've heard. But he's for Reform. He's not a friend of Mr. Mackenzie; they are too different in nature to agree on many things. But he does go around the country talking Reform to the gentlemen he thinks might be sympathetic. He does something like the work Pat does amongst us common folk. He'd be a great help with his military know-how if it ever came to fighting the Family Compact openly. He always gets together with Pat if they're in the same district. Don't worry your head any more about him."

That afternoon Doug saw four of his men on the Toronto road. Monday morning, he was up before the day broke. Minnie was ahead of him and had a breakfast of sausages and corn bread ready for him.

"You'll have a solid meal in you before you start out," she announced cheerfully. "I've packed you a lunch and there's a stone jug of milk to bear with you."

Doug felt very confident as he started out on the road. He knew exactly where he was headed. "I'll do the farthest farm first," he thought. "That's Pettigrew. I'll work my way back from there. I should finish all the Toronto road today and the rest tomorrow."

He was as good as his word. Luck was with him. He got a lift to Pettigrew's with a drummer driving a light-wheeled gig. The drummer had spent Saturday night drinking with Dawson, the storekeeper, and had been too drunk on Sunday to start back. His head was still not clear, but his horse knew the way and seemed clever enough to avoid the worst potholes.

Doug wondered about Dawson. Most men in the colony would take a drink only if the occasion called for celebrations. But if

Dawson were the drunkard that the drummer said, was he a good man to entrust with the secret of the meetings? What if he were to talk too much in his drink to a Tory sympathizer? What if the Tories caught Pat and his friends at the meeting? They would all go to prison for sure. Maybe worse. Doug tried to shrug off such thoughts. Pat must know the men he could trust. Dawson would have to be told of the meeting.

Chapter 14
A Traitor in Boltontown

It was quite early when Doug approached the last house on the Toronto stretch. This was bigger than most about, a two-storey stone structure with gables let into the roof. The clearing was large, too. The land from the road to the woods in the distance was not only cleared, but stumped as well. The earth looked rich. The green stalks of wheat were well up and strong. It made Doug homesick for Da's small fields. There was a fine barn on this place, built on a stone foundation. All that land and the buildings meant wealth. 'Twould be long before the Lachlan farm looked like this.

He consulted the map in his head for the name of the owner. For a moment he panicked. Homesickness and envy had driven the name out of his memory. Then it came to him: Horrocks. Benjamin Horrocks. Confidence restored, he marched up the elm-shaded lane to the fan-lighted door and knocked.

There was a long silence. Doug raised his fist to knock again. The door swung open before he could rap. A woman stood framed in the opening. Beyond her he could see, through a wide hall, a white room with shining brass and the soft gleam of silver. He realized why he had not heard the woman come to the door. The door was heavy and there was dark red and blue Turkey carpeting right up to the door sill. This was surely the home of gentry. Had Pat made a mistake?

The woman before him was tall, thin, and all angles. Even her red curls on either side of her face, under a frilled cap, stuck out in stiff planes from her face. Her sandy brows went up high above the sharp triangle of her nose. Doug felt his courage slip out of the ends of his suddenly too big hands.

"What is it?" The words were as sharp as her nose.

"Does . . . does Mr. Horrocks live here?" Doug stammered.

"And if he does?" The head tilted back insolently.

"I'd like to speak to him Ma'am, if you please." Doug knew she wasn't going to let him in on her Turkey carpet.

"What for?" Doug winced visibly under the acid question.

"I have a message for him, Ma'am."

"Give me the message."

"I was supposed to deliver it to Mr. Horrocks himself, Ma'am."

"Well, you will not, boy." The woman was adamant. "Mr. Horrocks is not home to the likes of you. You will tell me the message instantly. I will decide whether to deliver it or not."

Doug could not argue. He had no defences against this woman. He gave the message in a dull voice. "Hmph!" the woman sniffed. "Reformers! You tell your trashy Pat Rafferty that my husband is a gentleman. He does not mix with riffraff. Not if I have to lock him in his room. Where he gets his disloyal ideas, I do not know. Now, be off with you." The door shut without a bang, but with a sense of great finality.

Doug's feet made short work of the miles back to Boltontown. Jim would know if he had made a mistake in going to the Horrockses. Jim was in the smithy. Doug could hear the ring of iron as he turned into the yard. The smith looked up from the anvil, built especially high for his long body, as Doug stood panting before him.

"Trouble?" he asked in such a casual tone that Doug found his fears subsiding. Doug told about his encounter with the she-dragon.

"I know the lady," Jim nodded. "Too bad you couldn't have seen Ben. He's not a bit like that. His wife was maid to a lady who came to the colony on a visit. She set her cap for Ben when she learned he had come into some money. Got him, too. Hates this country. Always trying to get Ben to take her back where she can lord it over her old friends. Don't worry. We'll see that Ben hears of the meeting somehow. A pleasure to out-fox that red-haired vixen." He grinned at Doug.

Doug's luck held. That night Limpy Shaw, Pat's lame host, came to the Grissler home. Doug took to him instantly. After the first shock, you forgot the twisted figure of the man. His sideways bobbing walk caused by the one short leg didn't seem important. Nor did his humped back. His wise eyes that shone with interest above his bright smile were all that mattered about the man.

"So this is Pat's hero," Limpy said softly for Doug's ears alone. He did not go on about the "hero" business. Doug was glad. "Pat wondered if you had done the King road yet. I have to drive up there tomorrow with a load of lumber. I can take you. I won't be long in King. You can see Peebles and Barrett in the village and then I'll drive you back and we can stop at the places on the way. I'll be along at sun-up." He turned away, then turned back. "Oh, by the way, it's been arranged for me to drive you back to Toronto when you're finished here."

Doug was watching from the doorstep before dawn. Limpy drove up perched high on the wagon seat behind a four-horse team of big dappled greys, powerful and eager to go. Nothing would do but that Limpy should climb painfully down and introduce Doug to each of the team. They were named for Greek gods: Apollo, Hermes, Poseidon (Posy, for short), and Zeus. Doug wondered if owning these horses was Limpy's way of forgetting his crippled state. They certainly could go. Aside from the fine talk of books, for Doug learned that Limpy was a great reader, the very speed of their journey left him almost unaware of the country between Boltontown and King. In no time at all, it seemed, they had reached the village, done their business, and started back.

Indeed, they made such good time that the sun was still quite high, Jim was still in the smithy, and Minnie was just thinking about supper when Doug dropped down from his perch at the Grissler door. "Good-bye," he offered, suddenly shy. "Thank you. I'm glad I'm riding back to Toronto with you."

"A pleasure I'm looking forward to," Limpy assured him.

Doug decided not to waste the hour or so until supper. He still had to see George Pym and Nicholas Tupper, as well as Dawson, the storekeeper in the village. When he told Minnie his intention, she approved. "When you go to Dawson, fetch me some blackstrap. I didn't discover that the barrel is almost empty until this afternoon. Jim will take the wagon down tomorrow to get a new barrel. I'll give you a jug to carry some in for now. You'll be sure to see Dawson alone then, if you go out back with him where he keeps his molasses.''

Doug found Pym in his tailor shop. It was a depressing meeting. The tailor lifted short-sighted eyes to Doug as he entered the shop. He shook his head. "Not a customer, I can see. The gentry once thought me a fine tailor. Now they go to Toronto for their coats. All I get are their seams to mend. Like this one for Major Bolton.'' He lifted disconsolately the green cutaway he was working on. "Well, you have a reason for coming into my shop, I'm sure.'' Doug told him. "Very well, I'll be there, though Tory or Reformer in the Assembly will not help my business.''

Tupper was very different. He was home from his farm outside the town when Doug knocked at his door. His rosy English face beamed self-assurance and optimism. In a loud voice that made Doug start and peer into the street to see if anyone heard, he assured Doug of his support for the enterprise. "I'll be there all right. With bells on. Fool's bells, I suspect. Bolton would scalp me if he knew. But then, I'm not beholden to Bolton or any other of the gentry. Maybe I'll run myself in opposition to the Major. Tell Pat he's got a candidate.''

Doug hurried away lest Tupper indulge in further loud-spoken indiscretions.

Dawson's store was kitty-corner across the street from Tupper's house. As Doug entered, a bell over the door jingled. The two men at the far end of the store did not even turn around. They were too intent on their conversation. One was elderly and stooped, the tails of his plum-colored coat bulging out behind as he stooped to listen. This was Major Bolton, founder and Squire of the town; Jim had pointed him out in church. The other, coatless, with brownish-yellow nankeen sleeve guards from wrist to elbow, would have to be Dawson. His gingery beard was wiggling earnestly as he talked.

Doug slipped behind a pile of unopened boxes to wait for the Major to leave. He peered around the crates at the two men.

"I tell you," Dawson was saying, shaking a finger at the Squire. "I tell you Rafferty's somewhere hereabouts. Mrs. Horrocks was certain of that when she came in this morning. He's got a boy with him to run his messages. He's lying low so that you won't see him. I haven't seen any strange boys about, but I don't get out of the store much. Ask about. You'll find him. He can be made to tell where Rafferty is. Anyway, you can get your men together to break up the meeting on Thursday. That's what Mrs. Horrocks said, Thursday at dark in Shaw's mill.''

Doug had heard enough. He tip-toed to the door, pulled it open, and ran. The bell jangled madly behind him. He must get to the mill at the far end of the street. "I mustn't be seen,'' he thought. He swerved, dashed between two buildings just as the shop bell jangled again. That would be Bolton and Dawson looking out to see who had been listening.

Doug kept to the back of the buildings all the way to the lumberyard. Limpy had shut down for the day. His men had gone and all was quiet. He stopped behind a tall stack of boards and scouted the lay of the land. There was no one about. Limpy's house stood at a little distance from the mill itself. Doug scooted from lumber pile to lumber pile and at last made a dash across open ground to the carved, oaken door. He knocked quickly and waited impatiently for someone to come. He listened for sounds of pursuit. Nothing. Limpy himself opened to him. As he took in Doug's frightened face, he reached out and fairly lifted him inside. As he shut the door behind him, he called out, "Pat! Pat! It's Doug. Something's happened.''

He led Doug to the back of the house to a large primrose yellow room. Bookshelves of walnut gleamed in the sun that still reached across the sills of the west-facing, long windows. Those shelves stretched from floor to ceiling and they were crammed with books. Doug stared, fascinated. It was the finest room he had ever been in, finer even than the room he had glimpsed beyond Mrs. Horrocks's front door. The thought of Mrs. Horrocks brought him back to his worry. A closed door beyond him, to the left, opened and Pat slipped in.

"Bedad, and what's the matter?'' he demanded. "You would not come for nothing.''

Doug told his story slowly and carefully. He began with his interview with Mrs. Horrocks, and led up to the conversation he had just overheard. He knew from the concentration of the two men that they thought what he said was important. When he had finished, Pat was silent for a long minute. When he spoke, his manner was very grave and the words came out more slowly than usual.

"You've told your story well, Doug boy, and you were right to come. We have tonight and tomorrow. I must start out immediately. I'll have to cover as much ground as I can between now and midnight. There's no use hiding any more. Our enemies know I'm here. Jim can help. And he'll find us horses. Between us we'll see everyone. We'll change the meeting to tomorrow night.'' He fell silent, thinking. A wicked light sparked his black eyes. "We'll hold the meeting in Horrocks's barn. I know Ben Horrocks is a staunch friend of Reform. My guess is he knows nothing about this. And he shall have the chance to put a stopper to his wife's evil intentions. Ah, 'tis masterly, so it is.'' Pat capered about the room in delight at his own smartness. "We'll get enough men to appoint Mr. Mackenzie as Reform candidate. I'll come back at voting time and ginger up the electors. Come, Doug me lad. Don't look so glum.''

"I'll help too, Pat,'' Doug offered, trying to be as optimistic as Pat seemed. "It's all my fault for telling Mrs. Horrocks.''

"No, boy. I would have done the same. Someone should have warned us about her.'' He turned to Limpy. "Did you know what she was like?''

Limpy shook his head. "No, I didn't. Oh, I know she tried the manner of a great lady. But I've heard old Ben state his sympathies with Reform many a time, and in front of her. She never showed herself against him. Someone amongst the gentry has got at her. Maybe she sees a chance of getting into genteel society if she plays along with the Tories. It's Dawson that shocks me. He's always been openly one of us. I never thought he would betray us.''

"There are always some who try to play both ends against the middle,'' Pat commented wisely. "Dawson depends on the gentry for trade.'' He turned to Doug. "Your job is done. And you've done it well. You have no call to blame yourself. You are going back to Toronto in the morning. You will stay here until Limpy drives away with you. He can take you to Yonge Street to catch a stage. I don't think any of the Major's bullies would hurt a boy, but they'd want to question you. They might be carried away with enthusiasm for their inquisition. We'll take no chances. I'll let Jim and Minnie know.'' He swung back to Limpy. "You stay with Doug. Don't open the door to anybody you aren't sure of. Let them think you away from home. I'm off now.''

Doug was asleep when Pat came in, and Pat was still sleeping when Doug and Limpy set out in Limpy's wagon behind the four dappled grey gods on the road to Toronto. In spite of his anxiety and disappointment at the outcome of the work he had done for Pat and Mr. Mackenzie, Doug looked forward to the miles he would share with Limpy.

"Will the stage be waiting when we get there?" he queried, hoping that it would not.

"It doesn't matter," Limpy returned gravely. "I'll not set you down till I have you safely in the street outside Mr. Mackenzie's house." Doug smiled happily.

That night in bed Doug thought again about the crippled man and his horses. He felt he understood Limpy as if he had been inside the man's head and had thought Limpy's thoughts. He wished he understood himself as well. All this talk about rebellion against the Government — which was the King, really. Jim. Pat. Captain Anderson. Mr. Mackenzie. They all felt it was right to fight for Reform. He wished he could feel that sure. Da' would never rebel against the King; he was certain. Should a boy like him do what he thought Da' would want, or do what Mr. Mackenzie wanted? Da' had said, "Obey Mr. Mackenzie." Doug fell asleep, his thoughts still muddled.

Chapter 15
Doug Plays A Game of Rugby

The morning after Doug's return to Mr. Mackenzie's house was bright and warm. Summer was by-passing spring as he and his redheaded host, a high-crowned hat covering the wig, stepped out of the house on York to walk to the print shop on Yonge Street. Mr. Mackenzie walked much as he did everything else, and Doug had to lengthen his stride to keep up. He was full of stories of Toronto. Every street and every house brought forth a memory. A savage bear on Bay Street, as recently as fifteen years before, frightening the inhabitants until it was shot. A house, not far from his own shop, to which he had driven the death cart during the cholera plague. That had happened when Mr. Mackenzie was Toronto's first Mayor. So many people had caught the plague, so many had died, that Mayor Mackenzie could find no one to drive the cart that picked up the dead bodies for burial. He had done the job himself. Doug wondered if he would be brave enough to risk his life that way. His admiration for Mr. Mackenzie grew.

Outside the print shop Mr. Mackenzie stopped and faced Doug. "Have a good day seeing the sights," he urged. "Don't forget to take a look at Fort York. 'Tis a historic landmark. And our House of Parliament and the Governor's Mansion." Mr. Mackenzie fluttered a hand at him, and disappeared at a run into his place of business. Doug began to whistle happily. He put his hands in his pockets and stared at the sign above the shop: "W. L. MACKENZIE," printed in big, fancy letters. A whole day to himself! He hoped he might find Laurence. Laurence could show him the city.

Doug had been more than a bit nervous the evening before. But Mr. Mackenzie had neither shouted nor had thrown his wig. He had listened quietly, smiling a little when Doug imitated Mrs. Horrocks's grand lady manner and speech, frowning sternly over Dawson's betrayal. His anger had been for the storekeeper, not for Doug. And when Doug had finished, Mr. Mackenzie leaned forward and patted his arm. "You've done well, laddie," he praised. "I might have had my own toes pinched, had I been in your shoes. We'll learn by our mistakes. The next time we'll do better."

Doug was relieved and felt happy at Mr. Mackenzie's encouragement. "Next time." Exciting words. Even though underneath he worried a bit about being able to do the job. "Oh, well," he told himself as he turned toward the lake, "next time is not yet. And Mr. Mackenzie told me to enjoy my day." He felt good enough to want to shout. His whistle had died away as he stood remembering that interview. Now he pursed his lips and let the sound burst out to pierce the ears of the passersby.

The whistle was answered from behind him across the street. He turned his head sharply. I was Laurence. Both boys started running at once. They almost knocked each other over in the centre of the road. They pounded each other like two boxers in the ring.

"Where have you been?" Laurence demanded. "I've been here or at your house every day looking for you. The measles are still raging among the boys at school and we may have another two weeks of holidays. I didn't want to waste them."

Doug felt himself grow wary. How could he tell Laurence what he had been doing? How could he keep from telling? Laurence and he were friends. He couldn't have secrets from him. He knew Mr. Mackenzie would say, "Tell no one. Not even your best friend." And Captain Anderson would sneer, "I told you so." Bragging, he would call it. Laurence had been eyeing Doug quietly. He smiled. "Reformers' plottings?" he suggested. His smile widened. "It's all right, Douglas the Black. Not your secret to tell, I'd say. Just the same, I'm a Reformer myself."

Doug looked his surprise. Before he could speak a strange voice broke in on them. "Out of the road, you idiots! Keep me back, will you!" Doug and Laurence swung about. A red-faced carter was standing in his wagon, long reins in one hand and a long whip doubled in the other. Neither boy had heard the wagon approach. "Jump, blast you!" the carter ordered. "I'll lay my whip about your legs." He lifted the stock of his whip threateningly. The boys jumped. "A man can't drive down the street without the gentry taking up the road," the carter complained loudly, his eye on Laurence. He was still grumbling as he started his horse.

The boys looked at each other. Fright turned into grins, and the grins grew to laughs and presently they were supporting each other helplessly as they rocked with laughter. "Blasted gentry!" Laurence wheezed at Doug. "Idiot!" Doug threw back at him. They were still laughing when Laurence tugged Doug by the arm. "Come on," he suggested. "Let's go and sit on the church steps and I'll tell you about being a Reformer."

The churchyard was deserted. The boys made their way to the steps at the back of the building. Already the bent grass had grown high around the first riser. Doug plucked a stem to chew as he sprawled out on the step below Laurence and prepared to listen.

"When I left you last week, I began to think. Actually, all I knew about the Reformers was what I had heard Father's friends say. And believe me," Laurence added wryly, "they never say any good about Reform. You should hear the Robinsons. 'Hanging is too good for the likes of Mr. Mackenzie and Jesse Ketchum and the Lounts.' " Laurence drew an imaginary rope around his neck, stuck his tongue out and made choking noises. Doug laughed at him. "Well, anyway," Laurence continued, "I decided to find out for myself. Father is a newspaper hoarder. Never throws any out. We have *The Upper Canada Gazette*, *The Observer*, Mr. Mackenzie's *Colonial Advocate* and his new *Constitution*. Stacks of them piled in our attic! So to the attic I went. I read and read — both sides. When Father came home, late from a meeting, he made me go to bed. I couldn't sleep. Not for the longest time. I did at last, of course. When I woke up in the morning, I was a Reformer." Laurence pounded the step beside him for emphasis. "Mr. Mackenzie is right. It's not fair that a few people should have all the say and all the best Government jobs in the colony."

"You're right there," Doug agreed.

Laurence went on. "Now some of the things Mr. Mackenzie says about people just aren't true. I know these people. I know they aren't the criminals he makes them out to be. But aside from all those nasty attacks on individuals, Mr. Mackenzie makes a great deal of sense. There must be a change. I was downright angry when I read how, after being elected by the people, he was thrown out of the Assembly. More than once, too. No wonder he hates the Compacters."

"I didn't know about that," Doug admitted. "But I can imagine how mad Mr. Mackenzie must have been. Anyone would be. Mr. Mackenzie can certainly get mad, too. He throws his wig when he's excited."

Laurence threw his head back and shouted gleefully. "You're making that up, Douglas the Black," he accused, still chuckling.

"No, Scotsman's honor! I got his wig in my face the first time I saw him. But the point is, he cares about justice and people. I'm sure of it. And he's great fun at night after work. He plays all kinds of games with his girls and me. He's the best sport of us all." Doug was breathless when he finished. He realized that he had developed a strong loyalty and affection for his little host even this soon after meeting him. He was suddenly embarrassed by the depth of his feeling. "But you haven't told me what your father said about your being a Reformer." He brought the conversation back to Laurence. "Did you tell him?"

"Of course I did. First thing after breakfast. I think, you know, that Father is a bit of a Reformer himself. At any rate, he told me what he always tells me, that I must think for myself. 'Be sincere, Laurie,' he always says, 'and I shall respect your beliefs.' He even agreed that there would have to be a change. He did say, though, that Mr. Mackenzie is heading for armed rebellion. Father would never approve of that." Laurence shook his head.

"No more would Da'," Doug put in quickly. "And no more would Mr. Mackenzie, I'm sure." And then Doug found himself telling Laurence all about Pat Rafferty and Limpy and his stay in Boltontown. After all, he assured himself, these things were not secret from true Reformers.

"Jove!" Laurence exclaimed when Doug had finished. "You don't half have adventures. I wish I could be with you next time, but I would have to tell Father and no one must know except the friends of Reform." Doug agreed. He began to worry a bit about telling Laurence. After all, it's easy to say, "I'm a Reformer." But Laurence was a rich man's son.

"Now!" Laurence jumped up from the steps. "It's getting on toward noon." He took a gold watch from his waistcoat pocket and looked at it. Doug's eyes were glued to the timepiece. Imagine, a boy — no older than himself — with a gold watch. His very own. He felt suddenly shy of Laurence. How could Laurence, who inhabited this other so different world, really be his friend? His doubts swept back.

It was almost as if Laurence read his thoughts. "Do you like my watch?" He unfastened the fob from his waistcoat buttonhole and passed the chain to Doug. "It belonged to my uncle, John Todd. It didn't work. Uncle John said if I could make it go, I could keep it. It went." He swung it around the chain triumphantly as Doug passed it back. "I have to admit that Father did most of the putting wheels back. Father is frightfully good with his hands. It was decent of him to help, wasn't it?"

Doug's shyness was gone. Laurence might be rich, but he did not force you to remember his father's money all the time.

"What I started to say was that I'm taking you home for a meal of bread and cheese and the end of last year's cider. Afterward, I want you to come and play in a rugby match. Peter Robinson has a team and he has challenged my friend, Archie Ridout, to get up a team. We could use you. You play, don't you?" he put in as he saw Doug's reluctance.

"Oh, yes," Doug assured him. "We play rugby at school. Mr. Vicars taught us. He went to Rugby School. He never lets us ignorant colonists forget it either."

"Good," Laurence approved. "Then it's settled."

"Maybe your friend won't want me on the team." Doug was doubtful of anyone who was acquainted with Peter Robinson.

"Of course he will. With your weight, I expect you play forward position. I do myself. Archie says I'm fast if I haven't quite got the weight. And he hates Peter Robinson. We all do. You'll be more than welcome. Will you do it?"

Doug thought a minute. "Well," he agreed presently, "if you're sure the team won't mind, I'd like to."

"Good!" Laurence was thrilled. "Come on. I'm hungry." He led the way at a run down the steps and out of the yard on Church

Street. On the path outside, he turned left. Doug followed on his heels. He wondered how it would feel to be in a rich man's house.

The most difficult moment was in following Laurence through the fine oaken door with its heavy brass knocker. One glimpse of the rich velvet draperies on the windows in the front of the house, and he turned shy. But Laurence didn't seem to notice and he dragged him along, directly to the kitchen downstairs. There he bullied a large and busy Irish cook into setting out, on the servants' table, a quick luncheon of crusty bread with butter and cheese — all to be washed down with foaming golden cider. It did not take the boys long to demolish a loaf between them and put away healthy wedges of cheese. Laurence jumped to his feet, picked up his mug to toss off the last mouthful of cider, swallowed noisily and urged Doug up. "Come on. We'll founder if we eat any more. We've got to get to the field." He dashed for the hall with Douglas crowding him behind.

"We're meeting in the grounds of Upper Canada College," Laurence explained as they left the house. If we're early, you can look over the place. There won't be anyone around. There may be a couple of masters about. I hope there are. We won't have a referree if we can't find somebody there who knows the rules. I can hardly wait to see Peter's face when he meets the Lachlan again." Laurence laughed loudly at the thought. Doug grinned a little anxiously in return. He wasn't looking forward to his reunion with Peter Robinson.

They were not the first on the field. Archie Ridout, captain of his fifteen, was ahead of them. He shook hands with Doug as he looked him over. He smiled approvingly. "You'll do nicely in the scrum with your weight and breadth." He clapped Doug's shoulder confidently.

Very soon both teams assembled. Archie, who knew nothing of the fight behind the church, introduced Doug to Peter and his two cronies, Rob and Jamie. "Peter, Rob, Jamie" — Archie hardly looked at Peter as he spoke — "this is Doug Lachlan. He's offered to play wing on our forward line."

Young Robinson did not speak. He had learned well the aristocrat's art of ignoring the lower orders. Doug said nothing either and Archie did not notice. Three of his team arrived at that moment and he darted away to greet them. Peter and his cohorts moved away. Rob and Jamie could not help looking slyly and smugly over their shoulders. But Peter moved, not as if he were leaving someone distasteful, but as if there were no one there at all. Doug's face burned red with anger. Underneath he was envious of the older boy's lordly manner. Doug turned away to look over the field to avoid seeing the ugly spark in Rob's dark eyes.

All the boys of both teams had arrived by that time. Peter and Archie knelt down to spin a coin to see which team would kick the ball into play. Archie won. He called his team together. Briefly he introduced Doug and assigned positions. Doug felt warmed by the friendly smile he received. As he moved across the field to take up his position on the left wing, he felt Laurence's slap still between his shoulder blades. For the first time since Da' had gone, he was with a group of boys his own age. It was a good feeling.

They were going to play without a referee. Archie had tried to find a master in the college building who would act for the game, but all the doors were locked and the whole place had a deserted look. "All the masters are taking advantage of the measles outbreak to have a vacation from us monsters, by the looks of it," Archie told the boys. "We're lucky really. At least there's no one to chase us off the field. And it's still in pretty good condition. Even the lines are still pretty fresh. We can see them, anyway. We don't need a referee."

"Agreed." Peter's voice was bleak. "We don't need a referee when gentlemen are playing. You may have to look to your side today, though." Doug knew Peter meant him. Archie was quick with a comeback.

"None of my boys is a cheat, Robinson," he retorted. "Look to your own team." Peter offered no reply. He moved to join his team on the other side of the halfway line.

It was in the first tight scrimmage that Doug realized that Peter was going to ignore him as much as possible. He was out to get Laurence. The ball had gone out of touch on Archie's five-yard line. The scrum was formed with Laurence as hooker, the man whose job it is to hook the ball with his feet and get it to his own team. Rob was in the front line of scrum supporting the hooker on his team. Doug in the back line on his side heard Laurence yelp in pain. "Rob, you beast, you kicked me," Laurence shouted indignantly. Another cry, another shout of anger from Laurence. "Rob, you punch me once more and I'll push your teeth through the back of your neck."

Archie spoke out, his voice tight and angry. "Shut up, Laurie. We've no referee. Play the ball. They aren't going to win, no matter how they cheat. Put the ball in play!" Doug's hot anger prickled from head to foot. Archie was right, all the same. Without a referee there was no sense in protesting, no matter what fouls were committed.

As the game progressed toward the end of the first half, it became evident that the other team had been ordered by Peter to ignore Doug and to damage Laurence as much as possible. Doug had to watch his friend, again and again, taking brutal punishment. He was taking it, too, without a murmur.

The rough treatment was most evident when Laurence began to dribble the ball toward the opponents' goal at their five-yard line. Archie shouted, "Bunch and take!" Laurence's teammates immediately closed the gap on each side as he expertly dribbled the ball toward the touch line. Rob was playing a defensive position. He rushed in on Laurence . . . bulled his way past Archie's guard . . . forced Laurence to fall on the ball. Rob's great foot swung back and forward like an iron sledgehammer. Again. Yet again. Laurence cried out once.

"Foul!" Doug shouted and threw himself forward at Rob.

Archie was ahead of him. He squared up to the bully as if he would fight him then and there. "Rob, you're a dirty player!" He eyed Peter's henchman with contempt.

"Don't, Archie!" Laurence from the ground cried out to stop the fist that Archie held before Rob's face. "I'm all right. It was an accident."

Peter pushed in between Archie and Rob. "Of course it was an accident," he declared. "It's too bad." He bent down to help Laurence up. "Rob, watch those big feet of yours." He pushed Rob away from Archie. He looked back over his shoulder. For a flashing moment the steely glint in his eye rested on Doug. "Accidents are bound to happen to traitors." He laughed lightly.

"Traitors? What are you talking about, Peter?" Archie was genuinely puzzled. Peter did not answer.

"I know what he means," Doug put in quietly. "I'm going to leave the game."

Laurence caught him by the arm as he turned away. "No, Doug," he argued. "See. I'm not hurt." He clowned around his friend, sparring at him in a sham bout like a fighter in the ring. "Stay and let's beat 'em," he urged.

"It's no use, Laurie." Doug was adamant. "I couldn't stay and see you take this sort of thing again because of me. You won't be short a man. There's a laddie over there on the grass." Doug pointed to a heavy-set boy crouched on the perimeter of the field at the halfway line. "He's been shouting for our team ever since he came to watch. He can take my place."

Laurence cast a glance in the boy's direction. "Oh, that's Tony Bellew. He's played with us before. He didn't think he could get here today."

"Good. Then I won't be letting anybody down. No. . . . " Doug put up a hand to stop Laurence's protests. "I'm going. I'll see you soon."

"I don't know what this is all about," Archie broke in, "but Lachlan knows what he's doing. I like your style, Lachlan," he said, turning to Doug. "I hope you'll play with us again some day." He offered his hand and Doug shook it hard.

"Thanks, Archie. Now I'm off. Let me know when we can get together again," he called to Laurence as he drew away.

"Tomorrow!" Laurence was quick to answer. "I'll call at Mr. Mackenzie's for you."

Doug moved off the field without looking back. Behind him he heard the game begin again. He felt sad, yet happy, too. Peter and his friends might be his enemies, but Archie and all the team had become his friends.

Chapter 16
Doug Receives New Orders

August came. Doug had been with the Mackenzies for more than four months. He had received no word from Da', but he comforted himself with the thought that the Red River colony was far away and it was still early to expect to hear from his father.

There had been no more trips to help Pat, but Doug had been kept busy. He demanded regular chores and got them. Teaching Barbara every day was one job he enjoyed. She was bright and learned quickly. There were ordinary chores, too: weeding the garden, chopping wood for the four stoves over one of which — on cool days — old Mrs. Mackenzie huddled for warmth. Running messages was an important part of his work. He soon came to know Toronto like a native. But the Mackenzies always saw that he had hours in each day to himself. Most days he spent his free time with Laurence.

School began in August and he saw Laurence less often. He began to wish he could go to school himself. Laurence urged him on. He wanted Doug at Upper Canada College with him. "Tell Mr. Mackenzie you want to come to the College," he argued. "He must want you to get an education as your father would." Doug was reluctant. School cost money that Da' would have to pay when he came back from Red River. He held out against Laurence for more than a week. One evening he decided to try Mr. Mackenzie out.

He chose a time when Mr. Mackenzie was in a very good humor. He and Doug were playing hide-and-seek with the girls. Doug hid himself under the Mackenzies' big four-poster bed. Mr.

Mackenzie had the same idea. By the light of the candle in the hall, he could faintly see Mr. Mackenzie's friendly grin as he crept under the curtains that screened the bed. This seemed the right moment to ask.

"Sir," Doug whispered.

Mr. Mackenzie put a finger to his lips warning him to be quiet. "What is it?" he whispered back.

"I would like to go to school. To Upper Canada College. Da' would pay for me when. . . ." The game came to an end. With a high-pitched snarl, Mr. Mackenzie bounded out from under the bed. The snarl turned to a roar. When Doug, white with fear, followed his host, he found the little man hopping about the hall like an angry gamecock, his face as red as a gamecock's comb.

"Traitor!" He howled at Doug. "Dare ye ask to go to that sink, the sewer of narrow, bigoted Anglicanism? That foul nest of tyrants' offspring?" Doug flung up his arms about his head as if every harsh word were a stone. Janet and Barbara clung to each other at the head of the stairs, and reproached him with sorrowful eyes for spoiling their fun. Doug fled to his attic room.

Mr. Mackenzie's anger was soon over. A few minutes later there was a rap at Doug's door. Mr. Mackenzie entered. Doug was ashamed to feel himself trying to push his frightened body through the head of his bed.

"You were right, Douglas," Mr. Mackenzie began pleasantly. "It does you credit that you want to further your education. I shall teach you myself. Come. We shall go down to my den and I shall set out a list of studies for you to begin on."

There the matter ended. But Doug had learned his lesson. Never again, if he could help it, would he be the target of that ferocious temper.

As a matter of fact, Doug had begun to notice that Mr. Mackenzie's temper was growing shorter. He noticed the change in the little Reformer after a meeting in Doel's brewery on Newgate Street on July 28, and again after a meeting there on July 31. Mr. John Doel and Mr. Mackenzie were old and fast friends. Their families were in and out of each other's homes several times a week. Mr. Doel was as gentle and patient as Mr. Mackenzie was fiery and impatient. They were an odd pair to be such close friends, but both were deeply concerned in Reform. Mr. Doel's brewery was the meeting place for all the friends of

Reform in Toronto, and it was Doug's job to carry the summons to the meetings to all these men.

Mr. Mackenzie seemed a little strange on both July evenings. His face was flushed when he came home, and he had scarcely put his foot across the threshold when he began to talk in a loud, hard voice to his wife, to his children, to his mother, to Doug — to anyone he could persuade to stop working and to listen to him.

"We must be alert to seize our chance," he told Doug in his new, hard voice. "We'll show 'em. Force! Physical force! That is our lever to open the door to freedom!'' For the first time since coming to the Mackenzies', Doug wanted to get away from his Da's old friend.

Four days after the second meeting, *The Constitution* published a list of grievances that read like a challenge to war. Mr. Mackenzie praised the revolutions of the past: the battle against King James II, The American Revolution. The whole editorial frightened Doug. The Compact would call it treason. Even to Doug it seemed as if Mr. Mackenzie were urging the people of Upper Canada to armed rebellion. Soldiers would come. They would learn about the treasonous meetings at Mr. Doel's brewery. They would find out that Douglas Lachlan had carried the summons to the meetings: *Lovers of liberty will meet tonight at seven of the clock at Doel's brewery*. The soldiers would put a rope around Doug's neck and pull him into the air to kick his life out. His face would turn red, then blue; his tongue would be pushed out of his mouth. Da' would lose the farm as father of a traitor.

He was standing in Mr. Mackenzie's den, but gallows hill was more real at that moment than the pleasant little room. When the door opened suddenly, Doug was sure the soldiers had come. His legs gave way. It was only good luck that his calves had been pressing the chair edge behind Mr. Mackenzie's desk. He fell into the seat.

"Well now, laddie." It was Mackenzie himself who came in. "I see you've been reading our editorial. What do you think of it? 'Twill make our Tory friends start looking to their guns and ammunition. They'll want to start out hanging rebels."

"Aye." Doug sounded scared, even to himself. "It will do that all right."

"Lachlan, laddie," Mr. Mackenzie went on unaware of

Doug's fright, "we're going to make a progress about our constituency. Our plans are laid. We shall travel up Yonge Street to Newmarket and then swing across to Lloydtown. Eventually we shall end up in Boltontown where you had your first experience of the world of politics." His voice dropped to a secretive whisper. He looked about him as if there might be a crowd of listeners hiding in the room. "Rafferty's going ahead to alert our well-wishers and the Reform societies. He will arrange the meeting places. I've come deliberately to seek you out. Would you go with Rafferty? You could save him a good deal of the leg work and so save time. Will you join him?"

For a moment Doug could not answer. Was this trip to be used to stir up rebellion? He had to know what he was getting into. "You are not plotting violence against the Queen's peace, Mr. Mackenzie, Sir?" Mr. Mackenzie's eyes glittered coldly at him. Doug wished he had not asked the question. He waited for that frightening high-pitched roar and for the wig to fly. Then Mr. Mackenzie smiled.

"Are you afraid, Douglas?" He reached out and put a friendly hand on Doug's shoulder. "You have the right to ask what you are getting into. You have my word. We will offer no violence unless the Tories start it. Does that ease your mind?"

"Thank you, Mr. Mackenzie. It does." Doug felt as if he could breathe again. "I'd like to work with Pat."

Mr. Mackenzie nodded, but it was as if he scarcely heard. "Understand, Lachlan" — he leaned closer to Doug — "there are men in the Family Compact who would stop at nothing to keep me from speaking to the people of this colony. Indeed, just today, I found nailed to the door of my shop, a threat to kill me. It was not signed and perhaps I should ignore it. But somehow, I think it was a genuine warning. It is to prevent an attempt on my life, laddie, that I'm asking you to go with Patrick ahead of our little band to smell out, if you can, threats against me. Pat can then decide if we must have a bigger escort to guard us."

All Mr. Mackenzie's strange looks, his secretive whispers, were gone. He spoke simply. Doug felt a rush of affection for this man who had so generously taken him into his house. "I shall be proud to serve you, Sir." Doubt and fear had vanished. Doug offered his loyalty with open hands. He wanted to offer his life. Then he felt silly. He looked away.

Young Margaret saved him. She came dancing into the study. "Papa!" she commanded. "Come! You promised you would be funny tonight. Come and be funny. We are all waiting."

"Ye're right, my Meg. I did promise. In just a moment, child."

He turned back to Doug as Margaret skipped from the room shrieking to her sisters, "Papa's coming! He's coming!"

"I've arranged the use of a horse for ye, Douglas. Tomorrow morning ye'll set out for Newmarket where ye'll meet with Rafferty. I'll have a letter for him. Now let us go and be funny men for the children."

Chapter 17
Doug Meets An Old Acquaintance

Doug cantered down the Newmarket road astride a bay rented from a livery stable. It was no thoroughbred, but it had a noble head and Doug felt like a knight of King Arthur or one of King Charles's cavaliers. The livery man had called the nag Ned, which disappointed Doug. Such a horse should have a finer name than plain Ned. Besides, he and the horse were set for adventure. With a little shiver of dread Doug remembered the serious look on Mr. Mackenzie's face as he had said good-bye and warned him: "Talk to no one on the way, Douglas. No one! Not even the time of day." Mr. Mackenzie had been threatened with death. Did he think someone might try to kill those who worked for him?

Doug's own eyes swivelled half-fearfully as he heard a clip-clop of hooves behind him. He looked back, but a bend in the road hid the horse — and its rider. He dug his heels into Ned's sides and encouraged him with cluckings into a fairly quick canter. But livery horses aren't noted for keeping up speed for long, and Ned slowed down in spite of all Doug's urging.

Doug listened. There it was again, that steady clip-clop behind him. He turned in his saddle. Against the wedge of blue sky between the towering trees he glimpsed the shape of a shovel hat — a huge black silhouette against the narrow opening of the road behind. The Reverend Alfredo Barnes. The Methodist preacher who had preached a sermon to a congregation of one, back on the road to Toronto.

"Douglas Lachlan! Douglas Lachlan! Rein up, boy, and wait for me." The powerful voice rumbled like thunder through the wooden tunnel of the road. In spite of Mr. Mackenzie's warning, Doug felt forced to wait. "Now then, boy" — the preacher's voice was sharp with accusation — "what are you doing this close to Newmarket and astride a fine horse? When we encountered before, you were riding shank's mare and glad of a ride on my poor Ira who is getting too old to take double burdens. Explain yourself, boy."

"I'm meeting a friend in Newmarket," Doug replied, and felt his cheeks grow red. "Mr. Mackenzie hired the horse for me," he hurried on, hoping the Reverend would not see the blush. Barnes narrowed his black eyes at Doug and was silent a moment.

"So," he said at last. His voice took on that false sadness that, in Doug's experience, men of the cloth often assumed. "You are still with that black vassal of Satan? Have you no word from your father?"

"No, Sir," Doug answered. No harm in admitting that. "The road is long to the Red River and the post infrequent."

"True, true. I hope, for your soul's sake, that your father will soon return and snatch you from the house of that rebellious man, that seditious editor of lies, before it is too late. Take care, take care, boy, that he does not lead you into the ways of treason. He is a disloyal subject of our new Queen. He will hang yet. See if I am not right. Beware, lest you hang with him."

Abruptly, Barnes's tone changed. It became sweet and companionable. "And who is it in Newmarket whom you ride to visit? I know most folk who live there. Perhaps we are headed for the same good Christian household."

" 'Tis a man friend. He doesn't live in Newmarket." Doug cast a sidelong glance at the big face under the hat and saw the black brows come down, the thin lips tighten.

"Are you ashamed, boy, of the company you keep? What is the man's name?" The accusing voice was big enough again to fill a large hall.

"I am not ashamed, Sir," Doug retorted stoutly. "I but thought you would not know him, Sir." Doug knew that he was all too afraid that Barnes would know Pat very well.

"His name, boy?" It was a command that Doug did not dare refuse.

"P—P—Pat Rafferty, Sir."

"Rafferty! Another traitorous scoundrel. A troublemaker of the worst sort. He turns good men against their masters. Against those, whom God, in his wisdom, has set over them. This is evil company you are keeping. Did you meet him in Mr. Mackenzie's house?"

"No, Sir." Doug's Scottish ire was up for his friend. "I do not know that Pat is a traitor or a troublemaker, but I do know that he has been badly used by gentlemen who should know better."

"You are impertinent, Douglas Lachlan." Barnes's cheeks were puffed and purple with anger.

"What is your business with this ruffian?"

"You will have to ask Pat that." Doug clapped heels to his horse, and soon Ned was far ahead of the ancient Ira. Doug drove the horse until he galloped into Newmarket village. The first person he saw was Pat. The little Irishman was lounging against the upright that supported the roof over the door of Baget's Inn. His wrinkled bottle-green coat was held open by hands plunged deep in his trouser pockets. His waistcoat was undone, revealing a none-too-clean frilled shirt. The dirty white stock about his neck was coming undone. His cheerful grin was as bright as ever as he spied Doug. Doug's anger and anxiety vanished under the warmth of it.

"Ah, 'tis me own broth of a boy, Douglas Lachlan," Pat trumpeted for all the street to hear. What a voice Pat had! The tenor, which could be murmurous as any mourning dove, could also be a clarion to rouse men to action. Doug felt it stir him. "In good time you are, me boy, and 'tis under happier circumstances altogether that we meet again. How are ye? And how is our good friend whom you left this morning?" Pat closed one eye in a prodigious wink.

"Well, Pat, well!" Even as he answered, he was climbing stiffly down from his saddle. It was a long time since he had ridden a horse and his legs felt the strain. In a moment the Irishman's thin, hard arm was about his shoulders, pressing him tight against his lean body. "Ah, but it's a fine thing to see you again. And there'll be no traitors this time to spoil our foregathering."

Doug thought of the preacher. "I hope not, Pat." He told Pat about Alfredo Barnes and his rude parting from the man. Pat's flute-like tenor laugh echoed up and down the street.

"Bedad, 'tis a beautiful tale that. The ould spalpeen. Traitor and troublemaker, am I? Well, 'tis trouble his Riverence will be having, does he interfere with you and me, me lad."

"But why does he dislike you and Mr. Mackenzie so?"

" 'Tis politics, me darlint, politics. Sure, he thinks that, by making friends with the Compact, he'll earn the gratitude of the powers-that-be and so get more in the long run than could ever be gotten from the Reformers. 'Tis as simple as that."

"The Compact have kindness for none but their own," Doug returned hotly.

"True for you, Doug! True for you!" Pat agreed. "But don't you be worrying your young head about Barnes. He can't make trouble for us. Come along into the inn. We'll have a bite-and-a-sup before we get to work. I've a room taken for us where you can wash the dust off."

After Doug had washed up, Pat led him down to the public room where a number of men were already seated and eating. Pat looked about, then led the way to a corner where they could have a small table to themselves. While Doug attacked a mountainous meal, Pat took out the letter that Doug had given to him. When he finished reading it, he put it away into an inner pocket.

"Do you know what's in this note from our little friend?" he asked. Doug could not help but smile to hear small Pat call Mr. Mackenzie "our little friend."

"No, not altogether. Mr. Mackenzie did tell me," he confessed, "that someone had threatened his life. He told me he was leaving it to you to decide whether he needed a guard."

"That's the most of it," Pat said, nodding agreement. "The rest is mostly what road he will take to Lloydtown and Boltontown and whatever. He reminds me to arrange for a platform. He's a small man and is hard to see in a crowd unless he stands high. Bedad and we have a nice little wagon for him. Herman Schmidt, who farms north of here, owns it. It's painted in the German fashion. Bright colors. William the Lion will love it." Pat beamed with pride.

"Mr. Mackenzie will be pleased," Doug agreed. He likes things different and new. What will we do. . . . I mean . . . will *you* do about a guard for him?"

"You were right to say 'we.' We're partners in this. I think no guard will be needed here in Newmarket, though you and I must find men for a guard farther on.

"Now," Pat continued, "if you've eaten your fill we'll go up to our room and work. I have a list of names and a map for you. You will take the south road, while it's meself will call on our good friends to the north. Och! We'll have a crowd out to hear him. The Compacters will be shaking in polished boots."

Doug had not realized until that moment how dark it had grown in the corner where they were sitting. The lamps had not yet been lit, and the high-backed benches cut off most of the light that came in through the smoky-looking bottle-glass windows.

A similar arrangement of table and high-backed benches was set up against the other wall of their corner. As Doug scrambled after Pat he was vaguely aware of two dark figures pressed against the wall in the shadow of the bench backs. Although he caught only a glimpse as he hurried past, he felt a disturbing sense of recognition. Yet neither man was Reverend Barnes. He was sure of that. Should he go back? Pat was on the stairs beckoning. Doug shrugged his shoulders and wove his way quickly through the tables to join him.

Next morning Pat and Doug were up before the sun. They sat at the same table for their breakfast. From the kitchen behind them came the rattle of dishes, the banging of pans, the rich smell of frying ham, and the sound of eggs cracking into a pan.

Doug remembered the men in the shadows at the next table. He craned around his seat to see. The table was empty. He thought of speaking about them to Pat, but the Irishman was spilling plans at a great rate. Plans for Mr. Mackenzie's coming. Plans for the "Day" — when the Compact would be beaten. Doug did not like to interrupt. When the chance came to speak, he forgot.

Chapter 18
Doug Is Captured By The Enemy

Breakfast over, the two went out to the stables behind the inn to saddle their horses. The August morning was cool. Doug was glad of his old homespun jacket. They mounted and rode out of the yard into the main street that stretched north and south. Pat held his steed on a light rein, for the black he rode was eager to go. "Take care, Douggie boy," he cautioned, "and don't be talking to any Mrs. Horrockses." He grinned. "Ye'll do fine, laddie. I don't think there are any of her kind hereabouts. We'll meet at supper time, but don't forget I've planned that you'll be at the Wilkinsons about the time of the noon meal. Mrs. Wilkinson is the cook of the county. She loves to feed good appetites. She'll look after you. Bless you, and away with you!"

Doug turned his horse's head to the south and cantered down the dusty street that led to the outskirts of town. As he rode, he took off his cap and looked under the band for the folded map Pat had given him. It was there when he needed it. Pat had not encouraged him to memorize it this time. "There's not the hard feelings about Newmarket district that are to be found in Bolton-town," Pat had assured him. Doug put his hat back on his head. For the present he had only to ride five miles along this road to Josh Barrow's farm, with not a turn or a sideroad to lead him in a false direction.

Beyond the town, a mile or a bit more, the road ran through a stand of maples. Here and there, a glint of red showed in the sun. Soon, Doug knew, all the leaves would turn, and the glint of red would change to a blazing glory. Doug kicked Ned's sides and pushed him to a gallop. It was good to be alive, to have a horse under you. To be free on such a beautiful August morning. Ned was ready to go. He pounded down the way, raising a fine trail of dust. In no time at all they were in the shadows of the trees.

Suddenly Ned shied. Two figures had jumped out into the road. Ned reared on dancing hind legs. Up, up he rose until Doug felt himself sliding back over the saddle. He kicked his feet free of the stirrups and jumped clear. Everything happened at once. One moment he was shouting to Ned, urging him on; the next, he was rolling over and over on the dusty path. His cap flew from his head into the bushes at the side of the road. His last roll brought him sitting upright — looking at Ned who trembled and whinnied with fright, his bridle held tight in the large hand of the Reverend Alfredo Barnes. Doug had no time to wonder. He was seized under the arms from behind and jounced to his feet. He cast his eyes up to look into his captor's face. Dawson! Dawson, the storekeeper from Boltontown. The man in the shadow of the settle in the inn parlor. He knew now who the other had been. He should have remembered that huge bulk. Colonel Golightly. He looked around for Porker. He was nowhere in sight.

"Got you!" Dawson snapped and grabbed Doug's wrist. In a trice Doug's arm was behind his back. His fist was pushed painfully up between his shoulder blades. "Now then," Dawson barked, "no tricks, my lad. Turn the horse loose, Reverend, and give me a hand." He needed help. In spite of the pain, Doug was kicking out with his heels at the storekeeper's shins.

When the preacher let the bridle go, Ned bolted down the road. Doug fought harder as, from the edge of his eye, he saw Barnes start toward him. Dawson's grip tightened. He gave Doug's arm a savage jerk. Doug felt fire run from his shoulder to his fingertips. The fire burned away his resistance.

"In my pocket," Dawson panted. "Rope. Tie him up. Ankles first." Doug forced himself to struggle again. His flashing heels got the minister somewhere. He heard the man groan. The end was inevitable. He had no chance against two grown men. The rope bit into the cords above his heels. His wrists were lashed together in front of him. Dawson and Barnes on either side of him jostled him into the maple grove. He made it as hard for them as he could. He arched and flexed his body at every step. He soon saw their goal: the low, sugaring-off shed in the centre of the maple bush. It was a stout building of logs. There was a door in

J. MERLE SMITH

the side and one small window up under the eaves. The broken parchment that had been used to cover the frame in place of glass was broken. Some dry rags of hide rattled in the morning breeze. Doug's fear made him strangely aware of that sound, and of the panting of the two men.

Dawson took the peg out of the hasp of the heavy plank door. The hinges whined and screeched as the door swung open. Doug's nerves jangled with the noise. It sounded like the snarl of some threatening beast. Dawson pushed him into the dim, sticky, sweet-smelling shed.

"I'll teach you to turn my town against me with your spying and tale-bearing. See if I don't." Dawson gave Doug a thrust that sent him toppling into the cleared space of the hut. All about the walls were piled the oaken sap buckets and the iron kettles.

It was the preacher who helped Doug to his feet. "You will come to no harm, Lachlan," he murmured as he hoisted Doug up. "We simply want some information which you can give us. The map which Rafferty made for you. It has the names of the people you were riding out to contact."

"Aye, the map," Dawson broke in. "You have it, so don't lie about it. I heard Rafferty last night at supper say he had one. Where is it?"

Doug blessed the luck that had knocked his cap off his head. Perhaps his captors would not think of it.

"I haven't got it." Doug tried to keep his voice bold but he was disgusted to hear it come out in a quaver. He tried again. "I haven't got it and I wouldn't give it to you if I had." That sounded better. He tossed his hair back out of his eyes and tried to glare at his tormentors.

"We'll see whether you have or not," Dawson threatened. Quick hands dived into the side pockets of Doug's jacket. Buttons flew as Dawson tugged at him to search pockets. Angry fingers pinched his thighs cruelly as the man felt for papers in the trouser pockets. Finding nothing, Dawson cuffed Doug across the side of the head. "He hasn't got it," he confessed angrily.

"It would seem that you are telling the truth, boy." Barnes's voice was almost gentle. "That means you have memorized the names and places. Colonel Golightly would like to know who are rebelling against the Queen's governors. You do not want to be thought a rebel, do you, Lachlan?"

"I'm no rebel!" Doug's voice was firm. He was angry now, not afraid. "Nor are my friends rebels," he added.

"Good," Barnes cut in smoothly. "Then you will not mind telling us who these friends are."

Doug said nothing.

Dawson snatched the loose end of the rope that bound Doug's wrists. He unwound it from around Doug's shoulders and threw it over the cross-beam. He caught the dangling end and pulled viciously on it so that Doug's arms were jerked above his head and he was yanked up on his toes. Dawson snagged the end over a peg set in the wall. Without another word he turned and strode out of the hut. Doug felt Barnes's hand clap down on his shoulder.

"Be persuaded, Lachlan," the soft voice coaxed. "Mr. Dawson has gone to cut a stick. He will beat the names out of you. He has orders from the Colonel. I doubt I can restrain him. He is very wroth with you because of what happened at Boltontown. Tell me the names. I will try to save you from a drubbing."

Doug could hear Dawson hacking with his knife just outside the door. To his horror he felt his whole body shudder under Barnes's hand. The preacher felt it, too. He hastened to take advantage of the body's betrayal. "I don't wonder that you shake, Lachlan. A beating is a fearsome punishment for doing what evil men have persuaded you into. You are too innocent to know their wicked purposes. You have been used, Lachlan. Now you are alone to face the consequences. Quick, tell me the names! Mr. Dawson is returning."

Doug heard Dawson's foot inside the door. "Now we'll get those names, Reverend," he gloated.

"Wait. Let me reason with the boy," Barnes begged.

"No. We must have the names." The voice came from the doorway. Doug could not turn to see, but he had no need. No one could forget the Porker's fruity tones. Now that the dirty work of catching the quarry was over, the Colonel could appear without dirtying his soft, pudgy hands. "Beat them out of him." There was nasty anticipation in the words. Doug wondered if the Colonel had yet connected him with Jim Grissler's "cousin." He hoped his back was just another boy's back to the fat man. The Colonel's next words destroyed that hope. "I want to know his connection with Grissler as well. I'll have something to take back to Major Bolton that will persuade him that Grissler is a traitor. Then we can drive him out of our town.''

"All right, you young jackanapes. Let's hear you sing." Dawson brandished the stick under Doug's nose. It was about four feet long and as thick as the man's thumb. He beat the air with a sickening swish. His lips smiled, but his eyes were as hard and flat as chips of charred wood. "When I finish with you, you'll tell us everything you know.''

"Lachlan! Speak!" Barnes cried out, and Doug was surprised to hear real anguish in the man's voice. He only braced his shoulders as well as his bound wrists would let him and hunched his head down to save it as much as possible.

Dawson grabbed the tails of Doug's jacket and pulled them roughly up over his head so that the skirts of it covered his face, smothering him in the folds. There was another swish, but at the end of it came a thwack that made the pain shoot in streaks down Doug's back and flanks to his toes, then up his arms to his fingertips. Swish! Thwack! The pain and the smell of maple sugar together made a sweetness in his mouth. Again, and again, and again. Never twice in the same place. Each blow radiated out over his body like a bright red explosion. Suddenly his stomach heaved and he was sick into the folds of his jacket. The light went out. He felt himself pitch forward into an avalanche of darkness.

Chapter 19
Doug Finishes His Job

When Doug opened his eyes, he was alone. It was almost dark, for the door was closed. His wrists and ankles ached from the tightness of the ropes. He was half-lying, propped up against a pile of sap buckets. His tormentors had at least let him down from the beam. He shifted a bit and the hard edge of a bucket bit into the welts on his back. He stifled a groan. He could taste and smell his own vomit. He was close to sinking back into darkness. He fought the black mist and forced himself to an erect sitting position. The movement hurt him almost more than he could bear. He made himself listen. No sound. The three had gone. Or were they standing silent outside the door, waiting for him to make a move? If they were there, they must move sometime. He held himself straight and put his whole being into his ears. Not a whisper. Even the breeze seemed to have died down. It was stiflingly hot in the hut.

"I can't stay here," Doug told himself. "I've got to let people know about Mr. Mackenzie. Pat is counting on me. Even if they are out there, the worst they can do is beat me again. I've got to try to get away."

His first task was to free his ankles and wrists. He tried to turn his hands in against the bindings on his wrists. He could not get at the knots. "At least," he thought, "my hands are in front of me. I should be able to untie my feet." He bent forward. His back felt as if he were shredding the skin in strips from his neck to his waist. He had a picture in his mind of the skin hanging in rags from his spine. He forced the picture away and busied himself with the ropes about his legs. It was difficult to keep his balance with his hands tied together and his feet drawn up close under him so that he could reach the knots. Somehow he managed it. First one tight knot and then the second fell away under his fingers. His feet were free. He had moved too fast trying to rise and had to sit for a long minute to let the giddiness caused by the pain flow out of him. Slowly he struggled to one knee, then to his feet.

In the dimness from the small window beside the door he crossed the open space. Were Dawson and Golightly out there waiting for him? He had been so busy freeing himself he had forgotten to listen. He put his ear to the door. He stood unmoving. Not a sound. He put his bound hands to the handle of the door and pulled. It would not give. The oak peg had been dropped into the loop of the hasp. Perhaps if he were not so sore, if he could stand the flickering lightnings of pain, he might be able to break the peg.

He listened again. Had his rattling of the door alerted the men to his returned consciousness? Did they know he was trying to escape? Still no sound. They must have gone away. But surely they did not intend to leave him here. He did not know whether to be angry or glad that they had gone away. Did they intend to come back? He must be gone if they did.

If the door would not give, what about the window? It was small, but it looked big enough for him to wriggle through. Just. But how could he reach it? If only he could get the rope off his hands. He tried again to reach the knots. No use. And the rope was new. It would take a long time to rub it to the breaking point — even if there were an edge to rub it on. Whatever he did would have to be done with bound hands. He looked about him. The first thing to do was to reach the sill.

The big iron kettle, used for boiling the sap, stood overturned in the far corner. It wouldn't be high enough to allow him to crawl right out. But perhaps, placed under the window, it would allow him to see out, see how the land lay. Perhaps he would get an idea that would help. He crossed over to the big vessel and began to push and pull at it, as well as he could, to a place under the opening. He was forced to stop and rest. The bending and the movement made every inch of his back burn like fire. He knew now that the skin was broken in at least one place. His undershirt was stuck to it. Stooping pulled the wound fiercely.

When the weakness had passed, he scrambled up on the bottom of the kettle. He braced his feet against its wobble. His head and shoulders were even with the opening in the wall. He looked out. Everything was still. He heard a jay scolding at some distance, but that was the only sound from all the surrounding trees. He thought of shouting. Who would hear? At this time of year, no one. Except the men who had locked him in. He did not want to attract their attention. The wide eaves above the window kept him from seeing the sun as it shone into the clearing. From the shadow of the trees on the left side — the east side — he was able to judge that the morning was not too far gone. He could not have lain unconscious very long.

He turned his back on the scene outside. Bending backward, he thrust his head through the ragged hole of parchment. He looked up at the logs over the window. There it was, just as he had hoped — an oaken peg driven into the log just above the window at the left-hand corner of the frame, less than a foot above his head. A companion peg should have been on the right side to help support a shutter. Lucky for him it was missing. Otherwise the shutter would have been in place and escape impossible. The peg that was still in place looked sound. It should bear his weight.

He bent back farther to get his hands up and outside. The edge of the frame cut into his back. For a moment the pain made him so dizzy that he could scarcely see the peg. He forced his arms up and grasped the peg between his tied hands. He pulled. The peg was like iron. Good. He pulled harder so that his toes scarcely touched the iron pot under his feet. Da' had always been proud of having a son with such strong arms. How often Da' had held out his own arm when Doug was quite small; Doug, clinging like a bobcat, almost by his finger nails, would chin himself over and over. When he was older, he had used the door frames. Think of those days; think of Da' and the proud gleam in his eye. Think of anything except the pain that grew and grew until it was outside the body, was the roof overhead, was the whole world.

Slowly he scraped himself upward across the sharp edge of the window frame. The tears filled his eyes, ran out the sides down into his ears. He had to stop and shake his head to clear them away. He panted for breath. The pain burned out from his back to his fingers and toes. He waited until he could bear to move again.

Slowly, slowly. Up. Up. His hips rested on the sill. The pain was a little easier now. The worst was over. His head was above the peg. It was hard now to get leverage to lift his body higher. He jerked himself hard. The effort forced a muffled yell from him. But he had made it. He was sitting on the sill. He sat a moment and the pain flowed over him again. "You have to keep moving," he told himself. Dawson had not spared hips and legs with his stout staff, but the skin was sound. Doug wriggled his hips out, then his thighs, then his calves. His body made a big triangle from his hands almost straight out to his hips, then down and in to the soles of his feet that rested on the edge of the window.

This was the ticklish part. His hands were sweating. He could scarcely hold the smooth peg. If he slipped now, he would have a nasty six-foot fall on his sore back. He let one foot slip down till his toe caught a crevice between the logs. Then the other. An inch at a time, he lowered himself until his body was straight again. His weight was on the peg in his grasp. He let go and dropped the six inches to the ground. He was free!

He wasted no time celebrating his victory. He darted a glance from side to side, then stumbled for trees on the eastern edge of the clearing. Once among their shadows, he drew a long breath of satisfaction and headed toward the road.

When he saw the dusty track ahead of him as the trees thinned, he slowed and crept quietly to the edge of the bush and peered out. As far as he could see either way, the road was empty. Fair enough! He stepped out on the road. He was a little above the place where the two men had caught him. He must look for his cap. Perhaps they had found it. Found the map with the names on it. Perhaps that was why they had gone away. With narrowed eyes he scanned the bushes on his left. "There it is!" he shouted out in his excitement. The cap was almost hidden in the long grass under a tree. He ran to it, picked it up awkwardly with his two hands, and tried to feel for the paper under the band. He couldn't manage it. He set it down again on the grass and knelt on the peak. The crackle of paper under his fingers made him smile with satisfaction. The map was safe. Now to get to the Barrows' farm. Before nightfall, even counting the time lost, the job would be done. He tried to run. Every pounding step, every uneven spot on the road, sent cold shivers of pain through his body. He gritted his teeth and ploughed on.

A sudden snort stopped him in his tracks. A horse. Dawson? Barnes? He sprang to the side of the road and hid behind a tree and waited. He listened. No hoof beats. So that was it. The two devils had expected him to escape. They were waiting hidden around a little bend in the road. They would follow and find out where he went. Well, they were going to be disappointed. Doug stood where he was, pondering the best course to take. Another sudden snort! Doug's eyes narrowed in alarm. Had they heard him? Were they coming to get him? A horse stepped into the middle of the bend. "Ned!" Doug shouted. The bay threw up his head, but he did not bolt. He stood even when Doug pelted out of his hiding place and caught the dragging reins. Doug caught the saddle-horn in his two hands. Somehow he got his foot up into the stirrup and sprawled over the saddle. Ned waited patiently. After what seemed a long time, Doug managed to swing his right leg across Ned's back. His foot found the other stirrup.

"Good old Ned!" he whispered shyly. "You didn't desert me. I thought you would be halfway to Toronto by this time." The horse snorted again. Doug swung his head in the direction of the Barrows' farm. Even though he had to stand up in the stirrups to save his back, it was much better than walking.

The excitement of planning and making his escape had sustained Doug so far, but as he rode into the Barrows' houseyard all the energy drained out of him. All he wanted now was to stop and lie down and give in to the pain. He knew that if he got down from Ned, he could never get up again this day. His throat was dry. It hurt to swallow. His mouth was sour from his vomit. Ned came to a standstill on the drive before the door. For a moment Doug hung over Ned's neck, trying to summon the strength to call out. At last, he raised his head. "Ho, the house!" he croaked.

The door opened even as he called. A kindly-faced woman stepped out. Her grey hair was drawn back so tightly to the knob at the back of her head that the weathered, brick-red skin gleamed whitely over her high cheekbones. She must have seen the horse and rider approach.

"Save us!" she exclaimed. "What has happened to you,

young man? You look fair beat. Climb down and come in. You could do with a spot of rest and food, I'd say."

"No. No." Doug tried to sound firm, though every impulse of his body argued to obey. "No, I mustn't. I've a long way to ride yet. But would you untie my hands? Are you Mrs. Barrow?"

The woman did not answer. Her eyes were on Doug's wrists. The skin was puffed and white around the rope. "Save us!" she exclaimed again. "Who has been mistreating you, boy?" She busied herself as she questioned, fighting the knots with work-roughened fingers.

"Are you Mrs. Barrow?" Doug asked again. He could scarcely hear the reply as the rope slipped loose and the blood rushed like hot knives into his dead wrists and hands. From a great distance he saw the woman nod and was aware of her tears of sympathy and the anxious look in her motherly eyes. His own eyes blurred with tears of pain.

"You must get down," she insisted. "You're not fit to go on."

"I must!" Doug almost shouted. The sympathy threatened to melt his resolution. "I've been delayed as it is." And then he found himself telling what had happened to him. He had to take a firm hold on himself to keep his story short. He knew that if he talked too long he would begin to cry.

"Ah, that Dawson!" Mrs. Barrow clucked with disgust. "My husband saw him yesterday when he went to town. All over my Josh, Dawson was. Tried to find out how Josh felt about Reform. We're Mackenzie folks hereabouts, but Josh gave Dawson no satisfaction, I can tell you. We heard about the trouble he got into with our friends in Boltontown. Josh was suspicious of him. But here I am talking away and you suffering. Are you sure you must away? I could easily call Asa, my son. You could give him your list and he'd notify all. He'd be proud to do it."

"No, I must do it." Doug was sure now. "If you would give me a drink of water, I'd not trouble you more. You have been most kind, Ma'am."

"Kind, you say! If I were a kind woman, I'd have seen you were dying of thirst." She began to hustle toward the door. "What you need is milk. Water is too cooling to the stomach on a hot day. Besides, 'twill give you strength if you're determined to see it through. I've baked some fresh bread. . . . " Her voice trailed off as she disappeared into the house. Doug put his head down against Ned's mane. He was almost asleep when Mrs. Barrow returned, a big pewter tankard in one hand and a plate heaped high with warm, yeasty slices of white bread and butter in the other.

"Now eat that. Every scrap of it," Mrs. Barrow ordered. "You need food, my boy. And while you eat, I'll call Asa in from the fields. He will ride with you. No," she interrupted as Doug attempted to speak, "I'll not hear another word. If you must go, you'll have my Asa with you. He's only seventeen, but anybody would think twice before tackling him. Wait till you see him. He's a giant. Never have been able to figure how I ever begot one as big as Asa."

Mrs. Barrow was still talking as she disappeared into the house, to pop out again a moment later with an old army bugle in her hand. "My husband's," she explained to Doug, seeing him eyeing the instrument. "He was a bugler for General Brock in the American war back in fourteen." She threw the bugle to her lips and three loud blasts rang on the still air. "Three for Asa, two for Josh. I can't play a tune on the plaguey thing, though Josh tried to teach me to play reveille when we were both young. But, save us, I can wake the dead with it when I want to. Now, don't you feel better?" The bread and milk had gone to the last crumb and drop. Doug realized he had been starved. He did feel stronger.

" 'Twas manna from heaven, Ma'am," he said simply.

"Have some more. It will take Asa a few minutes to get here and then he'll have to saddle a horse. You'll have time to eat if you can choke it down. I'd feel easier, though, if you would climb down off that beast and rest yourself." Doug shook his head. Mrs. Barrow rattled on over his protests. She rattled in and out of the house with more milk and bread. She rattled an encouragement as he munched steadily through the thick slices. Doug was grateful for her talk. It kept his mind from his aches and pains.

Asa was a giant and no mistake. He seemed to tower as tall as the house. Doug wondered how the huge blond ever got those massive shoulders through the door. Mrs. Barrow had not waited for Asa to saddle a horse. Without, it seemed, any break in the flow of words, she had gone to the stable to bring out a big roan with a blanket already on his broad back. She had lugged out a saddle and had heaved it up into place. She had cinched the girth strap, lifting a skirted knee hard to knock the air out of the animal as she tugged the belt tight. The horse was ready for Asa when he appeared. The rattling stopped the moment the big fellow rounded the corner of the house. Mrs. Barrow wasted no words.

"This is Doug Lachlan, Asa," she explained. "I want you to go with him. He'll tell you where. Mr. Mackenzie's business. When you're through, you'll bring him back for the night. He's been beaten to a frazzle and his back needs attention. But he's a stubborn Scot. He won't stop now. Be off with the two of you."

As Doug rode out of the yard, he felt a load of worry fall from him. Asa had said not a word in reply to his mother. He had simply mounted and waited for Doug to lead the way. Doug knew a security, the kind of security he felt with Da', in the company of this huge man. Not a man yet. It was hard to remember that Asa was only two years older than Doug himself.

It was a nightmare day altogether, but in spite of his increasing soreness and weariness, Doug felt a sense of accomplishment. He had finished what he set out to do. Pat would be pleased. Mr. Mackenzie, too.

In the last glimmer of summer light he slipped from the saddle into Asa's waiting arms. He let himself be carried into the Barrow's kitchen and finally up the stairs to a down-filled bed. He was asleep even as his head touched the pillow. He was not aware of Asa easing the clothes off his blood-clotted back. He did not feel Mrs. Barrow's fingers, gentle despite their roughness, working bear grease into all his aching muscles.

He missed Mr. Mackenzie's speech in Newmarket. He slept through it all. He had half-wakened, just enough to swallow the spoonfuls of oat porridge that Asa put into his mouth. He had slept through the family's preparations to go to town. At last, by the light of the lamp on the table by the bed, he opened his eyes to see two faces, Pat's and Mr. Mackenzie's, bending anxiously over him. He smiled at them.

"Ah, you're right as rain, me own fine hero," Pat said softly. "Go to sleep again, me bucko."

"Good laddie," Mr. Mackenzie whispered. "Thanks to you, we've had a wonderful reception in Newmarket." Doug snuggled down in the quilts. His last view was of the little Scotsman and the little Irishman fighting gently over the top quilt to see who would tuck it about his shoulders.

Chapter 20
The Reverend Barnes Makes A Visit

Because of what had happened to Doug, Pat decided to double the guard he had rounded up to protect Mr. Mackenzie. Some twenty staunch Reformers, armed with shot guns, old muzzle-loaders, ancient pikes, and just plain cudgels, went with the little Reform leader wherever he travelled. So ready were they to fight that in no town in the riding did any Tory dare to raise a voice. Not so much as to heckle.

Though Doug missed the first speech and the one at King next day, by the third day he felt able to travel again. Mrs. Barrow did not think so. She said as much.

"I cannot bide this bed another hour, Mrs. Barrow," Doug protested. "You'll make a babbie out of me. Besides, Mr. Mackenzie needs me."

"Rubbish!" Mrs. Barrow retorted. "Mr. Mackenzie has twenty men at his beck and call this minute. My Asa among them. If he cannot do with that many henchmen, the Lord help him. If you had seen yourself when you rode up to my door, just a scant three days ago! You fair broke my heart. I didn't know what to say to you, and you so determined to go on. You aren't in any condition to be gallivanting around with a fit-for-a-fight bunch of men. Do rest easy, like a good boy. Just one more day."

"Not even half a day, Mrs. Barrow. I'm a fit-for-a-fight fellow myself. Right this minute. Please bring my clothes, Mrs. Barrow. I somehow remember that you took them away."

"They weren't fit to put on. I've cleaned them as best I can. They smell sweet again, at any rate. I've mended what needed mending. Put new buttons on your shirt and coat. Ah, I'd like to get my best iron skillet to work on those who abused you so.'' Her plain face grew fierce as she thought of his ordeal. "Well,'' she finished up, "I see you're determined. I'll not try further to persuade you. I'll get your clothes.''

She bustled from the room. She did everything in a bustle, Doug decided. In less than five minutes she was back. Her grey-brown eyes were as round and frightened as the tight-drawn hair at her temples would allow.

"You'll not believe it, Douglas,'' she burst out as she opened the door. "You'll not believe it,'' she repeated. She cast a frightened glance over her shoulder into the hall. "He's riding up to the door this living minute. As sure as my name is Hannah Barrow. He's coming here!''

"Who, Mrs. Barrow?'' Doug was puzzled.

"The Reverend Alfredo Barnes. That's who. And here's Asa with Mr. Mackenzie, and Josh in the fields. I'll lock the doors and call Josh in with the bugle. I'll blow out the back-kitchen window.'' She started at a run out of the room.

"No!'' Doug's fierce tone stopped the woman in her tracks. His heart was pounding with a mixture of fear and anger. His belly felt empty. His throat was tight. "No! Reverend Barnes would not attack us both. I won't run away from him. Da' would be ashamed. Let him in, Mrs. Barrow. I'll dress as fast as I can and be down before you have to say two words to him. Go on, Mrs. Barrow,'' he urged as he saw her hesitate. "I can't get out of bed till you do.'' He smiled at her and saw a flicker cross her taut face.

"I guess you've recovered,'' she said dryly. "You weren't so dainty three days ago.'' Doug blushed, but he began to put the covers of the bed back firmly. Mrs. Barrow looked startled. She hastened away. He still felt wobbly as he put his feet on the floor and it hurt to bend over, but he reached for his clothes and scrambled into them. He could hear the rumble of Barnes's voice and Mrs. Barrow's lighter voice. He could make out no words until he opened the bedroom door and stood on the landing.

"Shame on you! A grown man, too!'' The preacher was getting the rough edge of Mrs. Barrow's tongue. You could tell she was frightened, but she was gamely standing up to the big man. As Doug went down the stairs, he could see that Barnes's

eyes were on the ground. There was a sag to the wide shoulders. Indeed, there was a grateful look in the brown eyes that lifted to the sound of Doug's foot on the polished steps.

"Ah, Lachlan, I am happy to see you up and about," Barnes boomed in his best church voice.

"Hypocrite," Mrs. Barrow spat. There was a red spot on each of her wind-weathered cheekbones. Her lips were sucked tightly against her cheeks. Barnes said nothing. His broad brow furrowed, but whether with anger or pain Doug could not be sure. Anger or pain, it made no difference to Doug. He just wasn't afraid any more.

"You wanted to see me, Reverend?" Doug asked coolly.

"I have come most humbly to offer my apologies for what occurred the other day." The minister's voice was very quiet. He looked Doug straight in the eye.

"This must be hard for him," Doug thought. He was surprised that he could feel even a little sorry for the man. "I wonder how long it is since he apologized to anyone." He put out his hand as he saw Mrs. Barrow open her mouth to speak. Her teeth came together with a sharp click.

"You may find it hard to believe, but, as a man of God, I swear that I never meant that you should be hurt," Barnes continued. Every word seemed to knot the tongue that could be so glib. "I thought Dawson meant to frighten you with the stick. I realize now you could not be intimidated. You are a lad of courage. Your father should be proud of you." Doug felt the sandy ache of tears held back. He swallowed hard. "It seemed as if a paralysis overtook me, Lachlan, in the face of Dawson's vengefulness and the Colonel's wicked delight in your pain. I could not believe it was happening. Not until you fainted, did I muster my wits to wrest the stick from Dawson. I let you down. Then I forced both men to come away with me. I locked you in because I was afraid that someone, seeing the door open, might enter and, thinking you a willful trespasser, mistreat you further. I made them ride to town with me, but, as soon as I could I hastened back to succor your hurts. You were gone. How, I still cannot imagine. It all sounds very lame, even to me. But as God is my witness, it is the truth. I heard only by accident today where you were. I have wrestled in prayer for you night and day since the event. I beg you to forgive me so that I can make my peace with God. So that my sinful self-righteousness may be forgiven by the Lord of all.''

Doug could believe him. Barnes had black circles under his eyes. His face was anguished. He seemed to have shrunk even as he talked. Doug's fear had gone, now his anger died away. He pitied Barnes.

''I don't bear any grudge, Sir,'' Doug assured Barnes. He meant it — for Barnes. Dawson and the Porker were a different bowl of oats. He could never forgive them.

''Thank you, Lachlan.'' Barnes sounded as humble as you could expect from him. ''You have taken a load of self-condemnation from my shoulders. But I still cannot approve your companions.'' His tone was hardening into its customary ministerial boom. ''God will not be mocked, and it is the duty of all men who love God to hang a rebel.''

''Let us not quarrel again, Sir,'' Doug broke in as the sermon threatened to go on. ''I will not hear bad things of Pat and Mr. Mackenzie. Nor of Mrs. Barrow here. Not of any of my friends. I have forgiven you, Sir. Let us leave it at that.''

Barnes's face turned a dark purple. For a moment Doug thought that the preacher would have apoplexy. The corners of his mouth dribbled spittle. Doug could see the tongue working inside the stiff jaws. He turned without another word, threw open the door, and strode out into the yard. He left the door wide open behind him.

''Douggie, boy, I'm proud of you.'' Mrs. Barrow hugged him with strong arms. Doug tried not to wriggle but he was embarrassed. He did not feel proud of himself. Da' would say he had only been very impertinent.

Pat and Mr. Mackenzie and Asa were very interested in hearing of Barnes's call. They listened intently as Mrs. Barrow told of it, but soon their minds turned to details of the tour Mr. Mackenzie was making of the hustings. Doug was glad when they began to speak of a visit that Mr. Mackenzie was going to make to Samuel Lount, the Reform representative from Holland Landing.

''If you are recovered, laddie,'' Mr. Mackenzie offered, ''I shall be glad of your company. Asa is coming along and four or five other stout fellows who think I need protecting. Feel up to it, Douglas?''

"Oh aye, Sir. When are we going?" Doug was eager, but he could not help noticing how much satisfaction Mr. Mackenzie obtained from his armed escort. He had an uneasy feeling about it, though he could not explain why.

"Tomorrow morning, lad. Your bed is still awaiting you at the inn. When we have eaten that fine-smelling supper Mrs. Barrow is preparing, we shall all repair to the town for a good night's sleep. We shall make an early start in the morning. I want a good, long time with Sam Lount. If rebellion comes, and every day makes it seem more inevitable, Sam will lead his people to join us wherever we set up the standard of revolt."

"Don't speak like that, Sir," Doug protested. "You promised just before I left Toronto that there would be no rebellion. What has changed you, Sir?"

"Look at what happened to you, boy. When servants of Reform can be kidnapped and beaten in broad daylight, we must look to our defences. We must face facts bravely, Douglas," Mr. Mackenzie returned soothingly. "Without a show of force, the Tories will never grant us liberty and our rights. The common man must show himself ready to fight. Thank God we Canadians have spirit. Be proud to be remembered in the ranks of Reform.

"Now, I see Mrs. Barrow is ready for us. Let us go in and do justice to her hospitality." Doug rose with Mr. Mackenzie and Pat and the Barrow men and went into the dining room. His hunger had vanished, but he went through the motions of eating.

He did not bother to listen to the talk that went buzzing over his head. He frowned with the struggle to sort out in his mind what Mr. Mackenzie had said against what he knew of Da's beliefs. At last he shook his head and put the problem out of his mind for the time being. Da' was far away. For a moment Doug forgot Mr. Mackenzie and rebellion and let his mind dwell on that fact: Da' was far away — why had he not written? Surely, by now, there should have been a letter. Doug felt an empty feeling of sure fright growing in his chest. His breath came faster. Deliberately, he brought his mind back to consider Mr Mackenzie's attitude again. Da' had sent his son to Mr. Mackenzie. He had ordered Doug to obey Mr Mackenzie in everything. That was all he had to think about — his duty to Da' and the little Reformer.

With that thought there came a kind of peace in Doug's mind. And with that peace came a feeling of excitement. Who knew what adventures might come in this trip with Mr. Mackenzie?

Chapter 21
Doug Takes Part In A Battle

The next morning early they rode to Holland Landing. Mr. Mackenzie was put in the middle of the party with Pat on one side and Asa on the other. That is, they rode like this when the way was broad enough to ride three abreast — which wasn't often. Four other men, with guns across their saddles, had joined the party in front of the inn before setting-out time. They were farmers from 'round about who had volunteered to serve as Mr. Mackenzie's guardians for the expedition. Two of them rode well in front and two brought up the rear. All of them had grim faces and little to say. They had shaken hands warmly with Doug when he was introduced, and had inquired as to the state of his hurts. But when the company turned north, the men again set their faces grimly to the task, and that task precluded idle chatter.

Doug had a scary feeling as he watched them ride along. Their eyes darted at every thicket or tree large enough to hide an enemy. For the first time he could really believe Mr. Mackenzie's life was in danger. Even his beating by Dawson had not made him aware of the peril in the same way. That, up to now, had loomed only as a case of personal revenge for what had happened at Boltontown. Now it seemed to become part of a larger issue, and the outcome of that issue was growing clear: armed rebellion. The first time they stopped, Doug cut himself a stout stick. If others were to be armed, he would be, too. The excitement he had felt back at the Barrows' was growing.

Samuel Lount's smithy in Holland Landing was a busy place when they got there. Samuel himself was at the anvil beating a steady clangor on something that, to Doug's eyes, looked very like a pike head. He had three young men assisting him. The smith was a brawny man with a quick eye. He was soft-spoken, but very direct. You felt confident because he had such confidence in himself. You knew he could finish anything he put his hand to.

"Well, Mr. Mackenzie," he said, laying down his hammer and extending a hand like a spade to welcome the little man. "We aren't wasting any time. Two hundred pike heads ready for the Day. The Protheroe boys and Gordon Blakely are helping me. We'll be set to go the moment you send the word. I'm leaving it to you to let our friends in your part of the country know that they must come armed with a stout seven-foot staff that will fit my pike heads." He waved his hand toward the gloom at the back of the smithy. Doug could see dimly a dozen baskets that apparently held the finished weapons.

"Should they not be under cover, Samuel?" Mr. Mackenzie queried. "Should the Tories seize them 'twould be a great loss to the cause and put your life in danger."

"It would be a brave Tory would put his nose inside my shop, even if they knew what we were up to. There is not a man in Simcoe County who would tell them. Besides, the boys and I have taken to sleeping here nights. One of us is awake and alert in four-hour tours of watch. No, Mr. Mackenzie — our weapons are safe here. But come, we shall go to my house, you and I. We have much to talk of and to plan. Your companions will excuse us, I know. My wife will bring out ale and bread and cheese. You can do with refreshment after your hot ride." Lount took Mr. Mackenzie away with him, his big hand on the little man's shoulder as he conducted him out of the door.

Pat took Doug off by himself into the sunshine of the yard. They sat together under a spreading elm. "Out with it, me bucko," Pat ordered. "Och, I'm no sorcerer" — he put up a protesting hand at Doug's surprise. "If you could have seen your own face at the sight of those pikes you'd not be wondering that I question you."

"All right then, I'll tell you." Doug felt a little angry, though he could not have said why. "You knew. You all have known all along. You mean to fight. To rebel against the Queen."

"Now don't be going off half-cocked." Pat's voice held a soothing note. "We must be ready if the worst comes to the worst. Sure, Mr. Mackenzie doesn't like it at all — not at all — but lately we've despaired of achieving reforms without a show of strength. There are rumblings of discontent in Lower Canada. If the French there take up arms we must be prepared to support them. 'Twould be an opportunity straight from heaven above that we could not miss. A show of strength here at the same time and the governments of both Canadas would be forced to back down. And no fighting, mind! This is what Mr. Mackenzie plans. But we must show that we have the means to strike if we're not listened to. There's no more to it than that. By the memory of me own darlin' mother, I swear it to you."

Doug turned away. The excitement he had been feeling was at war with his fear of rebellion. Less than a week ago Mr. Mackenzie had sworn that he had no thought of taking up arms, but all the time he must have known that pikes were in the making at Holland Landing. What could he do about it? Nothing. Only believe in Pat's promise that threats would be enough.

The pattern of the days that followed was like that at Holland Landing. Hard riding, then long waits while Mr. Mackenzie closeted himself with the heads of vigilante committees. What they talked of Doug never knew definitely. There were words dropped here and there. He saw drilling going on in private meadows, squads of men — screened by trees and bushes — drilling with sticks and umbrellas in place of pikes and guns. Excitement was in the air everywhere. Doug felt his own excitement still at war with his fear.

In Lloydtown excitement won out. It was just past noon when they rode up the main street. A watch had been kept for Mr. Mackenzie's coming. The people were out in force. A large banner stretched across the street above their heads. On it in black letters that stood boldly against the bellying white cloth were the warlike words: *Liberty or Death?* Doug felt a little shiver of fear run down his spine.

Then Mr. Mackenzie began to speak from the wagon Pat had fixed for him. Doug tried to stand apart, to listen as if to a stranger speaking. He tried to watch the crowd to see their reactions. But soon he found his eyes glued to the fiery little redhead. He forgot his fears. He felt his blood pulse under the onslaught of the Reformer's words. Mr. Mackenzie began quietly enough. He spoke of injustices, of roguery, of misused public money. Then he began to speak of the violence of the Tories, of Doug's treatment, of the threats to his life. Doug flamed with fury when Mackenzie told of Pat's torment south of Toronto at the hands of Squire Collins. When the little Chief ceased, Doug could still hear the words go on. He wanted to fight. Now. Pat was beside him. He caught his friend's arm. "You're right," he shouted. "We must be ready for war!"

Pat hugged him to himself. "That's me brave boy!"

As the visit about the riding went on, Mr. Mackenzie became more open in his rebellious talk. At Caledon he proclaimed the rights of the colonists to defend themselves against this unjust Tory Government, as their ancestors had fought against the tyranny of kings. It was hard for Doug to connect this fire-breathing orator with the gentle, loving father who played hide-and-seek with his daughters. Even the Mackenzie who laughed and joked with his bodyguard as they rode from town to town was a different man from the Mackenzie who stood up on the platform in the villages and proclaimed a call to arms.

Doug spoke of the difference to Pat. "Can you see the Mr. Mackenzie we know leading an army against the Queen of England? Yet when he stands up to speak to the crowds, I can imagine him going before his army, a general leading his men to battle. What's more, I want to follow him."

"Aye, the speech of man's a wondrous thing," Pat returned. "But Doug, me boy, never forget, it's just talk. Talk will hurt no one."

Doug was to wonder soon whether Pat was right. Was it all talk? Was Mr. Mackenzie not only willing, but eager for battle? It happened when they had finished their tour and were starting for home. They came to a ford across the Humber River. Doug and Asa were near the end of the ragged lines of men. Only two other riders were behind them. Everyone was relaxed. The tension of the past two days was over. They had avoided an open clash with their Tory enemies. The bodyguard of twenty men, a constant watch at the meetings to guard against Tory infiltration, had been responsible for keeping the peace. There had been scares, of course. Rumors of armed members of the Orange Lodge, Tory fanatics, had increased the tension more than once. Still, nothing untoward had really occurred. Now the men were

strung out in long lines without scouts and without any attempt to keep in touch with those before and behind.

As Doug and Asa drove their horses into the water of the ford, the last riders ahead of them were scrambling up the bank on the other side. Doug heard the quick clop-clop of the two men behind him as they speeded up their mounts to catch up. It was the speed that was to save them.

There was a sudden whoop and the bushes on either side of the path came alive. Men — a dozen perhaps — erupted into the road, cudgels brandished as they leaped to cut off the two riders. The Reformers were just too fast for the attackers. They splashed into the stream. Doug turned in his saddle in time to see a man, in a flying leap, land behind one of the riders and try to wrestle him off his horse. There was no mistaking that face. Dawson! Three or four others had surrounded the second man and were trying to pull him down.

"Ride on, Doug!" Asa shouted. "Bring help back." Even as he shouted Asa had turned his horse's head and was forcing his way into the melée. Doug had turned Ned at the first sounds of attack. He began to tighten the rein to head the horse for the farther shore, when a man leaped into the middle of the road, a gun to his shoulder, aimed at Asa. No mistaking that great girth either. The Porker. Scarcely thinking, Doug raised his stick, drew back his arm, and flung it straight at the Porker's face. The Colonel ducked, the gun went off in the air, and Doug tugged Ned's head around. He dug his heels into Ned's sides and dashed for the far bank.

"Attack! Attack!" he shouted. "To Asa! Help!" Even as he plunged up the bank he met men returning. He drew aside to let them pass. He had no weapon now. He would only be in the way. The shouting vigilantes plunged into the stream, but not before a little grey figure on a black horse wove in and out among them, to the very fore, waving a riding crop and yelling at the top of his voice: "Patriots to the rescue! Down with the Tory tyrants!" Mr. Mackenzie led the relief party.

It was over almost before it began, but not before the ambushers suffered some broken bones. At least two of the skulkers were lying motionless in the stream. One was Dawson. Asa stood close by him. The Tories had fled up the bank. "Best come and pick up your mate before he drowns," Asa bawled after them. "He's not dead, though he'll have a sore jaw for a week or two." Doug saw the second man reel to his feet and begin to scale the bank. He fell on his knees in the mud and clawed his way upward weakly.

Mr. Mackenzie and his vigilantes drew back into midstream. It was a sheepish lot of men that crept down to the river's edge and fished out their fallen comrades. They kept wary eyes on the men sitting so still, watching. A horse stamped a foot, splashing water up. One of the Tories jumped at the sound and hastily stumbled shoreward. A laugh went up from the Mackenzie men. Golightly shook a fat fist at them. The Reformers turned as one and resumed their journey. There were no more jokes or songs. Everyone was sobered by the incident. There was a taste of war in it that made everyone think seriously of the future. Instead of leaving Doug and Mr. Mackenzie on the road to Toronto, the guards conducted them all the way to Mr. Mackenzie's door in the city.

Chapter 22
Doug Hears Exciting News

The last week of August and the whole of September were quiet weeks in the Mackenzie household. Quiet, that is, for the Mackenzies. No place that held William Lyon Mackenzie was ever really quiet. Mr. Mackenzie talked all the time — even when he was alone reading, or writing his articles and letters, or editing his paper. He groaned, he sobbed, he shouted. The calm with which his gentle wife tried to surround him rocked to the blasts of his emotion. Sometimes Doug, sitting at his lessons in the big kitchen, would catch Mrs. Mackenzie's eye as a loud yell vibrated the walls between the kitchen and Mr. Mackenzie's den. They would smile at each other, Mrs. Mackenzie a little apologetically, Doug with delight.

It seemed quiet only because Mr. Mackenzie was not rushing off madly about the country. Not that he wasn't busy; he called three meetings of the Reform Party leaders in those five weeks. From each of the meetings Mr. Mackenzie returned with a red spark of anger in his eye and with his mouth working as if he were chewing up words. There was no doubt that he was angry about something. Doug wondered if the other leaders were not as brave as Mr. Mackenzie was about taking a stand with the Government.

He knew about the meetings because Mr. Mackenzie sent him to deliver the notices to attend. Part of Doug hoped that Mr. Mackenzie was having trouble urging his friends to rebel. But part of him felt anger that anyone would refuse to obey Mr. Mackenzie, and still another part was disappointed at the thought that perhaps there would be no more adventures like the crossing of the ford on the Humber. Doug wondered if anyone else ever had as many mixed-up feelings as he did.

After the last meeting it happened that Doug was in Mr. Mackenzie's den looking for a book when the little master of the house came home. Doug was standing at the window when a movement on the path outside caught his eye. Mr. Mackenzie was lurching toward the door. His hands stabbed the air. It was plain that he was almost beside himself with rage. Doug hurried into the hall. The street door burst open. Mr. Mackenzie swayed on the threshold. He was shouting, though Doug could not make out the words. His hat flew one way. His wig followed, slapping into Barbara's thin little chest as she and Janet and Margaret came running down the stairs in their nightclothes.

Mrs. Mackenzie appeared quietly from the back of the house. Old Mrs. Mackenzie hung over the railing at the top of the stairs. Mr. Mackenzie ignored them all. He strode to his study door and stepped through. The door slammed behind him.

The three girls sat on the bottom step, weeping. There was scolding and banging of books and furniture behind the closed door of the study. Doug crowded down on the step beside the girls and did his best to hug them all.

"It's all right, Margaret," he whispered. "Janet, Barbara, you're older. You must stop your crying. You're frightening Margaret. Your father is not angry with you."

"I know," Barbara sniffled. But she jumped just the same and cried noisily again as another sound from inside the den told of another object hurled to the floor.

Mrs. Mackenzie passed them on the way to the closed door. She turned and smiled encouragingly at the huddle on the stairs, then she tapped lightly on the panels. She did not wait for an invitation to enter; she turned the knob and went in. She closed the door behind her. From the steps they could hear her gentle, clear voice and Mr. Mackenzie's high-pitched snarl. Presently the door opened and Mr. Mackenzie came out. He smiled at them and came close enough to pat Margaret's head. The seven-year-old turned her face from its hiding place against Barbara's breast.

"See!" Mr. Mackenzie's smile widened. "Papa is not angry any more. I'm a lucky man to have such daughters and a fine young friend like Douglas. And most of all, fortunate to have a wife like your mother. Now off to bed, the three of you. Don't worry your heads any more. I'm not going to, I promise you. We'll have a game tomorrow night for sure."

Doug never did find out why Mr. Mackenzie was so angry that night. At any rate, the explosion seemed to clear the air. The little man was gentler, more ready to play. Until October 9. Doug would never forget that day. In his milder mood, after that one explosion, Mr. Mackenzie had seemed to put away all thought of rebellion. At least, he said little at home about it. But on October 9 all that changed.

Doug was in Mr. Mackenzie's study with a pile of history books before him. Mr. Mackenzie had set him the task of reading. Doug heard his host come down the stairs in his usual clattering run. He heard him shout, "Isabel! Isabel!" He heard Mrs. Mackenzie's voice grow as she came hurrying from the kitchen regions. "Yes, William. Is anything wrong?"

"No, no!" Whenever Mr. Mackenzie had some plan afoot, he sounded impatient, even when he was not. Not even Mrs. Mackenzie was exempt from that tone of exasperation. He went on: "I'm going to ride up Yonge Street this morning. It's time I checked on the vigilance committees. They'll stop training for the Great Day if they are not kept up to snuff. I shall probably go as far as Gibson's place above Eglinton. I shouldn't be late home." There was a brief silence as he kissed Mrs. Mackenzie good-bye. Then the front door slammed. He was gone.

Doug's heart sank and then leaped with excitement in that complicated way it seemed to do these days. Doug had told Laurence how mixed up his feelings were lately. Laurence didn't seem to find such a mixture of fear and excitement extraordinary at all. "Anybody would be afraid of rebellion, Black Douglas. Nobody wants a war. Not even Mr. Mackenzie. He's said so. But you have to admit that you would never have had so much excitement back on the farm at St. Catharines. Admit it." And Doug had to confess that Laurence was right.

It was hours after Mr. Mackenzie had left. Doug was still sitting, thinking of his talk with Laurence instead of doing his studying, when there came a quick, hard knocking at the front door. He heard Mrs. Mackenzie answer the summons. He heard her and the visitor, a man, in excited, low-voiced conversation. Then Mrs. Mackenzie called him. "Douglas! Douglas, come quickly." Doug tumbled the books from his lap to the desk and hurried into the hall. Mrs. Mackenzie was standing close to a square-built man. Dark of hair. Both of them had their eyes fixed on him as he came out of the den.

"This is the lad?" The man's voice was quick, almost impatient.

"This is Douglas Lachlan. He is a bright boy and greatly in my husband's confidence. Douglas. . . ." Mrs. Mackenzie had never taken her eyes from Doug's face. He felt uneasy under the joint stare that was on him. "This is Mr. Jesse Lloyd. He must see Mr. Mackenzie on urgent business. As soon as possible. Do you think you could take him to find my husband?"

"I'll try, Ma'am. Shall I go to the livery and hire Ned?"

"No time," Mr. Lloyd cut in. "You can mount behind me. My horse can take us both though he is weary. I've ridden him hard, poor beast." Mr. Lloyd looked weary himself. His hair was spriggy as if it needed combing. There was a dark stubble on his face. His clothes, though they had come from a good tailor, were crumpled badly.

"I'll just get my jacket and cap, Sir." Doug turned to the stairs to his room even as he spoke. Mr. Lloyd looked as if he did not want to wait even that long.

In less than five minutes Doug was mounted on Mr. Lloyd's great hunter behind the man's square back. He was still buttoning up his jacket when they turned and headed for Yonge Street.

They ran Mr. Mackenzie to earth about eleven miles north of Toronto. He was in the centre of a knot of men. As usual, Mr. Mackenzie was holding forth, talking too fast and with such energy that a cloud of spray stood about his head in the crisp October air.

Mr. Lloyd did what Doug would not have dared do. He interrupted Mr. Mackenzie in the very middle of one of his long-worded sentences. Mr. Mackenzie hated to be interrupted. Doug waited for a violent outburst. It never came.

"I must speak to you at once, Mr. Mackenzie," Mr. Lloyd said forthrightly. Mr. Mackenzie's hot eyes grew cold for a moment, then he spoke. "Very well, Mr. Lloyd. Gentlemen, you must excuse us. Here is a messenger with news that, unless I miss my guess, will affect you and me and every man, woman, and child in the colony." He moved out of the circle as Mr. Lloyd dismounted stiffly from his saddle. The two went apart.

They spoke in tones so low that no one could hear, though Doug saw heads cocked and ears fairly flapping to catch what was said.

From that moment on it seemed as if Mr. Mackenzie were involved in some sort of race. He called for his horse and mounted as if the Governor's soldiers were at his heels. He rode like a madman toward Toronto. Doug and Mr. Lloyd on the hunter trailed behind.

They were near enough to see Mr. Mackenzie jump nimbly down from his horse in front of his house. Mr. Lloyd had whipped his animal to keep up, though the poor beast was blowing and gasping so badly that Doug feared it would founder at every step. They were not far behind the little man as he burst into the house and slammed the door behind him. Even as Mr. Lloyd took his feet from the stirrups and Doug slid down over the horse's tail they could hear Mr. Mackenzie's voice shouting inside the house, "Isabel! Mother! Everyone! It's come!"

As Doug and Mr. Lloyd entered, Mrs. Mackenzie was appearing from the back of the house wiping her hands on her apron. She was smiling indulgently at her prancing spouse. Old Mrs. Mackenzie was hurrying down the stairs as fast as her ancient legs would carry her. Mrs. Mackenzie's little maidservant had her frightened face in the door at the end of the hall. Mr. Mackenzie did not even look around at Mr. Lloyd and Doug. He had forgotten them completely in his excitement. "The Great Day has come!" Mr. Mackenzie's voice broke as he uttered the ominous words. "We must be ready for it. It's war to the end now."

"Hush, William," Mrs. Mackenzie urged. "You'll have one of your headaches again."

He stopped his hopping about the hall and seemed to bring himself out of some waking dream of glory. He looked about him. His eyes, which had been glaring madly at nothing a moment before, focused on Doug and Mr. Lloyd. He pointed like an actor at Mr. Lloyd.

"Our good Mercury here," he began. "Our good Mercury," he repeated, "has brought the news I have been awaiting. Lower Canada is up in arms and ready to strike a blow for freedom, for independence. My bon ami, Monsieur Papineau, has sent us word and bids us to rise here in the upper colony in support of the glorious revolution. I wish we had a Liberty Tree here in

Toronto. I would dance about it.'' He proceeded to dance a highland fling about his wife who still smiled indulgently at her capering husband.

He stopped abruptly. ''We must not celebrate too soon. There is much to be done. Lloyd, I know you are weary, but do one thing for me before you go to your rest. Go to the old garrison. See the situation there. Number of guards. The arms. The ammunition, if you can. Take someone with you who can come back and report to me. I have heard rumors of a stand of some four thousand weapons there. Test those rumors. No, not Douglas,'' he went on as he saw Mr. Lloyd turn to Doug with a question in his eyes. ''I need Lachlan for other errands. Away with you, the sooner to get your sleep.'' He swung to Doug now. ''Douglas, you must go to Pat Rafferty and ask him to hasten to Fort Henry. 'Tis a long way to Kingston, but I must have an early report on the situation there. The size of the garrison. What preparations, if any, are being made to send men to Lower Canada. Afterward, I want you to look up your young friend, Laurence. We shall see if he is the Reformer he claims to be. As the son of an important banker, he has entry where you would have none. I want to know where his lordship, Sir Francis Bond Head, is at this moment.''

''Where shall I find Pat?'' Doug put in before Mr. Mackenzie could think of more things for him to do. ''I didna' know Pat was in Toronto.''

''No. We thought it best that Rafferty lie low a while. He has kept close to Mrs. Wilson's house on Peter Street. You will find it easily. It is a big stone house set back from the street with several fine maples in the yard in front of the house. The only one so situated on the street.''

''Yes, Sir.'' Doug turned to go.

''And Douglas. . . . '' Mr. Mackenzie stopped him. ''Go to Mr. Doel and have him round up our most trusted friends for a meeting in his brewery tonight at seven of the clock. Say nothing more to him now. Only stress the urgency of the gathering. Off with you now. And run, boy, run. 'Tis the hour toward which we have all yearned. We must not be caught sleeping like the hare.''

Doug found Pat without difficulty. When he told the little Irishman about Mr. Jesse Lloyd and his news, Pat seized him fiercely by the shoulders and swung him 'round so that the light from the open door fell on his face. "Is it the truth you're telling me?" he demanded. Then in the same breath he whispered, "Holy Mother, I thank thee. 'Tis the best news since his Satanic Majesty welcomed the spirit of Oliver Cromwell to Hell. What does our little Chief want me to do?" Pat's face shone and his black eyes were like two glowing pools. Doug gave him Mr. Mackenzie's orders. Pat darted away into the depths of the house. "Tell the Mackenzie I'm on my way," he shouted as he went. Doug retreated to the street and made his way toward Laurence's house.

Chapter 23
Doug Visits The Governor

Doug found Laurence just starting out armed with a satchel of books for his afternoon classes. Doug's eyes widened with disappointment. "I forgot it was a school day," he burst out. "You won't be able to help."

"Help with what, Doug?" Laurence looked puzzled.

Doug explained. Laurence was afire at once. "Wait," he ordered. He ran 'round the house by the carriage drive. When he came back the books were gone. "In the coach house," he explained. "The best place for them this day."

"But Laurie, you can't miss school. Your father will find out. You'll get a beating besides when you go to school tomorrow. They'll get out of you why you played truant."

"Not from me. Not ever. And it will be worth every stroke of the cane. It will be my suffering for the cause of Reform. I'll be a martyr like you and your Pat Rafferty." Laurence grinned. "As for Father, I have given him fair warning of my Reformist sympathies. We understand each other, Father and I. If I take my caning like a man, he will feel justice well satisfied and ask me not one word of reasons. Where's your spirit, Black Douglas? I do believe that you don't welcome this day as much as I do."

"You know how I feel. Part of me is screaming, 'Run! Run for your life.' Part of me is shouting, 'Up the rebels!' The trouble is I don't know which part to listen to. Rebellion is treason, Laurie. You can hang for treason."

"Father would have something to say to that. And he is an important man in this colony, remember. Come. Be cheerful. We shall win. And then who will cry treason at us? Tell me about the fight in Lower Canada. Is it because of the Family Compact there, too?''

"Same sort of snooty Tories. They call them the Château Clique. Mr. Mackenzie said there would be trouble if the Clique pushed through the Ten Resolutions. That's a kind of law they passed that took the control of the money in Lower Canada away from the people and gave it to the Clique. And then, too, the French are angry at the idea that they can't speak their language any longer in their Assembly. When there are more Frenchmen in the Assembly than Englishmen, it does seem unfair, don't you think?''

Laurie agreed that the Tories, wherever you found them, had no idea of fair play. "They're a bunch of Peter Robinsons, the whole lot of them.''

Meanwhile, as they talked, the boys had been covering ground. Mr. Mackenzie had been right. Laurence had no trouble finding out the information he had been sent to gather. When they arrived at the Governor's palace, Laurie simply walked up to the sentry standing inside his box out of the brisk chill wind.

"Good day, Tim," he greeted the big guardsman. "Is Sir Francis at home? I'd like to speak to him. It's not too soon to begin thinking of the Christmas ball. I have some ideas I'd like to put to the Governor about the young folks' fun.''

"He's out riding, Master Todd," Tim replied very politely. Doug wondered if he would have been as polite to farmer Lachlan's son.

"When will he be back, Tim? Do you know?''

"That I don't, Master Todd. You never know with His Excellency. In this wind he may not go far. But on the other hand, the sun is shining and he may stay out for hours. Why do you not go up to the door and ask if he has any engagement that will bring him back early?''

"I'll do that," said Laurence. "Come along, Doug." He led the way up the drive to the broad steps and mounted to give the knocker a resounding thump. A big footman in knee breeches and powdered wig opened up the heavy door. He looked down his nose from a back-tilted head at the two boys, but there was a hint of a smile as his eyes met Laurence's merry grin.

"Ah, Derwent. Still with that bad crick in your neck, I see. You really ought to do something about it," Laurence greeted the man pertly. The hint grew into a real smile.

"You and your jokes, Master Todd," Derwent chuckled. His voice was a light tenor that went oddly with his broad shoulders and giant frame. "Your father would dust your breeches, Sir, if he heard you."

"Oh, no he wouldn't, Derwent," Laurence retorted. "He would go out and purchase some horse liniment to loosen up those muscles.

"Do you know when Sir Francis will return? Tim tells me he's out riding."

"About five, Sir. I heard him tell Captain Nicholson. Sheriff Jarvis is due to come to speak to His Excellency at five-thirty. Something about these cursed rebels, I heard the Captain say. Sheriff Jarvis thinks there's rebellion brewing here in Toronto, but we discount the rumors." Laurence jerked a wink aside at Doug at the pompous "we" of the servant. "We believe," Derwent went on, his eyes raised above the horizon beyond the door, "that the people of this colony are loyal and happy subjects of the Queen, God bless her."

"No rebels could panic you and Sir Francis, Derwent," Laurence nodded wisely.

"No, indeed, Sir," Derwent agreed. "Could you return about six, Master Todd? I would guarantee His Excellency will be free then. He'll soon make short work of Sheriff Jarvis's fears. And there will be no one in to sup. I happen to know that. The master promised the mistress they should have a quiet evening at home together."

"Thank you, Derwent. I may do that, if my father doesn't need me." Laurence turned away and Derwent closed the door behind him.

"It's no' very honest, Laurie," Doug objected as they moved down the driveway. "I don't know how you do it," he continued laughingly. "I'm no good at telling lies. I'm always found out."

"Nor am I, Doug," Laurence retorted. "That's why I told the truth. I do want to see Sir Francis about the Christmas ball. I have some real ideas about livening it up. And I may come back this evening and talk to him about them. Besides, who knows? Mr.

Mackenzie may want me to come back to see how the land lies. I might hear something of Sheriff Jarvis's fears."

Mr. Mackenzie was pleased with the boys. "A fine, clever job, Laurence," he praised. "You have done the Reform Party and me a great favor. I hope I may, one day, return it to you."

Laurence looked quickly at Doug, and then back to Mr. Mackenzie. "You can, Sir. Right now. Let Doug and me come to the meeting with you."

Doug gasped. He would never have dared Mr. Mackenzie's anger. Doug looked sharply at the little man, waiting for the wig to fly. But Mr. Mackenzie was not angry. He was smiling. "Two such loyal supporters of Reform have a right to know what is going on. Aye, you may come with me, Douglas and Laurence."

The two boys sat in the shadows behind the group of worried-looking supporters who gathered in Doel's brewery that night. When the last person arrived, Mr. Mackenzie stood up and began a long speech about the thirteen colonies and the American Revolution and the glorious rebellion of 1688 against King James II. Doug found it wearying, but Laurence drank in every word.

It all took a very long time and his older listeners were stirring restlessly before Mr. Mackenzie got down to the real business of the meeting. Laurence was furious with them. He turned shining eyes on Doug. "Can they not see," he whispered, "how magnificent Mr. Mackenzie is? He's the greatest orator in the colony."

"And now," Mr. Mackenzie was asking at that moment, "how does all this affect us here this October evening of eighteen thirty-seven in the city of Toronto? I will tell you, fellow Reformers. A messenger is on his way to Fort Henry to discover the situation there. There is every reason to believe that he will find the fort empty, the garrison on its way to Lower Canada. A steamer, sent at once with men from Dutcher's and Armstrong's, could take the place without striking a blow. What is more, the Governor has stored in the City Hall a stand of several thousand arms with ammunition. All this guarded by but two constables. Before our loyal men leave for Fort Henry, they could seize those arms, and — with artillery from the old garrison — create a fortress that not the whole British army could take away from us.

"But that is not my plan. On the way to the City Hall we will capture the person of His Excellency, the Governor, and hold him prisoner. He is at home this very minute with only one sentinel to guard him. We will force him to give us an Executive Council responsible to the Assembly, newly elected after we get rid of this 'Bread and Butter' Parliament that has ruled us too long.''

There was no doubt that he now had the attention of everyone in the room. Doug, watching the faces, saw that the group was stunned by Mr. Mackenzie's plans. Laurence squirmed with excitement. "Go to it, Sir! Give it to them!" he whispered violently, jerking his clenched fists as if he were fighting a battle this very minute.

There was a long silence. Then one man spoke in a breathless, frightened voice. Doug strained to see who it was, but his face was hidden in the shadows. "And if the Governor refuses our demands?''

Mr. Mackenzie's voice cracked like a whip over the last syllable of the fearful question. "Then, friends, we will go for independence.''

Laurence could restrain himself no longer. "Hurray!" he shouted. "Long live the Republic of Canada!''.

Chapter 24
Doug Has Bad Dreams

Laurence's shout stirred up the meeting like a stick in a nest of ants. Everyone started talking at once. Some men jumped out of their chairs and crossed the circle to argue with others loudly and angrily. They shouted at Mr. Mackenzie, who stood with arms folded and simply looked at them one by one. The hubbub went on for a long time. In the end the followers went away with no plan agreed on. Nothing done. Mr. Mackenzie's shoulders slumped wearily when the last one left the brewery, and only Doel himself was left behind to lock up.

"You go too fast for them, William," Mr. Doel said quietly to the little Scotsman. "They're good, and true to the cause of Reform. But you can't expect them suddenly to become soldiers in battle. As well expect my fat, old spaniel to fight a lion. These men and my dog are both too comfortable. Here in Toronto we are too far from our pioneering parents and grandparents whose courage was constantly being put to the test. They have no stomach for rebellion."

"They are cowards, every man jack of them," Laurence put in indignantly.

"Now, now, lad. You must not put the name of coward to honest men," Doel scolded him.

"I agree." Mr. Mackenzie straightened his shoulders. "You are young. You have no responsibilities. To lose the battle with the Compact would be to lose everything for those men. Homes, businesses, lives. Tomorrow they will find their courage. You will see. I took them by surprise tonight. Tomorrow is still not too late.''

But tomorrow came and went. Day followed day and the men of Toronto would not give the word to carry out Mr. Mackenzie's plans. Mr. Mackenzie was not idle, though. Messengers came and went at the house and the bookstore. He himself was out, day and night, coaxing, pleading, arguing for immediate attack.

Doug's lessons were forgotten and Doug had no heart to remind Mr. Mackenzie about them. The poor man's face was often grey with weariness and despair. But only if he thought no one was watching him. With everyone, even his family, he was cheerful. Only Doug saw the little Chief's effort to be gay. He went everywhere with Mr. Mackenzie, ready to run errands or do anything he could to help. The fact that sensible Toronto businessmen, who had looked on Mr. Mackenzie as a leader, were against him roused all Doug's old fears and feelings about rebellion. He felt guilty that he had slipped back from feeling excited and right about helping Mr. Mackenzie to feeling that rebellion was all wrong and a fearful mistake.

He knew he was a disappointment to Laurie. Laurie came almost every day after school and if he and Doug were left alone, even for a minute, Laurie would argue.

"Be strong, Doug," he urged. "Why, you and I, with Mr. Mackenzie to lead us, could capture the City Hall ourselves. Then all those cry-babies around Mr. Mackenzie would be shamed into taking a stand."

"They're not cry-babies," Doug would protest. "They're successful businessmen. They must know when the odds are against them."

"What about Mr. Mackenzie?" Laurie would retort. "He's a successful businessman, too." Doug never had an answer to that. He would stare miserably at Laurie's triumphant grin and try to think of a telling argument.

"Maybe," Doug offered once, "the Governor will hear how near he's been to open war. Maybe he'll reform the Government himself."

"Old Bone Head?" Laurie scoffed. "He tells people every day that this is England's most loyal and contented colony. I've heard him. Reform? From him?"

Sometimes Laurie would bring Da' into his arguments. "If your father were here, he would be in the very thick of the fight." When Doug did not answer, Laurie would persist. "Wouldn't he?"

Doug did not know how to answer. He knew Da' would not want to fight unless he had to. "Fighting solves nothing," Da' had often said. But if he told Laurie that, Laurie would class Da' with all those others he called cowards. Always it ended the same way. "I'll do what I have to," Doug would make his peace-offering. "Fight if I have to. But I hope it doesn't come to that."

"Oh, it will come," Laurie would return, and laugh at Doug's discomfort. Then he would slap Doug on the back. "I haven't any doubts about your courage, Douglas the Black. You'll fight when the time comes."

In the first week of November Mr. Mackenzie took Jesse Lloyd and Doug north with him to Samuel Lount's place in Holland Landing. They were joined by Captain Anderson who, all autumn, had been trying to make soldiers out of the men of York County. There were other men, too, whose names Doug never heard. They all met in Sam Lount's smithy. Everyone looked very serious as Mr. Mackenzie got up to speak.

He told them frankly of the situation in Toronto. He told them he could not get the men of Toronto to attack the City Hall, to capture the Governor. "If I could persuade Dr. Rolph and Mr. Morrison to agree to my plan, all the others would go along. Those two are the leaders. They are respected and I must abide by their decision. They are wise men, wiser than I am, perhaps. We cannot move without them. We need men whom the city men will follow."

"Come, come, Mackenzie," Mr. Lount interrupted. "You are too modest. All the Reformers in our colony will follow you. You know that is true."

"I trust they will." Mr. Mackenzie sounded humble, but there was a spark in his eye that had been missing since the meeting at Doel's.

"He's got his confidence back," Doug thought. "I don't need to feel guilty and sorry about him any more." He was relieved. In fact, as the men about him plotted and planned, he began to feel the excitement creep into that spot in the middle of his chest that seemed to have something to do with the way his breath came more quickly.

He started to listen to Mr. Mackenzie again. "With your aid, gentlemen" — Mr. Mackenzie was smiling wickedly at them all — "I intend to give the men in Toronto a needed push. I propose we set a date for our revolt. A date not later than December seventh. That gives us five weeks to be ready. What do you think?"

Fists banged on the table. There was a shout of "Aye!" and "Yes!" and "Agreed!" and even "Bravo!" Doug was thrilled with the men's excitement, glad for Mr. Mackenzie, but a little terrified too.

Captain Anderson rose as Mr. Mackenzie sat down. He bowed to the little Chief. "You would make a good soldier. A clever plan. Those men will not dare back out if we set a date. They would lose the faith of those who believe in them. I congratulate you." The Captain saluted Mr. Mackenzie. Mr. Mackenzie beamed. His own hand flew up in a kind of salute. "December the seventh it shall be," he shouted.

Doug pushed down the excitement in himself to consider his fear. He scarcely heard the talk about five thousand men. About Montgomery's Tavern at Eglinton crossroads. He dimly knew that there were plans to seize the Government arms that Mr. Mackenzie had set his heart on. Doug realized that the very setting of a date meant that the rebellion had started. Now. This moment. He had never liked fighting very much. But he had never avoided a fight either. He had to decide. Now! This very moment! Was he going to tell Mr. Mackenzie that he was going to leave him? Mr. Mackenzie had his confidence back. He didn't need Doug any more. Where would he go? Not to Laurence. He could not fit into a rich man's house. And Laurence would think him a coward like the men in Toronto. And Da' had sent him to Mr. Mackenzie. He couldn't go against that. Da' had said, "Obey Mr. Mackenzie in everything." Well, he would. He felt better. He let the excitement sweep his fears away. He knew that they would come back. But he would go on helping the rebellion in any way he could. He began to listen again. Mr. Mackenzie was arranging for messengers to go to London and St. Thomas, to urge that all men of good will should join him and Mr. Lount and Captain Anderson at Montgomery's on the big day.

The return to Toronto brought no let-up in excitement. Doug was on the go constantly with messages to this one or that one. More than once he was scolded by the people he was sent to for Mr. Mackenzie's high-handed setting of a date for action. Doug took the scolding in silence. He did not know how to answer. The effect of the scoldings was to make him more sure that Mr. Mackenzie was right. A deep loyalty to the Reform leader warmed his heart.

His growing loyalty, however, did not prevent him from having bad dreams at night. There was one that repeated itself over and over. Peter Robinson knelt and grinned wickedly as he pressed bony knees into Doug's chest. He never said anything in the dream, but the pressure of his knees would cut off Doug's breath. Doug would struggle to cry out. The knees pressed harder so that he had not enough air to make a sound. He would waken gasping and cold with sweat. It was hard to fall asleep again, and when he did, often he dreamt again of Peter's hated face looming over him.

The dreams, the daily excitement, and the worry that he had deliberately pushed down inside him showed in dark circles under his eyes. He found often that when he sat down to eat, he was too tired to have any appetite. Mrs. Mackenzie worried over him. She urged him to eat and looked anxious when he could not. Finally, she took him to the parlor, just the two of them, to question him.

"Is there something bothering you, Douglas?" she pressed him. "I am anxious about you. You don't seem yourself. You look so tired. Are you not sleeping, Douglas?"

Doug could not meet her eyes. "I'm all right, Ma'am," he mumbled.

"But that is what you are not, Douglas. Please tell me at once. Are you concerned for Mr. Mackenzie?"

Doug nodded miserably. It was true, he was worried about her husband. But that was not the whole truth. He could not say to the Chief's wife, "I don't know whether Da' would agree with your husband. I don't know whether Da' would be on the side of those men who resisted Mr. Mackenzie's call to fight." Where *was* Da'? Why, why did he not write? Had he disappeared like Graham? What he would not give to see Da' walk into the house this minute.

Mrs. Mackenzie was speaking. Doug tugged his thoughts back from Da' to listen.

". . . Good and loyal boy, Douglas." Did she mean him? "Let me assure you that Mr. Mackenzie has a way of landing on his feet that keeps me from too great fear for him. All his life he has managed somehow to come out on top when things have gone against him. He will this time, too, I do promise you. Come to me with your fears any time. I am sure I can drive them away." She let him go then, though she still looked anxious. Doug noticed that he was not sent on quite so many errands. Mrs. Mackenzie must have spoken to her husband about him.

Doug's faith in the rebellion and the excitement of being part of it was always helped by being with Laurie. "Cheer up, Douglas the Black," Laurie would tease. "Your face is almost as black as your name. And twice as long." Doug would grin and immediately feel cheerful again. And the dream of Peter would stay away on the nights after he had seen Laurie.

"You watch," Laurie would say. "Mr. Mackenzie will have old Bone-Head Sir Francis on the run in no time. He's clever, your little Chief. Look how he has bound all these scared Toronto men to him now that he has set the day for the uprising. He'll win. Your father will be proud of you." Doug would believe Laurie while he was there. But if a day went by without a meeting of the two boys, Doug's dreams came back to haunt him.

J. MERLE SMITT

Chapter 25
Stones Are Thrown And
Mr. Mackenzie Faces Arrest

On the evening of the twenty-fourth Mr. Mackenzie summoned Doug to his study. "I am leaving for the north tonight, Douglas," Mr. Mackenzie informed him. "I must hasten the recruiting and see that all as in readiness at Montgomery's. With James still away on business, I must leave you in charge of the house. You are a sensible laddie and I know I can trust you. My mother, and my wife, and the girls will feel more secure to have you around. I anticipate no trouble. Sir Francis and his cohorts are either ignorant of our plans, though this I doubt — I am sure there are informers among us — or they despise us so much that they do not fear us. In any case, they are making no move to protect themselves. It will be an easy victory. The Compact will scuttle like a flock of nervous old hens when our army comes marching down Yonge Street. You do not fear the responsibility, Douglas?"

"No, Sir. I shall be happy to stay." He had had one of his dreams the night before and he felt so weary that he was glad to stay quietly at home.

Mr. Mackenzie left just after six of the clock. He had been in high humor during tea which Mrs. Mackenzie laid on just before his departure. He ate enormously and made everyone laugh when he bulged out each cheek with a scone and tried to whistle at the same time. Even the baby in her cradle giggled with delight at the funny face he made.

After Mr. Mackenzie had gone, Doug settled down in the study to read. Mrs. Mackenzie was up in her room. The old mother retired to bed shortly, and by seven-thirty the girls were in

their rooms making ready in their boisterous way for the night.
The house grew as silent as Doug's own home in the St.
Catharines woods. Doug read on, lost in the fantastic adventures
of Lemuel Gulliver, and consequently he was startled when the
clock in the hall chimed ten. Almost on the last stroke there was a
sudden shout in the street. Glass crashed upstairs. The shouts
were right outside the house. "Rebel! Traitor!"

Doug jumped to his feet. Swiftly he blew out the lamp. A rain
of stones. More smashed glass. A man's voice shouted, " 'Ware
the watch!" Feet pounded down the road. Doug ran to the
window and parted the draperies. Black night smothered the
view. He left the den and ran up the stairs. In the light of the
candle that burned on a table in the upstairs hall, he saw Mrs.
Mackenzie, still dressed, quickly cross the hall to Barbara's and
Janet's room. She carried a candle with her, shielding the flame
with her hand. Only then Doug realized that the whole attack had
lasted no more than a minute or two. The senior Mrs. Mackenzie
opened her door and put a nightcapped head into the hall.

"What is it?" she demanded. Her voice was cracked with age
but there was no fear in it. "What happened?" she demanded
again.

"Someone throwing stones, Ma'am, I think." Doug became
aware of the girls chattering excitedly and of Mrs. Mackenzie's
voice, calm as always, dominating the chatter. He realized, too,
that there was no sound from the other girls' room. Margaret and
Helen had apparently slept through the ruckus. He was grateful
for that.

"Douglas!" Mrs. Mackenzie called.

Doug stepped to the doorway of the girls' room and hesitated.
Mrs. Mackenzie was standing in the middle of the room. Her
outstretched hand held something, though the shadows from the
flickering candle masked the object. "Look," she said. He
advanced into the room and took the object from her. It was a
stone the size of his fist. "I found it on the bed. At the foot." She
looked at the girls sitting up against the pillows, the clothes
drawn up under their chins. Mrs. Mackenzie shuddered. "If it
had struck one of them, Douglas!"

Doug, meeting the girls' wide, shocked eyes, made himself
smile. "No real harm done, Ma'am. Tory pranks. That's all. I'll
go down and fetch hammer and nails. You find a blanket,

Ma'am. I'll nail it over the window for tonight. Tomorrow I'll fetch the glazier.''

There was no more trouble in the week that followed. No trouble, except that Laurence stopped coming. Doug had waited impatiently the day after the attack for Laurence to drop in after school to tell him about it. He did not come. Not that day. Not the next. Not at all. Had Laurie changed sides? At the end of a week he decided he must know. He went to Laurie's house. But there, on the doorstep, his nerve deserted him. If Laurie had turned traitor it was better not to know. He turned and trudged slowly home. He never felt lonelier. Not even when Da' had left.

For days Doug clung to his wretchedness. His bad dreams came every night. On the thirtieth the shadows vanished. He could scarcely remember how bad his loneliness had been. Laurence came that afternoon. Doug opened to a knock and there he was.

"Laurie!" Excitement and joy made Doug's voice crack.

"Hullo, Douglas the Black. I've been away. To Buffalo with Father. He had business down there. Sorry I couldn't let you know. Father likes to surprise a fellow. He hardly gave me time to pick up my portmanteau. Tell me what's been happening."

Doug told him. Not once did he mention his doubts of Laurie. Those were thoughts he would never tell anyone. He felt his face burn with shame. Laurie thought it was a flush of anger. "I don't wonder you're red in the face. Too bad you hadn't a good old blunderbuss filled with nails to blast them. I'll try to find out who was back of it all. I wonder if Peter Robinson had anything to do with it. I wouldn't be surprised."

"I wondered myself," Doug agreed. "But it's over now. The window is fixed and no one was hurt. Perhaps you should keep still about it. Especially right now with Mr. Mackenzie away recruiting. You might make trouble for him."

"I'm going to find out just the same," Laurence persisted. "Even if we can't do anything about it."

Find out he did. By next afternoon he had the list of names. "Peter was in the mob," he told Doug with some satisfaction. "Not the leader. He just tagged along. He's been very busy these days rushing about as Defender of the Tory Faith. The other boys at school are weary to death of hearing about the responsibilities of the upper class. *Noblesse oblige*, Peter calls it. To him it means stamping on the face of anybody he thinks his inferior. Makes me sick to listen to him.''

The next day Laurence had more news. "There's a Colonel Fitzgibbon here in the city. Ever hear of him?'' Doug shook his head. "Well, he was a bit of a hero in the war with the States twenty-five years ago. It seems he captured a whole battalion of Americans with only a single platoon of our men. Anyway, he seems to be the only one who believes that rebellion is coming. No, not the only one. Peter Robinson thinks so, too. Colonel Fitzgibbon has made him his aide. Or so Peter says. But we may have to take the Colonel seriously before we're finished. He's been urging the Governor to keep some of the soldiers here instead of sending them all to Lower Canada. He also wants the militia called out and armed. Old Bone Head won't hear of it. An insult to the loyalty of his dear subjects and all that, don't you know?''

"Good thing for Mr. Mackenzie,'' Doug interjected.

"Yes, Sir, my Black Douglas. Of course, Bone Head can't admit there could be any rebellion here. He likes to believe that everyone loves him like a father. Good King Francis! That's old knucklehead for you. Father says he's afraid he'll be sent home. He says he doesn't know how Sir Francis ever got the appointment. Father knew him a bit at home. Thought he was a proper joke even then.

"But to get back to Fitzgibbon. The old chap's convinced that everyone with less than a thousand pounds a year is just waiting to rise up and slaughter all us rich folk in our beds.'' Laurence grinned. "Please don't come too early in the morning with your little axe to chop off my head, Black Douglas. I do hate to be wakened early.''

Doug returned the grin. "It's going to be hard slaughtering you, Laurie. Your father lets you stay up so late that we lower classes are all in bed for hours. And now you say I can't disturb you at a decent waking hour. It's hard on us rebels. Pity, too. I've been working day and night to put a good edge on my axe.''

Laurence laughed till the tears ran down his face. How good it was to laugh with him again! It was Doug who put an end to the fun.

"Stop it, you fool,'' he ordered. "You'll have old Mrs. Mackenzie in here. And she can be a tartar. I like the old lady though. Now," he went on when Laurence's mirth subsided, "finish telling me about this Fitzgibbon fellow."

Laurence sobered. "There's not much else to tell. Fitzy and Peter have been all over Toronto telling people, like Father, to keep their firearms loaded and be ready to use them. Father just laughed at him when he came to our house. Fitzy turned purple. He was really angry.

The very next evening Laurence came with truly grave news. A warrant had been issued for Mr. Mackenzie's arrest.

"Why?" Doug demanded. "You said Sir Francis didn't believe the stories about the rebellion."

"Fitzgibbon's doings. There was a meeting today of all the Compact heads with the Governor. They were all agreed that Fitzgibbon was nothing but a troublemaker. At that very moment Fitzy burst in on them. He was dragging along some man from up north, where Mr. Mackenzie is, who swore that the rebels are making pikes for an attack on the city. No one believes him. But Fitzy made such a fuss they appointed him Acting Adjutant General of the Militia. Then he ordered Mr. Mackenzie's arrest. Father told me at supper. You can imagine how I gobbled my food to get over here to let you know. I think Father knew I would pass the word. He didn't say so, but he had that spark in his eye he always has when he knows exactly what he's doing. I think Father thinks that arresting Mr. Mackenzie will make people sorry for him and make more people join him. Anyway, Father admires Mr. Mackenzie. I've told you so before. He says Mr. Mackenzie is right when he insists that those who pay the taxes should have more say in running the country. What are you going to do, Doug? I have to get back. I'm supposed to be in my room studying tomorrow's lessons. Though I expect Father knows I'm not there."

"Mr. Mackenzie ought to be told. . . ." Doug began. Suddenly there was a tap at the door of the study and Mrs. Mackenzie put her head in.

"I'm sorry to disturb you, Douglas," she apologized, "But Dr. Rolph is here. I think we're going to need you to go up Yonge Street to find Mr. Mackenzie."

"Is it about the warrant, Ma'am? I've just been hearing about if from Laurie."

The door of the study was pushed open and Dr. Rolph brushed

by Mrs. Mackenzie. He was a good-looking man, well turned out. A man to have confidence in. Doug liked him. Now his manner was icy, challenging. "How do you know so much, young man?" he demanded. "Who told you?"

"Dr. Rolph, this is Laurence Todd . . . " Doug's introduction was interrupted at that point.

"Todd, the banker, is your father?"

"Yes, Sir," Laurence answered.

Dr. Rolph wheeled on Mrs. Mackenzie. "Surely this is the height of folly to discuss Mr. Mackenzie's affairs before young Todd."

Mrs. Mackenzie drew herself up. "Your pardon, Sir. You must let me be the judge of that. Mr. Mackenzie knows of Douglas's friendship with Laurence. Indeed, Laurence has been useful to my husband's plans. If the leaders in Toronto had backed my husband when he offered them the opportunity of capturing guns and hostages, he would not now face danger of prison. Laurence helped my husband to formulate that scheme by the information he obtained for my husband."

Dr. Rolph reddened under Mrs. Mackenzie's stare. "You know best, Madam," he mumbled. Then he collected himself. He ignored her thrust about not backing Mr. Mackenzie. "You are right, Douglas. Mr. Mackenzie must be informed of his danger. Since Mr. James Mackenzie is not at home, and the staff at the bookstore might be known to those watching the roads, you must go. I took the liberty of bringing one of my horses with me, saddled and ready. You should leave at once. Do you know where to find him?" Rolph looked from Mrs. Mackenzie to Doug. He was careful not to see Laurence at all.

"He may be at Gibson's above Eglinton. I know he plans to be there tomorrow," Mrs. Mackenzie put in.

"We need not name names or places." The doctor was amusingly pompous. It was evident that he could not get Laurence out of his crop.

"I shall go and get my coat," Doug offered.

"See you when you get back." Laurence lifted a hand in farewell. "I'll be off now. Good night, Ma'am. Dr. Rolph, your servant." Laurie made a truly magnificent bow. Doug envied him his ease of manner. There were advantages in being a rich man's son. You could put older people in their places so well if you had fine manners. "Good luck, Doug. Give my best wishes to Mr. Mackenzie." Laurence turned and marched to the door, his back very straight.

In a few minutes Doug himself was out in the cold, black December night. He was mounted on a strange horse. He pulled the horse's head in the direction of Yonge Street. He was off to find Mr. Mackenzie.

Chapter 26
Doug Rides With A Warning

Doug had a long, lonely ride ahead of him. He could not hurry his horse; the road was too dark and icy. He found himself nodding over the horse's neck. He took off one mitt, licked his finger, and rubbed the spit on his eyelids to drive away sleep. "The Governor may have spies set out anywhere along this road to watch for messengers to Mr. Mackenzie. You'd best stay awake, Lachlan," he warned himself. But even the wet finger did not help much. He fell to nodding again. Not even trying to scare himself with imagined soldiers behind distant tree stumps could keep him alert. He could not really believe in them. The road was deserted.

If there were no watchers on the road, there was no Mr. Mackenzie either. No one at any of the settlements Doug passed through knew the little man's whereabouts. As soon as people recognized Doug as Mr. Mackenzie's boy, they were quite willing to talk. They were curious, too, to know what message Doug carried that made a night journey necessary. Doug told them nothing. He was pretty sure there were no Tories present, but just the same. . . . He felt a fierce protective loyalty toward Mr. Mackenzie. He was not going to talk to possible enemies about a man who had been so kind to him. And Mr. Mackenzie was the Chief. Without him there would be no Reform Party, no one to lead the fight for people like Da' and Mr. Doel and Pat Rafferty. Tonight, Doug realized that he had given himself, with no turning back, to Mr. Mackenzie and the rebellion.

At Montgomery's Tavern, which was still open and crammed with men finishing off their last drinks before taking the icy road home, every man had a guess at where Mackenzie might be. David Gibson's house up the road. Samuel Lount's in Holland Landing. Lloydtown. Even London, in the west. All these suggestions thrown at him by men, each of whom tried to make everyone believe that he alone knew the Chief's plans. Doug, drinking the hot chocolate that the innkeeper set before him, eating fragrant fresh bread and tangy cheese, felt his head buzz with the noise.

"If I was you, which I'm not," Montgomery, the landlord, said softly in his ear, "and I never knew a young 'un that wanted to take an oldster's advice, I'd try Dave Gibson's first. He'll know where Will Mackenzie's got hisself to, if anyone does. And if he ain't there, I'd go to Sam Lount's. He's going to be one of the bosses of this show, I hear. He's bound to know. Don't quote ' me though. I'll be more help to the Reformers as long as the Tories think I'm taking no sides. Better for business, too." He smiled, then added ruefully, "Not that I'll be in business long. Tell Mr. Mackenzie I've sold the inn. I'm sorry, but I had no choice." He winked solemnly at Doug and moved unhurriedly away to wait on someone else.

Doug followed the landlord's advice. At Gibson's everyone had gone to bed. Doug was a bit shy about pounding on the door and waking the Gibsons up. He made himself do it. It was Mrs. Gibson who opened the door. Her thin, colorless hair was covered by a frilled white nightcap. She huddled a big, dark shawl about her thin body against the December wind. She whined a bit at first about being disturbed until she learned who was at the door.

"I don't know what to tell you, Douglas." She sounded worried. "A boy your age should be home in his bed, not traipsing the highways at this hour." She turned her head to answer a shout from inside. "It's Douglas Lachlan, Mr. Mackenzie's helper," she called. "He's looking for Mr. Mackenzie. An urgent message, he says. That's what I'm telling him," she protested impatiently. She turned back to Doug. "My husband says he doesn't know where your master is either. Though he's due back here tomorrow. Do you want to come in and stay the night? We can put you up."

Doug shook his head. He was tempted. The warm air that came through the half-opened door was inviting. He turned away at once. The warmth made him realize how chilled he was. He stamped his feet though they were so cold that stamping hurt. "I must go on. Mr. Mackenzie may be at Mr. Lount's place. If he comes before I get back, tell him to be careful. There is a warrant out for his arrest."

Mrs. Gibson's scream startled the horse. It was lucky that Doug had already taken hold of the reins. He mounted and steadied the animal down. Mrs. Gibson was out on the step in the full strength of the wind now. "Did they mention my husband?" she demanded, her voice shrill with fright. "He's been hand-in-glove with your Mr. Mackenzie. Are they going to arrest him, too?"

"He wasn't mentioned, Ma'am," Doug called as he swung the horse's head toward the road.

Lount's house was lighted. Doug breathed a sigh of relief. Mr. Mackenzie must be here talking, talking, as he so often did, while his listeners nodded and longed for thier beds.

He was wrong. Mr. Mackenzie was not there.

Mrs. Lount answered the door. To his eager question she shook her head. "No, Douglas." Doug was glad she remembered him. "Mr. Mackenzie is not here. Neither is my husband, though I expect him at any minute. When you knocked, I thought it was someone with a message from him. He and Mr. Mackenzie are together somewhere. I believe he was not going to return here. I rather think he was heading for the Gibsons'." Doug turned away, more discouraged than he had been before, because he had been so sure that the house lit up meant Mr. Mackenzie.

"Wait a minute, Douglas." Mrs. Lount's voice was one to be obeyed. "You aren't going a step further this night. No." She put up a hand to stop him as he started to speak. "You will put up your horse in the stable and come into the house and wait for my husband. You're simply trembling with cold. I'm sure you must be hungry. Now, do as I say. My husband will know how to act when he comes."

Doug could not resist her. He stabled Dr. Rolph's horse and returned to the house. Its warmth closed 'round his chilled body like a quilt as he stepped inside the door. He felt silly because his eyes would not stay open. Even as he crossed the room to a chair by the potbellied Franklin stove, he felt himself falling asleep. He sat down and leaned back. He fought sleep for a moment or two.

His eyelids dropped. He slept. He struggled up to the lights in the room and the sound of voices. Mr. Lount was there, giant-size in his greatcoat. He smiled at Doug. There was another man with him. Doug, still struggling with sleep, took a moment to place the man in his mind. He remembered the previous meeting with Samuel Lount. This man had been present. He looked small beside Mr. Lount, though actually, Doug realized, he was as tall as the blacksmith.

"Well, Douglas. It's good to see you. I think Mr. Mackenzie was not expecting you though."

"No, Sir." Doug scrambled to his feet. He was wide awake now. "It's the warrant for Mr. Mackenzie's arrest, Sir."

"Warrant? Arrest?" Mr. Lount's big face hardened and his eyes were black with consternation. "What are you talking about?"

Doug told him. The big man lurched across the room, pounding the floor with angry heels. "This is the very devil. It means changing our plans." He said nothing for a minute or two, but his pacing continued as if he were stamping his thoughts into the floor. He stopped and looked at his companion who stood silently by the door. "Crocker," he snapped. "Go and fetch Captain Anderson. Tell him it's urgent. We will have to gather the lads together and march for Montgomery's without delay." Crocker turned and flashed out of the door. Mr. Lount stood still. His eyes turned inward. His lively face worked with his plans. Doug hated to interrupt him.

He finally nerved himself to speak. "Where is Mr. Mackenzie now, Sir?"

"Eh? Mr. Mackenzie? Oh! He stayed the night at Newmarket. He'll be at the Gibson farm tomorrow. He's safe enough for now. You must be bone-weary, boy. Mrs. Lount will bed you down somewhere."

"Not without a proper bite to eat before he goes," Mrs. Lount put in from the doorway to the back of the house. "I've put a kettle on the fire and I'm heating up some lamb stew we had for dinner today."

"A happy thought, my dear. I'm hungry myself. Crocker and Anderson will want something, too, I'm sure."

"I thought as much." Mrs. Lount's eyes twinkled. "I would worry greatly if you weren't hungry. There will be plenty."

Mr. Lount grinned sheepishly at Doug. "A fine reputation you're giving me, wife," he chuckled. But almost immediately he went back to his inward musing.

In a very short while Captain Anderson, Mr. Crocker, Samuel Lount, and Doug were seated at a table. From the steaming dishes before them wafted up the hunger-making smells of stew and hot biscuits, cinnamon-apply pie, and hot spiced cider. Doug was so empty he had a pain in his belly. He wished the men would stop talking and begin to eat. He felt a touch on his shoulder. Mrs. Lount bent over him. "Don't wait for them," she whispered. "When they're full of plans, they won't even know what they're eating when they do start." Doug waited for no second bidding. While he helped himself to the dishes that Mrs. Lount, going about the table, snatched up and pressed on him, he kept his ears open to the talk.

Captain Anderson seemed never to use one word more than he had to. When Mr. Lount told him of Doug's long night ride to warn Mr. Mackenzie, he gave Doug a warm smile and a pat on the shoulder. "Bravo!" That was all, but the word and the smile made Doug feel that this soldierly man had become a close friend since the first meeting in Boltontown. Now he was saying: "Agree with you. Must march on Monday. I hesitate to say how many men we will have. Spread the word tomorrow. Hope for the best."

"We'll have to see Montgomery about victualling." Mr. Lount, nodding in agreement, carried the plan further. "I hope he has prepared ahead of time. We did say Thursday, you know."

Doug remembered Mr. Montgomery's message. "Mr. Montgomery has sold the inn, Sir," he offered shyly. "He told me when I stopped in there tonight."

"What?" Three open mouths.

"Disaster!" cried Captain Anderson. "Fellow's mad. Need the inn for headquarters. Need someone to feed us. Planned meeting place. Can't change that now."

"He said he had to," Doug offered in defence. He liked Mr. Montgomery.

"No business to do it. Should have told us," Captain Anderson retorted. "Have to make arrangements with the new man. Wonder who he is?"

Doug could offer no help there. He subsided and ate until he could eat no more. Mrs. Lount must have been watching him, because as soon as he pushed his plate away she called him to follow her and led him to a room at the back of the house, and to a clean, soft, warm bed. Doug put on the clean nightshirt that must have belonged to one of the Lount sons, for it fitted not badly. He fell into bed and was asleep in moments.

Chapter 27
The Rebellion Begins

Early the next morning Doug rode back toward the Gibsons'. He rode alone. Mr. Lount, Captain Anderson, and Mr. Crocker had started out before Doug was awake — indeed, before daylight, with no sleep at all — to rouse the countryside for the march on Montgomery's Tavern.

Doug had one bad scare. He was pushing his horse along down a hill and into an open valley when he heard a loud "Halloo-oo!" from behind. He looked over his shoulder. A party of perhaps eight or ten men were pounding down the slope toward him. It needed only that one glance to show him that these were gentlemen. Their horses, their clothing, everything about them showed wealth. They were on him before he could do more than swing his horse to the side of the road. There was no place to hide. Doug's heart pounded madly. Did they know Mr. Mackenzie was at Gibson's house? Were they going to seize him?

The leader threw up a hand and the party stopped with a mad thrashing of hooves and rearing horses fighting their bits. "Seen a fox cross the road, fellow?" the leader — a young man in a red hunting coat — threw at Doug.

Doug shook his head. For the life of him he could not get a word out. He could hardly breathe for the pounding of his heart.

"We've overrun the pack." The young man turned in his saddle to face his friends. "We might as well wait here till Crowther brings them up."

Doug touched his cap and began to move away. He felt with every pace of the horse that someone was going to shout at him,

"Where are you off to?" Nothing happened. Doug put his horse to the slope ahead of him. He broke into a canter, a gallop. He only breathed easily again when he topped the hill and, looking back, saw the hunting party still milling about in the valley.

As he turned into Gibson's yard he saw Mr. Mackenzie dismounting at the door. "Wait, Sir! Wait!" Doug called. His guardian turned and waited for Doug to ride up.

"Douglas, what are you doing here? Is there aught amiss at home?" Mr. Mackenzie was instantly anxious. "My mother? Has she taken ill?"

"No, Sir. She was well last night. It's you, Sir. You are in trouble." He told Mr. Mackenzie about the warrant and his search and Mr. Montgomery and Mr. Lount and all the rest. Mr. Mackenzie laughed.

"I wonder that my good wife would send a young laddie to consort with so dangerous a criminal. I shall speak to her about it." He laughed again. "But this other news you bring me is a serious matter. To march three days before the hour appointed is madness. They should have awaited word from me. 'Tis a gey foolish decision. Well, they must change it, that's all. We cannot have this shifting and bargling about. 'Twill ruin our chances. We must send you back to Lount. He must cancel his orders. The men must not march."

The Gibsons, apparently, had seen Mr. Mackenzie arrive. They stepped out to greet him while Doug was pouring out his story. Dave Gibson spoke up now. "Douglas was riding about half the night to find you, Will. Let him stay here. I'll send a servant. He may have to do considerable riding to locate Lount and Anderson." He turned away. "Henry!" Gibson bellowed. "Henry! Saddle a horse and be ready to ride at once." He disappeared in the direction of the stable still shouting orders.

Doug felt a shadow of worry darken his spirits. Things were going wrong. Mr. Mackenzie might laugh at the order for his arrest. Would he still laugh if soldiers came riding up the road this very minute? He was not laughing about the change of plans. His face looked grey and anxious. It seemed as if the little man in the brave red wig felt the shadow, too. Red hairs fluttered about the collar of the grey greatcoat. The wind was rising. Mr. Mackenzie drew the coat about him. Was that drawing-in gesture only to shut out the cold? Was he shutting out the feeling that Doug had — that things were going badly?

They spent that Sunday with the Gibsons. For once, Mr. Mackenzie had little to say. Most of the day he sat at the window looking out on the road, speaking when spoken to, but offering nothing. Doug wondered if he were watching for Henry, the Gibsons' man, to come back with a message from Mr. Lount. Henry did not return that night.

On Monday morning Dave Gibson took Mr. Mackenzie to an old building at the back of the barn. Doug went along. He hated to let Mr. Mackenzie out of his sight. In the big, unheated interior of the shed some half-dozen men were busy casting hot lead into shot moulds. There would be plenty of ammunition for the muzzle-loading guns that the farmers and tradesmen would bring to the muster at Montgomery's. They were still in the building when Henry appeared. He looked pale and tired. He was obviously newly out from the old country and unused to the hard living of the colonists. His face was very grave as he gave his message.

"I was too late," he reported softly so that only the three — Mr. Mackenzie, Dave Gibson, and Doug — could hear. "Mr. Lount and Captain Anderson say they can't turn back now. The first companies will be at Montgomery's tonight, shortly after sundown."

"God save us," was Mr. Mackenzie's only reaction. He turned away so that they could not see his face. After a moment he swung back to Dave. "Will you ride with me to Montgomery's? We must be sure that a mess is established to feed the men when they arrive. Douglas, you will come too. I wish Rafferty were with us. He has a quick mind. He would be a great help to us in this muddle we're in."

"Where is Pat, Sir?"

"At Newmarket, recruiting. Perhaps he will get the word and bring his company tonight. I hope so." Mr. Mackenzie stamped back toward the house. Henry and Dave took Doug with them to saddle the horses.

"I have never seen the Chief look so discouraged," Dave said to Doug, shaking his head. Doug wondered if he were beginning to question the outcome of this uprising.

At Montgomery's, Doug's feeling that everything was going wrong became a certainty. As they had cantered along the crossroads where the inn stood, Doug wondered if the new owner would help as Mr. Montgomery had done. He felt he had to know Mr. Mackenzie's thoughts on the matter.

"What will you do, Sir, if the new landlord is a Tory?" he asked as he jogged beside Mr. Mackenzie's grey. The only answer was a mumbling that did more to depress Doug than a wig-throwing rage would have done. He got his answer as they drew up before the inn door. Mr. Montgomery himself was standing outside the building talking to a knot of men, each of whom carried a musket carelessly at his side. He left his listeners immediately when he saw Mr. Mackenzie dismounting.

"Mr. Mackenzie, Sir," he began. Mr. Mackenzie stood stone-faced and cold before him. Doug saw the rueful look that passed over the tavern-keeper's face. "I'm sorry if you think I have failed you. You must know that the deal for selling the tavern has been going on for months. Long before there was any talk of a mustering. I fully expected it to go on for months more. Lingfoot, the new owner, turned up, without warning, Saturday. He had his solicitor with him. All the papers were ready to sign. I could do nothing to stop the sale then. It was too late. I could only hope that Lingfoot would be sympathetic to our cause, would carry on as I had planned. I fear my hope was ill-founded. He is as arrant a Tory as you could find in a day's travel. A great toady. You will get little help from him. I couldn't be more sorry, Sir."

Mr. Mackenzie's face softened at the sincere tone of regret in Montgomery's voice. "I do not blame you, John." He put out a hand and took Montgomery's in a firm clasp. "But you must help me to persuade your successor to prepare for I know not how many companies of men who arrive this very night."

"I will do what I can, though I am not hopeful. And, Mr. Mackenzie!" Montgomery's other hand closed warmly over Mr. Mackenzie's. "I will fight at your side in this cause, though I had expected only to serve in the rear as provisioner."

"We shall have need of you." Mr. Mackenzie accepted the offer simply. "Now, who are those men you were conversing with?"

"Friends! Every one! They will do what you command, Sir."

Montgomery's round face beamed with pleasure, knowing that Mr. Mackenzie was not angry with him.

"Good. Let them fall in behind me. We may have to put a bit of the Lord's fear into yon Mr. Lingfoot."

Mr. Mackenzie was overly optimistic. The surly man who met them inside the door of the tavern was hard and unfrightened under Mr. Mackenzie's threats. "But this is war, man," Mr. Mackenzie shouted up into the tall man's obstinate face. Lingfoot fairly spat at the Chief.

"It is rebellion! Treason! I will not give one atom of help to rebels. You may force your way with your armed rebels into my premises. You cannot force me to serve you. I will not. That is final."

In the end they could only retreat. Not even Mr. Mackenzie's final thrust — "We will be back, fellow!" — saved it from being a complete defeat.

Outside, Montgomery faced them again. "I feel responsible for this. I will go about and see that food is collected to look after the men's needs tonight. Further than that I cannot promise."

A man on the outskirts of the group spoke up. "I have my team and wagon, Sir. They are at your and Mr. Mongomery's service." Doug swung about at the first word. He knew that voice. A path opened through the press. Limpy Shaw hobbled toward them. He smiled at Doug and took the hand Doug offered, but he did not speak.

Mr. Mackenzie nodded. "Thank you, Mr. Shaw. 'Twill be of enormous help." Doug wanted to go with Limpy and Mr. Montgomery, but Mr. Mackenzie kept him beside him. "I need you, Douglas," he explained.

The Chief said nothing more until the men came, and then he was transformed. He was everywhere at once. He snapped out orders. He shouted. He screamed sometimes. He seemed to go a little crazy, Doug decided. Perhaps he had one of his fearful headaches. Perhaps he only wanted the men to feel welcome. To feel that someone was ready for them. Certainly no one else was. Montgomery had not come back with food for them yet. Lingfoot, with his angry glare, was making clear that he was not ready to welcome them. The men were beginning to look bewildered.

Doug had watched the first company march up to the inn.

Mostly young men, these were, though the companies that followed had quite a few oldsters. Grey-headed, grey-bearded men with bowed backs and knotty arms more used to pushing a plow than to carrying a gun or a pike.

That was another thing. No weapons had arrived to issue to them. A few had guns, mostly old army muskets. Another few had light fowling pieces, of no use against a well-armed enemy. Even Doug knew that. There were pikes, a scattering of them. Some men had bound hunting knives to an ash or hickory staff to make their own pikes. Some had simply sharpened a staff to a point. Doug felt more and more that the rebels were heading for disaster. Some of the marchers must have felt the uselessness of it all. Doug saw more than one, alone or with one or two others, sneak off in the darkness in the direction from which they had come. He was sure they were on their way home. He didn't blame them.

Chapter 28
Doug Sees His First Killings

It was better when Samuel Lount and Captain Anderson arrived. Better — and worse. They brought a feeling of authority with them that Mr. Mackenzie had not showed, in spite of his concern for the comfort of the men. For one thing, both men were more practical. They set the men of their companies to cutting down young trees to build bivouacs and to start fires going, around which the rebels could at least warm themselves. When Montgomery turned up with his wagon loaded with hams and corned beef and vegetables, things brightened even more.

The bad part of it all was the bickering that broke out between Mr. Mackenzie and the other two commanders. Mr. Mackenzie seemed to feel that Mr. Lount and Captain Anderson were taking away his authority. Doug knew how the little man felt. It had been that way at school sometimes when bigger boys took over in games that younger or smaller boys had started. He wished though that Mr. Mackenzie would not make himself seem small and petty. "Don't do it, Sir," he wanted to say. "We all know you are the Chief." But Mr. Mackenzie did not seem able to stop. Lount and Anderson had scarcely alighted from their saddles when Mr. Mackenzie rushed at them.

"Samuel, Captain Anderson, as soon as your men have eaten, I want you to be ready to march to Toronto. We must attack tonight before the enemy can gather his forces. If we capture the guns in City Hall, victory is assured." His voice was arrogant and shrill with urgency.

"Hold on, Will." Mr. Lount was quiet and reasonable. "These men have marched, some of them, thirty miles today.

Little in their bellies either. They could not fight tonight if they should meet resistance. I will not ask it of them.''

"You are refusing my orders?"

"Yes, Will. I must refuse."

"A joint appointment as commanders, Mr. Mackenzie. Be good enough to remember that," Captain Anderson put in. His voice, unlike Mr. Lount's, was as cold as the frosty air that turned each word into a puff of steam.

"But I am leader of the Reform movement. You forget that."

"You are not trained in military matters, Sir," Captain Anderson retorted. "Your very valuable contribution will be to keep alive the spirit of rebellion. With matters in the unhappy state of unpreparedness which we find here, that will be a very necessary part of the war, believe me. Leave decisions of strategy to us, Sir."

But Mr. Mackenzie, like the pestering fly he was, would not leave it. Silenced for the moment, he returned to the attack over and over. Finally, just before ten o'clock at night, Mr. Mackenzie tried again.

"We must attack tonight," he insisted. Doug, who had dogged the little man everywhere he went, saw an exasperated frown pass over Anderson's face. In a moment his face was bland again.

"Come, Mr. Mackenzie. Let us ride out, you and I, to reconnoitre. We have had no reports from our scouts for some time." Doug was glad that Captain Anderson was giving Mr. Mackenzie a chance to be a commander, too. He felt himself warm more than ever to the soldier.

Anderson organized the scouting party. He took two other men with him. One, Doug recognized as the leader of the Richmond Hill vigilance committee. The other was completely unknown to him. Pat Rafferty had arrived moments before with the company of volunteers from Newmarket. Mr. Mackenzie ordered him to ride along, too. Doug was able to take Pat aside before the party set out.

"Look after Mr. Mackenzie, Pat," he urged. "I am worried about him. If something does not happen soon, I fear he may go almost mad."

"Now, don't you be worrying your head at all — *at all* —

about the Chief. 'Tis never his reason will go,'' Pat reassured Doug.

Doug watched the riders set out. As he moved to the side of the road out of the way, he wished that he might have gone with them. It wasn't that he was going back on his determination to be loyal to Mr. Mackenzie, but he felt surer about the rightness of this rebellion when he was with Pat. He wandered down the road. He was too worried about the way things were going to stay in one place. He just had to be on the move. His eye caught the silhouette of the rebel guards who were watching the highway. He decided to go and talk to them. Perhaps they did not feel things were going badly. Perhaps they could make him feel better in his mind. One of the men turned quickly on hearing Doug's footstep on the icy verge of the road.

"Who goes there?" he demanded in his best military voice. Doug had a hard time preventing a laugh from bubbling to his lips. If he hadn't been so worried, he might have laughed out loud.

"Doug Lachlan," he answered as gravely as he could. "I'm with Mr. Mackenzie."

"Oh, it's the boy who runs errands for little Will," the man explained to his mates. "You're a right plucky 'un, too, from what I've heard. Taken some beatings from the enemy, they say."

"Just one." Doug felt foolish and a little proud that the man knew so much about him.

"Well, come along and talk to us. 'Tis a plaguey cold business standing here, waiting for an enemy that never comes."

Almost before the words were out of the man's mouth, there was the quick ring of hooves on the ice-hard road. The men of the party sprang to the alert. Not just one rider. Doug squatted to look for shadows against the stars. One, two, three. Stars were blotted out momentarily by moving shapes. Then they were upon them. Doug flung himself sideways. The leafless bushes whipped his face. A shout from the patrol. The horsemen swept through. Doug reared himself on his hands. Flashes from the guns of the guards stabbed the night. There was a sharp cry. A voice shouted, "Got one!"

The sentries pounded down the road after the fleeing

horsemen. Doug scrambled to his feet. He ran after the patrol. When he reached them, they were bending over a dark figure on the road. There was a clink of flint on steel. Someone lit a hank of tow. By its light Doug could see the huddle of a man, lying on his side. He was glad he could not see the face. But what he did see made him sag weakly at the knees. Beside the head, a sticky pool of blood reflected the light of the torch.

"Dead!" The voice — Doug could not see who was speaking — sounded awed and sick. Doug turned away. He did not want to see any more. His stomach heaved. His throat felt sore from the acid that filled it. "It's Moodie."

"Aye," another took up the comment. "Colonel Moodie of Richmond Hill. I've seen him often hereabouts." Still another voice, a very young-sounding voice, broke in. "Wonder which of our shots got him." Doug felt a shiver go through him. Whoever it was that asked the question sounded excited, eager almost. There was a moment's silence, then a deeper, older voice answered. "Guess we'll never know, son." The sorrow in the tone made Doug fight away the tears with an angry hand.

"What do we do now?" someone asked.

"Take him up to the tavern, I suppose." It was the sad man who took charge. Doug had the feeling it was the man who had challenged him. How long ago? Minutes, but it seemed hours. "Ian, you and Silas stay here on guard. The rest of you help me tote the Colonel." There was a shuffling of feet and a movement toward Doug. He couldn't bear to see that limp body again. He knew he couldn't. Without turning he could almost see a heavy body sagging in the middle of a square of men who tucked an arm or a leg under their armpits for better purchase. Doug fled south along the road. He could not go back to Montgomery's and listen to the men talking, bragging a bit perhaps, about this first casualty of this stupid war.

He did not know how far he ran. Perhaps not far, though he did not seem to have any breath. His eye caught the outline of a stand of firs at the side of the road. He swerved and dived under the branches to escape the wind that seemed icier now. His heart pounded as if he had run a mile. He panted hoarsely. Out of the wind, he was forced to open his coat. A hot wave swept up to his face and stayed there. He burned in spite of the December night.

He was still huddled there much later — how much, he had no

idea. He must have dozed off. The wind had gone down but the cold was more intense, more penetrating. He huddled his coat about him and struggled to his knees. His body was stiff, his feet numb. When he put his feet under him to crawl out of his hiding place, pains shot from his toes to his ankles. He stepped out into the open beside the road. He stretched, slapped his arms across his chest, once, twice. He stopped. Listened. Horsemen — it sounded like two — coming slowly. He started forward. Maybe Mr. Mackenzie would not be so silent. Unless — unless they had met with the enemy and some had been killed. Then they would be just this quiet. Doug dropped to one knee and squinted. He could make out two heads against the sky.

Suddenly, one of the men spoke. "Get on, Mr. Powell. Almost there." Captain Anderson. Doug could not mistake the clipped words. "Patrol just ahead." Doug could not see what happened then. There was a flurry of movement, as if the leading man had whirled his horse about. There was a flash. The clap of a pistol. Galloping. The sound faded out south toward Toronto. Doug could see the one man still sitting his horse, motionless. The horse had stopped. The figure in the saddle toppled. Doug heard the thud of the body on the road.

"Help!" Doug shouted then. Just once. Shouts and then he was surrounded by men as he ran toward the fallen horseman. They gathered around the man on the ground.

"Who is it?" somebody demanded.

"I don't know. I heard Captain Anderson speak to someone called Powell. I recognized the Captain's voice. Then one of them shot off his pistol." Doug's voice shook.

"Pray God it's not the Captain," a man muttered. "We're done for without him." And then in a loud voice, "Silas, give us a light."

It was Captain Anderson. Shot through the throat. Doug did not feel sick this time. Dead, was the word to describe his feelings. All dead inside. He could not really believe it. He went back with the patrol to the inn. They carried the Captain's body tenderly among them. They took him inside. Doug followed. They laid him on the floor. Someone put a coat over the body. Doug crept into a corner and stayed there. He could not take his eyes off the still form under the caped greatcoat. That and the other draped figure lying near the Captain. Why didn't everyone go home now? There was nothing left. That guard had said it. "Without the Captain we're finished."

Mr. Mackenzie found him there. The little man was very quiet, very gentle. "I'm sorry, Douglas," he murmured. "I understand you saw it all. No sight for a laddie. I'm truly sorry." Doug wished he would not be sorry. He wanted to cry.

"What will you do now, Sir? Give up?" Doug's voice sounded hoarse, even to himself.

"Give up, Douglas? No! Never!" Mr. Mackenzie's voice was stern, almost angry. "Captain Anderson's death was murder. His murderer must be brought to trial. You see, Douglas, Captain Anderson was killed for what we are fighting for: the right to be treated as men by these fine gentlemen who run the colony. Captain Anderson wanted to search Powell for weapons. I would not let him. Powell gave me his word as a gentleman that he was unarmed. He lied. But, don't you see, he would not have lied to a man he thought was his equal. He could lie to me because, in his eyes, I am less than a man. We must fight on so that we can change all that wrong thinking. If we can make the Family Compact see us as men, Captain Anderson will not have died uselessly. And I . . . I shall lose some of my load of guilt for his death."

Suddenly, Mr. Mackenzie was gentle again. "Douglas, I want you to go back to the city. Sleep until it is light, and then you must go. I am worried about my wife and family. They need a man with them. I cannot go. You must be the man of the house until I come. If James were in Toronto, I would not ask it. Will you go?"

Doug knew that that was what he wanted. To be away from this place where two men could die so violently, so quickly, one after another. He wanted to see Mrs. Mackenzie's calm face. Hear her clear, serene voice. No. He wanted Da'. Yes, Da'. Where was Da'?

"Yes, Sir," was all he said.

"Lie down here now and sleep," Mr. Mackenzie urged. He cleared the corner of chairs and the gear that some of the rebels had dropped there. The whole public room was cluttered with it. Doug lay down. Mr. Mackenzie put something under his head. Someone's knapsack. He covered him with a blanket. Doug closed his eyes. He did not want to look at Mr. Mackenzie now. He knew he could not sleep. But he did.

Chapter 29
Doug And Old Mrs. Mackenzie Fool Some Soldiers

There was only a thin line of red along the eastern horizon when Doug mounted and began the ride down Yonge Street to the city. He had had no breakfast. He wondered if the army he left behind him would ever get breakfast. Things were still at sixes and sevens in the camp. But it was not his hunger that made his stomach crawl as he jogged along; it was what he would say if soldiers stopped him and questioned him about Mr. Mackenzie and the rebels.

As it happened, he saw not one soul all the way. When he reached the city, he went directly to Dr. Rolph's house and left his horse with the stableman, who took the animal without any remark beyond, "I'll tell Doctor gelding's back." Doug made his way on foot to the Mackenzie home.

As he entered the door, he was instantly surrounded by an excited Mackenzie family. They threw questions at him all together until Doug shook his head and put his hands over his ears.

The younger Mrs. Mackenzie appeared at the top of the stairs. She carried a duster in her hand and she flicked it at the girls. "Be quiet," she ordered in her low voice that carried down the stairs and instantly stilled the clamor. "Douglas will answer your questions as well as he is able once he has had something to eat. We shan't have to wait long. You all know how fast Douglas can eat his way through a meal." She smiled down at Doug.

Doug hurried. Mrs. Mackenzie came down and prepared a hot breakfast for him. She sat with him, more, he felt, to protect him from old Mrs. Mackenzie and her daughters than to keep him company. She would not let him speak until he had finished. He pushed his chair back then and told them all he could. Mrs. Mackenzie said nothing for a moment when he ended. Doug had not tried to varnish over the truth. He was too worried himself to think of others' worries. When it seemed the chatter would begin again, Mrs. Mackenzie put up a hand. She turned a clear, quiet eye on Doug.

"Thank you, Douglas. I am glad you did not try to spare my feelings. We must not worry. My husband is a great man. He will win through, somehow." As he looked from her confident face to the fierce gleam in old Mrs. Mackenzie's faded blue eyes, he could almost forget the quarrelling and the sudden death, the lack of plan and organization out at Montgomery's. He could almost believe that Mr. Mackenzie would win his war. All he said was, "Yes, Ma'am."

Everyone tried to look cheerful, but nobody was fooled. The noon meal was late because no one wanted to eat. After lunch the little ones were put down for a nap, and Barbara followed Doug to the study. He was glad of the company.

"Read to me, Douglas," she begged. "I'm frightened."

"You mustn't be." Doug put an arm around her thin, young shoulders and squeezed. "Everything will be all right. Your mother has said so. She knows." He read to her from *Pilgrim's Progress* until it grew too dark to see the page.

It was truly dark when Mrs. Mackenzie came downstairs. She seemed her unworried self. But it seemed to Doug, as he met her at the foot of the stairs, that the light of her candle revealed dark shadows around her eyes. She went past him to the kitchen and presently she called the family to supper.

They were still at their meal, all a little subdued, when a furious pounding at the street door made the girls jump up screaming. Dishes were overturned. Only Mrs. Mackenzie did not move in her chair. "Sit down and behave yourselves," she ordered. The screaming stopped. Mr. Mackenzie's mother shamefacedly sat down, too. "I do not know who is at the door," Mrs. Mackenzie went on when quiet was restored," but no one is warring on little girls and women. And young boys," she added, looking at Doug. "Douglas, go and see who is there. We shall retire to the parlor and await your word." The girls scurried only a little under their mother's strong eye. Doug made his way to the front door. He took a long breath as he turned the handle.

As he opened the door, a boy tumbled into the hall. It was Hodges, one of the apprentices from the press and bookshop. His head was uncovered. The wind had turned his hair into a badly made bird's nest. He had no coat, no jacket. His ink-stained smock was torn. His whole body shook. Cold? Fear? Doug could not decide. Doug caught him by the shoulders and steadied him. At first it seemed as if he had lost the power of speech. He opened and closed his mouth. His breath rasped in his throat.

"What is it?" Doug urged. "Hodges!" He shook the boy a little. "What is the matter?"

"Alderman Powell!" Hodges panted. "The soldiers came with Alderman Powell. They smashed the press. Everything. They're on their way here. Right behind me. I got away and ran. They have the printer. A prisoner. Tell Mrs. Mackenzie." He turned, then rushed away through the open door as if the soldiers' hands were already reaching for him. Doug shut the door after him.

Mrs. Mackenzie appeared from the parlor. "I heard," she said simply. "My husband's papers are on the files hanging in the bedroom. They must be hidden. You and the girls attend to it."

Doug raced for the stairs. He remembered the files of papers hung on hooks from the ceiling in the Mackenzies' bedroom. Mr. Mackenzie liked to have them handy if he got an idea in the middle of the night. He would light a candle and clamber upon a chair in his nightshirt. He would take down what he wanted and scramble back into bed with a quill and inkhorn beside him on a convenient table. Sometimes he would work until morning. Mrs. Mackenzie scolded him gently about his "office on the ceiling." His mother scolded him for not getting his sleep. "Wasting candles instead of working like a Christian during the daylight hours."

Doug had not climbed three steps when the door burst open. The house filled with men. Alderman Powell, red-faced and loud-voiced, led the van.

"Mrs. Mackenzie!" he shouted. "I am authorized to search your dwelling. Your husband is an attainted traitor. I am here to seize proof of his treason."

"You are a brave man, Mr. Powell, to enter so boldly a house tenanted by two women and small girls and one boy, a house guest. I wonder you dare to come so lightly protected." Mrs. Mackenzie's eyes passed from Powell's purple face to the sheepish herd of soldiers, then on to two officers decked in plumed helmets. "We cannot defend ourselves. You must do as you please." She turned to re-enter the parlor. "Show the gentleman anything he wants to see, Douglas."

"Douglas?" The tenor was a soft, frightening sound. Doug felt his breath stop in his thorat. The Porker! Colonel Golightly! The massive figure in plum-colored coat pushed through the huddle around the door and immediately seemed to fill the little hall. "Let me handle this, Powell. This is the brat that has been running the traitor Mackenzie's errands for him. He is as miscreant as his master. I, myself, can give evidence that he was in Boltontown helping sow sedition, and I saw him again at Newmarket and at the skirmish at the ford on the Humber. Captain Bell . . . ." he turned to one of the plumed and helmeted officers. "Arrest this boy. Give me five minutes with him and I guarantee we will have enough evidence to hang Mackenzie as high as Haman."

"Colonel Golightly, I am in charge here. I have no warrant to arrest anyone except Mr. Mackenzie." This voice was as light as the Colonel's, but it had the reverse effect on Douglas. He began to breathe again. He could not forget that pleasant English tone. Bell! Bert Bell. No, Captain Herbert Bell. The young farmer with the broken-down wagon on the way to Toronto. "As a matter of fact, this lad did some work for me," Bert went on, "before I sold my farm and bought my commission. I have never heard him utter a seditious word. Now," he turned to his men, "search the house. You, Lachlan, come with me." He started for the stairs leaving a fuming Porker and a purple-faced Powell exchanging protests in the hall.

In less than a minute, it seemed, there was a man in every room, upstairs and down. They threw the furniture about. They thrust their heavy sabres into upholstery. They pulled down draperies, they dragged out drawers and flung contents on the floor. Wardrobes were emptied and turned over on their sides so that the men could search behind them. A hurricane could not

have caused as much wreckage. They did not stick to one room either. Where one had searched already, and gone, two others would appear and search again.

Upstairs in the master bedroom, Bert turned to face Doug. "I am sorry to see you in this house, Lachlan," he murmured gravely. "You must get away from here. Sooner or later the fat Colonel is going to get that warrant for your arrest. He's a nasty piece. He'll hang you if he can."

"Thank you, Bert. But I must stay and take my chances." With his words, all Doug's fears flowed away from him. He was committed now.

Bert straightened up. Doug held his breath as plumed helmet brushed the papers hanging from the ceiling. Bert never even looked up. "I must do my duty. I am an Officer of the Queen. Friendship cannot stand in my way."

He was thorough. He pulled the mattress from the bed and with his sabre ripped the ticking open, sending goose feathers like a cloud of snow all over the room. He flung open the clothes press and dumped the clothes on the floor and then with the pummel of his sword pounded the walls, the bottom, the sides, listening for any hollow sound that would tell of secret hiding places. The drawers of the bureau were pulled out and the contents scattered among the feathers. With every step the Captain took, his plumes started Mr. Mackenzie's papers to waving back and forth. Doug felt his skin crawl. When would Bert look up? He kept silent, afraid that some word might turn the Englishman's eyes ceilingward.

If he was silent, old Mrs. Mackenzie was not. She joined Doug as Bert once more attacked the mattress. He flung it over and began attacking it from the other side. "You Sassenach vandal!" she screamed at him. Doug was startled. It was not like the old lady to scream and call names. He did not change his slouching position by the door, but his brain sprang to the alert. Old Mrs. Mackenzie was bent on keeping Bert's eyes off the ceiling. He must be ready to help her when he could. She needed no help at the moment. "Barbarian! Do you know how long it took me to gather the goosefeathers that you are scattering to the four corners of the house? Addlepate! Shame on you. An officer and a gentleman! Pfogh!" She rushed on Bert and clutched his sword arm. Doug hustled after her to hold her back.

"You must excuse her, Bert," he offered quickly. "She is an old lady. She doesn't know what she is doing."

Mrs. Mackenzie rounded on Doug. "Old lady! Out of my wits! Is that what you are saying, Douglas Lachlan?" My son took you in because your father deserted you while he traipsed off to the West. How dare you insult the mother of your benefactor?" There was more, much more. Doug was not sure that Mrs. Mackenzie was pretending. Her pale eyes shot sparks. He began to back away from her, and only partly because of the game they were playing. He really was afraid of her. Two privates stopped in the doorway. They began to guffaw.

"Give it to him, granny," the one chortled. "Let there be no sparing of ingrates."

Mrs. Mackenzie turned on him then. "I'm no' your granny," she spat in her broadest Scots. "I'd be ashamed to own you, as your own grandmother must." She drew breath for a further attack. Bert interposed.

"Come," he said to the two men, "there is nothing here." He tramped out of the room and led them down the stairs. Mrs. Mackenzie stood still, listening. Then she turned to Doug, a thin-lipped grin on her wrinkled, old face. She grabbed his hands in her bony old ones. "We did it," she whispered. "We did it, laddie." She turned him 'round in a jig. "'Twas a great piece of acting on your part. You looked positively ashen with fear of me."

"'Twas not acting, Ma'am," Doug admitted. "I thought you meant every word of it."

"Ach, well. 'Twas good you thought it. I persuaded yon Sassenachs to leave off the search. Now my daughter-in-law is looking for an excuse to get the beasts out of the house. The minute they've closed the door behind them, you and Barbara and Janet and Margaret go to work. Burn everything." She cast her glance at the ceiling. "What my son will say, I hate to think. But there is no other way. The good Lord himself would not know what they might interpret as treason. Now, do you go out into the hall and listen has Isabel got rid of these robbers. I'll stay here lest some other bold Englishman might take into his head to make a search. They are all over the house. I don't know how many may still be upstairs."

Doug did as he was bidden. He tiptoed to the bannister to peer over. He could hear someone bumping and thumping about in Barbara's and Janet's room. As he peeped down into the hall, he could see Mrs. Mackenzie facing the Colonel, Alderman Powell, and Bert. Mrs. Mackenzie was quiet, but her straight back and pale, unsmiling face would tell anyone who knew her that she was armed for battle.

"I must insist. . . ." she was saying. "I cannot have my daughters, defenceless young girls, prepare for bed with a lot of rough men about. Search their rooms if you must. Then withdraw from the house for half-an-hour while I put my children to bed. You may then pull things about to your heart's content. But not in my daughters' bedrooms."

"It is a trick!" Alderman Powell was more purple of face, if that were possible, than when he first entered.

Golightly spoke as softly as ever, but every word held bane. "Do not listen to the female traitor, Captain Bell. I will have your commission if you fail in your duty. Arrest her. Arrest them all."

"Mr. Powell," Bert's voice was cold and sharp. "You are not in charge here. I am. As for you, Colonel, you are no longer on the active list, nor are you my superior officer. I do not allow anyone to call me derelict in duty. Mrs. Mackenzie's name is not on the warrant, which I carry, for the arrest of her husband. She has not been accused of treason." He took a short step toward Powell and Golightly as the Alderman and Porker began to splutter and protest once more. Powell backed away, leaving Golightly to face Bert alone. "Enough!" Bell snapped a warning. He swung back to Mrs. Mackenzie as the two older men subsided. His voice was still cold, but the snap was gone. "One half-hour, Madam. No more." He raised his head and opened his mouth. Doug dodged back from the railing. He ran back into the room with old Mrs. Mackenzie. Bert's voice thundered up the stairwell, making the old grandmother jump. There was movement in all the rooms around. Feet pounded the polished floors and clattered down the stairs. The front door banged shut. There was a moment's silence. A quiet rush up the stairs. Mrs. Mackenzie herded the girls, all very quiet and scared, into the bedroom. They all worked quickly under Mrs. Mackenzie's soft-spoken commands. She and Doug stood on chairs and handed down papers.

"The stoves in your two bedrooms are still burning. It is fortunate that I lit them earlier to warm up before bedtime. Margaret, you go with Janet and Barbara. Put the papers in one at a time. If you stuff them in, some may not burn." Mrs. Mackenzie did not stop working as she gave instructions. "Douglas and Mother, you will take yours downstairs. Mother, burn yours in the kitchen. Douglas, use the parlor stove. Be sure all the papers are in ashes before you leave them. Don't burn them too fast lest the men see an excess of smoke. We have plenty of time with four stoves going. As soon as you can, girls, get into your nightdresses and get into bed. I don't want to hear or see you out of your rooms this night. I shall come to see you as soon as I can."

All worked quickly. If the men outside noticed that the Mackenzie chimneys were being overworked, they gave no sign. Exactly at the end of the half-hour there were men back in the house, but not Bert's squad. The new gang pried and prodded and pulled furniture about, like the first party. It seemed as if it would go on all night. Men would tramp into the house, search, go away for a while, only to return and search all over again. At last old Mrs. Mackenzie had had enough. When a new batch stormed in, she was waiting for them at the door. Douglas and her daughter-in-law stood behind her.

"Stop!" Her old voice cracked with the rage in her. The men jammed up like cattle crowding into the door of a byre. "Brave men!" Her highland scorn burned like acid. The men nearest actually flinched. "Brave men indeed! You're a great threat to defenceless women and children, are you not? Are you, perchance, building up your courage to face my son and his men when they come?" The soldiers' faces took on shamed grins. They shuffled their feet and cast sidelong looks at each other. "You'll be a great defence for the Governor and his minions, that you will. An old woman's contempt on the lot of you. Be off! And don't let me see you spying about this house again. If you dare, I will march out, an army of one, with my daughter's iron griddle in hand, and beat you off myself." The men turned and went. Young Mrs. Mackenzie began to laugh as the door closed on the last retreating back.

"Mother, I never admired you so much. William would be proud of you." The old lady undid the ribbons of her cap and retied them under her chin more to her satisfaction. She did not speak, but there was a frosty gleam of pride in her aged eyes. Her thin, wrinkled old lips quivered at the corners. Just a little. Douglas was sure she was fighting back a smile. She marched past them, her spare figure as straight as a girl's. Up the stairs she went. They heard her bedroom door close. She had retired for the night.

The men did not come back.

Chapter 30
Captured!

Doug slept little that night. A creak or a crack of frost in the roof beams and he was wide awake in his bed, expecting the tramp of military boots to thunder again in the house with a warrant to hang him. No one came. Why would Alderman Powell and the Porker take all their men away? Did Bert simply override them? Would they wait to catch him in the street? No use to take chances. He would not leave the house.

No one went out. And no one came near them. They waited. For what, Doug wondered as he looked at the two women who sat with him in Mr. Mackenzie's study. Their faces seemed strange, unfamiliar. They just sat. Doug could not remember seeing the Mackenzie women with idle hands. Always they had knitting, patching, something to keep their hands busy. He would have been happy to see Mrs. Mackenzie coring and peeling apples for one of her tasty apply dumplings. Her hands, as if they missed a useful occupation, twined and twisted together. She saw Doug looking at them and hastily laid them in her lap.

Did the two women expect Mr. Mackenzie to march up to the door with his army of farmers behind him? Did they expect another raid from the soldiery? Doug felt impatient with them. He wished they would say what they were thinking. The silence of the room became a frightening presence.

At noon Mrs. Mackenzie rose, but with none of her usual lightness. She seemed almost as old as her mother-in-law. She went away. Doug guessed she had gone to feed the girls who were playing too quietly in the parlor. It was the only room that had not been wrecked by the searchers. Doug wondered why Mrs. Mackenzie had not attempted to set the place to rights. Perhaps she expected another raid. Presently she came back with a plate of buttered bread and a mug of milk for Doug. He had no appetite, but it seemed impolite not to eat what had been prepared for him.

"Shall I get you something, Mother?" Mrs. Mackenzie asked in a voice that, like her face, had no expression.

"No." That was all. Mrs. Mackenzie sat down again in the chair behind the desk. Nothing more was said.

Doug lost all sense of time. Even thought seemed to stop. He noticed suddenly that the light outside had grown dim. Dusk was coming. At that moment there was a light running in the street and a soft rat-a-tat on the front door. Laurence. Doug knew his rap. He hurried to open the door.

His heart sank. Laurence had no quick smile for him. "The news? We've heard nothing. Is it bad?" Doug whispered as he drew Laurence inside.

Laurence nodded. "Bad," he admitted. "There's been a parley at Gallows Hill. Dr. Rolph carried the message to Mr. Mackenzie and the rebels. They've offered a pardon if the rebels will go home."

"Dr. Rolph?" Doug's eyes widened with surprise and dismay. "But Dr. Rolph is on our side. He helped plan the rebellion. Is he being traitor to Mr. Mackenzie?"

"I don't think so. He was asked to go. I've been with my father at the Governor's all day. What could Dr. Rolph do, Doug? He'd have been arrested if he refused. They suspected him anyway. I think it was a kind of test of his loyalty to the Government. He came back for the Governor to put his offer in writing. So nothing came of the parley.

"I hear Mr. Mackenzie has moved his men up to the Bloor Street tollgate. If only he would march! The Tories aren't ready. They keep hoping something will happen. They argue and argue."

Doug thought of the arguments that had gone on at Montgomery's between Mr. Mackenzie and Captain Anderson. Perhaps neither side was ready to fight.

"The Tories can't seem to believe that Mr. Mackenzie means

to fight. Someone must go to him and tell him to march at once into the city. Now. Before it is too late. Let's go together, Doug.''

''No.'' It was Mrs. Mackenzie. Doug turned and saw her in the study doorway. ''You must not go, Laurence,'' she commanded. ''You have mixed yourself up in our cause enough, as it is. You will embarrass your father greatly if you persist in coming here. Oh, I know — '' she put up a hand to stop the boys' protest, ''Laurence has been very helpful in bringing us news. But it must stop now. Indeed, I wish Douglas might go with you and be out of all this, too.''

Doug turned and looked at Laurence. Did Laurence realize what Mrs. Mackenzie was saying? She doesn't expect Mr. Mackenzie to win. She really doesn't. But that was nonsense. She had said herself: ''My husband will win through, somehow.''

''No, Ma'am.'' Doug shook his head stubbornly. ''I'll not desert you and Mr. Mackenzie. Da' said I was to obey Mr. Mackenzie as I would himself. I'll not go.'' He knew now how strongly he wanted Mr. Mackenzie to win. He was a rebel through and through now.

Mrs. Mackenzie sighed. ''Well, Douglas, I'll not argue with you. Though your father did not know there would be this trouble when he bade you obey my husband.'' She smiled then, a sad smile.

''I must go to Mr. Mackenzie, Ma'am, and tell him what Laurence says.''

''You must do what you think best, Douglas.'' Mrs. Mackenzie turned and went back into the room. Doug fetched his coat. He and Laurence went out and closed the big front door behind them.

''I'm going with you,'' Laurence anounced when they started into the street. Inside, they had talked in hushed voices as if the silence and the fear in there had put a damper in their gullets. Outside, their voices rang freely again.

Doug shook his head. ''No. Mrs. Mackenzie is right. You can't get mixed up in the rebellion now. Your father would be hurt by you. If anyone found out you had even come here, your father's business might even be harmed. You can't do it, Laurie. You know that the reason I held back so long was because I was afraid of hurting Da'. I know now that if Da' were here, he would be with Mr. Mackenzie this very minute. But not your father, Laurie.''

''Listen, Doug. Mr. Mackenzie and the others would pay more attention to what I can tell him about what is going on in the Governor's library than if you tell him. I've heard them. I can remember the exact words of most of the men.''

''That's it, Laurie. Can you get back into the Governor's now that you've been away like this?''

''No trouble at all. Mr. Mackenzie could walk in and nobody would notice. Everyone's a little crazy there tonight, they're so scared.''

''Then you must go back. We need somebody who can find out what plans are made. I'll try to get back here at midnight. I'll meet you and you can tell me what's happening and then I'll go back again to Mr. Mackenzie.''

Laurie was silent a minute. It was too dark to see his face now. The winter night was settling fast. At last he spoke. ''Perhaps you're right,'' he said slowly. ''I'll be like Major André who was captured by the Americans in the Revolution. I would never tell the enemy anything, just like him.''

''You mustn't be caught. Promise you'll be careful, Laurie. If you can't get away at midnight then don't try. I'll wait for you.''

''Right.'' Laurie's voice was full of laughter. It made Doug feel strong and brave just to hear it. ''I'll remember every word. Wouldn't they get a shock to know that Laurence Todd was carrying messages to the nasty rebels! I'll be here. Don't worry. Where's your hand, Black Douglas?'' Hand fumbled for hand, met, and clasped tight. Laurie let go and Doug felt him turn away. He heard Laurie begin to run. ''You take care of yourself, Doug,'' he called. Doug turned himself then and began running toward the Bloor Street gate.

He was still running as he neared the edge of the city on Yonge Street. If Mr. Mackenzie had not retreated from the tollgate, Doug had not far to go now. He was loping down the middle of the road, lifting his feet high to keep from stumbling on the cobbles. His eyes were used to the dark now. There was enough light in the wintry sky to see anything that loomed up against it. He was safe anyway from obstacles as long as he stayed in the centre.

Doug swerved to the right. Something was there. Something that moved suddenly. A stray horse? A man? A voice ordered, "Halt!" The command was barely above a whisper. Doug slid to a stop. He waved his arm wildly to prevent a fall. Mr. Mackenzie must have begun his march. This would be one of the scouts.

"It's Douglas Lachlan," he called, keeping his voice low like the other. "I'm looking for Mr. Mackenzie."

The voice broke into a laugh. "Oh, you're looking for Mr. Mackenzie, eh, Lachlan? Well, you won't find him here." Doug's heart beat so hard he could feel it at the base of his neck. He knew that voice. Peter Robinson! What a fool he had been to take for granted it was Mr. Mackenzie's man. He swung on his toes.

"Don't try to run, Lachlan." The voice was hard now. "I've a gun, and I can see your head against the sky. I'll blow it off if you make a move. Put your hands up where I can see them, too, and walk toward me." Doug obeyed. Peter laughed again. "You can help us wait for your Mr. Mackenzie. There are twenty-seven of us here waiting with our guns ready for the dirty little traitor to make a move. I'll take you to Sheriff Jarvis. Lucky that I was just on my way back from taking a message for him into the city. Now, step!"

All the time Doug had moved slowly forward. Suddenly he felt the hard end of a musket jab painfully into his back just below his left shoulder. His legs felt weak. If he fell down, would Peter shoot him?

"No tricks," Peter threatened. "I'd love an excuse to shoot you, though it will be more fun to see you hang for treason. I'll enjoy that, Lachlan. I really will."

Doug believed him.

"It isn't far. We've got our little ambush set up in William Sharpe's garden."

As he talked, Peter thrust Doug ahead of him at arm's length. He got a vise-like grip on Doug's shoulder. Doug found himself constantly off-balance so that he stumbled at nearly every step. It was true that they had not far to go. A barrier loomed up, blacker than the surrounding dark. A hedge. Peter seemed to have the eyes of a coon. He propelled Doug along the hedge a bit, then thrust him through the opening.

"I've got me a rebel," he announced gaily.

"Hush up, you young fool," a voice whispered savagely. "Do you want to give the show away? Prentice has just come back from scouting the enemy. The rebels are stirring, ready to march."

"Sorry, Sheriff," Peter reduced his voice to the barest sibilance. "I forgot they were so near."

"Whom have you got there?" Even in a whisper there was no mistaking the flutey quality of the Porker's accent. He was caught by the two people in the world who hated him.

"Douglas Lachlan. He's been living with the Mackenzies."

"I know. We have met several times. You have done well. Only Mackenzie's self would give me greater satisfaction."

"He was looking for Mackenzie when I captured him. Thought I was a rebel, the fool. Carrying messages to the traitor, most likely from friends in the city. He'll hang for this night's work, won't he, Colonel?" Peter gloated in a voice that rose in volume.

"Shut up, Robinson!" The first voice came in irascibly.

"Sorry, Sir." Peter's tone was sulky. "But he will hang, Sir, won't he?"

"The courts will decide that. Not that there's much doubt. Treason is punishable by hanging. We'll question him when we have time. There's a tool shed over yonder toward the house. Lock him in there till we have time to deal with him."

"Shall I tie him up, Sir?"

"The shed is stout. It'll hold him. We may be in action any minute."

Peter shoved Doug into movement again. The structure that the Sheriff had recommended was not more than ten paces away. Doug gathered himself, ready to bolt, as Peter fumbled for the door. The grip tightened, each finger digging like a claw into his muscles. The door creaked open. Peter hurled Doug inside. The door slammed. There was the sound of a pole or log scraping the door as it was set as a brace. Doug was left alone.

For a moment Doug lay where Peter had thrown him. Up to this instant he had not really believed that he would actually be a prisoner. That they would *hang* him. Panic swept over him. He charged where he thought the door should be. He crashed into the wall with a jolt that flashed pain in every joint. He shook his head. His mind cleared as if the shock had driven the fear out of him.

"It's no good, Lachlan," he told himself. "Being scared won't help you *or* Mr. Mackenzie. Think, man. Think!"

First things first. Explore the prison. He began to move along the wall, feeling his way. The Sheriff was right. It was a stout, well-made place. He stumbled over a clutter of spades and rakes and buckets, all sorts of equipment for the garden. At one point he almost brought down on his head a scythe, hanging on pegs. There was no window. Of that he was certain. His hands had covered every bit of wall that he could reach. The door, when he finally came on it, was as solid as the walls. It did not even rattle as he shook the handle. There was no way out.

He picked his way to a clear spot on the cold mud floor and sat down. He realized that he had been sweating. Sweat of fear! Da' had spoken of that once, talking of the old war, back in 1812. Doug felt the cold settle in him as he became aware of the wetness of his body. "This is no good," he scolded himself. "I'll die from the cold before they can hang me." He grinned wryly to himself in the darkness and felt better that he could grin. He got up and made himself walk as vigorously as as the space allowed. Three paces forward. Three paces back. Three, if he shortened the last step. Back and forth. Willing himself to a warmth that would not come. His teeth chattered.

He must plan. Hard to plan in the cold. How let Mr. Mackenzie know about the ambush? If only he could get out. Not think about that. The very idea of a trap stopped all thinking. There must be a way. A sudden memory sent a wave of warmth through him. Laurie! When he didn't turn up at midnight Laurie would look for him. He'd get his father to help. The warmth drained out of him. Laurie would just think he had stayed with Mr. Mackenzie. He would go home to bed. By morning Doug might be in prison, a condemned rebel. He would hang as Peter had promised. For a few minutes Doug gave way to despair, before he could squeeze a little hope into his heart again.

It was such a very little hope. The Sheriff had said the rebels were getting ready to march. The minute he heard them, he would start to yell and bang on the wall. Now, cold or no cold, he must stand still and listen. Listen! He suddenly realized that he was straining even his eyes, widening them in the dark as if they would help him to hear. His teeth began to rattle with the cold and he snapped them shut to stop the sound. Was that a noise?

Nothing. He could not hear even Sheriff Jarvis's men, a few feet away. Were the boards too thick for any sound to get into the shed? If only he could see!

How long he stood motionless, listening, he had no idea. It was so still he could hear his heart. He tried to shut out the sound. Nothing. And then it came. The muffled sound of horses' hooves on the ice-hard road. Doug opened his mouth to shout his warning. It was lost in a roar from outside. "Fire!" The Sheriff had given the command. The ragged rattle of shots echoed inside the hut as muskets went off. There were screams. Doug could picture men clutching at legs or bellies as they tumbled to the ground.

He flung himself at the wall nearest the sounds. With the scythe in his hands he beat on the wall. Then, just beyond his prison, the pounding of feet. Again the voice, the Sheriff's voice, roared. "Stand, you cowards. Stand, I say!" The running did not stop. Even the voice disappeared into the distance as the Sheriff ran after his fleeing pickets. There was a distant firing. Then silence.

Doug waited. He would hear the rebels now. Mr. Mackenzie would be after the Tory cowards this very minute. A victory! Doug danced a little step and hugged himself. He would shout when he heard them coming. Somebody would open his prison and let him out. Saved.

He held still and listened. No sound. Well, that was natural. Perhaps the rebel scouts were moving up, seeking out the enemy. They wouldn't know yet that all the Tories had run. He could help. Let them know. He shouted once, then again. "It's all right! It's all right, I tell you. Let me out! Let me out! I'm Douglas Lachlan. Tell Mr. Mackenzie. Let me out! Please!" He called over and over until his voice grew hoarse.

He listened again. He was panting now, as if he could not get enough air in the dark, enclosed space of the shed. He forced himself to hold his breath, but his heart was thudding so loudly that he could not hear properly. In spite of the cold, his forehead was damp with sweat. He began to shake again. He could not stop gasping. His legs grew weak. He sank to the floor, no longer caring about the cold. He was deserted. No one could hear him. There was no one out there to hear him.

What had happened? Was it a trick, that flight of the Tories?

Had there been another Tory patrol that had circled the rebels and caught them in the rear? Something terrible must have happened. What else, but disaster, could explain the rebels' failure to follow up their victory?

That meant that Peter would come back with his friends. They would open the door. No matter how he fought, they would seize him. Drag him out. Put a rope around his neck. He could almost feel the rough hempen bristles of the rope scratching the tender skin of his throat. He put two fingers inside his scarf and shirtband to ease the sudden tightness. He could see himself at the end of the rope, kicking . . . kicking. He shuddered. Cold and fear settled down on him. Pushed his thoughts down into blackness that was all fright, leaving no room for conscious thoughts. He grew numb.

He must have slept. When he opened his eyes at last, the fear swept over him again. He tried to move. Every joint seemed frozen stiff. He ached. He tried to stand, but his legs wouldn't hold him up. There was still no light.

A creepy silence surrounded him. As if everyone were dead. Panic shook him. He could not stop the twitching of arms and legs, the chattering of his teeth. By a tremendous effort of will he stilled himself to listen. Not a sound. He swung his head from side to side and stared into the blackness. Suddenly he was aware of a faint line of light, close to the floor, on his right. That must be the door. It must be morning. He dragged his body over to the place and put his ear to the rough boards. He forced himself to concentrate on hearing.

Footsteps. He could hear footsteps. Peter coming back for him? He pressed his ear harder against the door. A voice spoke quite loudly . . . quite near.

"This must be the shed."

A blinding flash swept before Doug's eyes, as if hearing had turned to sight. Laurence! He heard the scrape of wood on wood as the stop was pushed away from the door. It opened. He squinted blindly into the light. He fell forward on his hands and knees, groping with numb hands toward his friend.

"Laurence! Laurence! Save me, Laurence!" He knew he was babbling. "They are going to hang me. They ran away. Left me. I don't want to hang." He scrambled forward, caught Laurence about the knees. Arms pulled him up. Not Laurence's arms.

These were big arms, man's arms. The arms continued to lift him, bodily like a babbie. Where were they taking him? To hang? Now? A voice spoke in his ear.

"Douglas, my son."

It couldn't be. But the voice was real. The arms were real. Doug opened his eyes to see better. A dark, bearded face above his. "Da'! Da'! I was so scared. I'm shamed, Da'! Peter and the Porker said they would hang me."

"No shame, son. I would be more than scared myself. What Laurence tells me makes me verra proud, my son. Verra proud indeed. But come" — Da' put him on his feet — "we must be out of here. The Governor's troops will be moving up and we must be far away before they come."

"Tell me, have we been defeated then?"

"I'll tell you as we go." Laurence was fairly jigging with excitement about the two of them. "I can only tell you what I have heard." Laurence took the other side of him from Da'. Da' was hoisting him along. His legs did not seem to want to work. Doug, between the two of them, felt as if he were flying. He tried hard to listen to Laurence. "I needn't tell you about the ambush. You know the cowards ran after they fired on the rebels. On the other side, Mr. Lount ordered his men to return the fire and then drop to the ground to let the file behind shoot over their heads. The second file thought the front men were being mowed down. They turned and ran, too, like the Tories. And that set all the rebels to running. They're back at Montgomery's. I only know what your friend Pat Rafferty told me."

"Pat! Is he safe then?"

"Safe as Father's bank. Rafferty was at the Mackenzies', with a message from Mr. Mackenzie, when I got there. Mr. Mackenzie is trying to rally the men to fight. Pat wasn't too happy about the prospects. He's probably back out there himself, helping."

"What were you doing at the Mackenzies'?" Doug managed to ask, though he felt breathless with all he had gone through, and the speed with which Da' was racing him through the streets.

"Peter turned up at the Governor's. Golightly was there, too. They bragged about capturing you. Wouldn't say where you were being held. Father got hold of Mr. Prentice. He told Father about the ambush and about your being in Sharpe's tool shed. I went to the Mackenzies' hoping you had been released and returned there. That's when I met your father. We came out together to look for you.''

''Da'?'' Da' knew what Doug wanted to know.

''Well son, when I got to Kildonan on the Red River, I found your brother, Graham, very ill with cholera. It took a deal of nursing to win him back from the grave. Then I began to hear rumors, way out there in the middle of the continent, of the rebellion brewing and of Willie Mackenzie's part in it. As soon as I could safely leave Graham, I started east. I had to know, son, how you were faring in the midst of all this trouble. I feared for you, laddie. Justly so, it seems.''

''Where are you taking me to now?'' Doug suddenly realized that they were heading down Bay Street close to the centre of the city. ''What about the Mackenzies? Ought we not stay and help them, Da'?''

''Willie Mackenzie has a host of people to help him. Even should the rebellion fail, as it seems to me it must, he'll come to no harm. Not should the Governor put a thousand pounds on his head. The people, the real people of this province, will not betray him, you may be sure. Barring accidents, the wee Chief will escape. But you have only Laurence and his father, bless him, and me to look after you — and you with the name of traitor on you. We must get you away before there's a warrant out for you. I packed your clothes last night for an early start today. There are horses awaiting us at the livery stable. We are starting for the States and then west to Kildonan. Best not to appear at the Mackenzies'. Yon Peter Robinson might hear of it. Mrs. Mackenzie sent her love and respects to you. She thinks well of you, son.''

''But the farm, Da'?''

''We'll sell it from our new home in Kildonan. I have taken up a hundred acres there, laddie. Wait till you've seen that black prairie soil. You cannot imagine. 'Tis the promised land, Douglas, I tell you.''

The promised land and Graham and himself and Da' all together. Doug could scarcely believe he was really awake.

''You're a lucky fellow, Doug,'' Laurence broke in on his thoughts. ''All that way into new country. What things you'll see. You'll write it all to me, won't you?''

"Dinna' doubt it, Laurence." He could almost grin now to hear the brogue on his tongue.

Lucky, he thought. Aye, verra lucky indeed. Laurence for friend. And Da'. Always Da'. Lucky to leave behind the Peter Robinsons and the Porkers. War and hangings behind him. Aye, lucky Douglas Lachlan!

*   *   *   *

A LETTER FROM LAURENCE TODD TO HIS FRIEND, DOUGLAS LACHLAN,

September, 1838

Toronto

Hail, Douglas the Black!

Your letter was carried to us by a peddler, Inigo Porter by name, who claims he had it from your own hand in far-off Fort Garry. I do not know whether to believe him; he seems a veritable rogue. At any rate, I was most happy to hear from you — to hear that you and your Da' are getting settled in the Red River colony. I hope one day that my father will have business there and that he will take me with him so that I may see your fine farm.

Father has sold your place at St. Catharines as your Da' requested. He will be writing himself to announce his success and to arrange financial details. Knowing Father, I am sure he got the best possible price. Your goods and chattels are on their way to you by a wagon train, which was to start from Buffalo in July or early August. Perhaps by this time you have received them.

It must be grand for you having Graham and your Da' together with you again. Graham seems a fine fellow to have as a brother. I envy you.

You ask for news of all those who took part in our adventure last year. I have news of some of them: good news and bad.

I must tell you that, when your Da' hurried you away that morning when we found you in William Sharpe's tool shed, utter confusion reigned here in Toronto. Foolish people ran about the city screaming, "the rebels are coming!" Nasty people accused their neighbors of taking part in the rebellion and had them arrested. Nobody could decide who was to lead the loyal armies of the Governor. It was Colonel Fitzgibbon who finally marched a reluctant band of volunteers north toward Montgomery's Tavern. He was successful — because of his weapons and his bigger numbers — in defeating Mr. Mackenzie's forces. Mr. Mackenzie, along with a number of his friends, apparently fled the field of battle.

Your Da' was right when he wagered that no one would betray Mr. Mackenzie to his enemies — not even for the thousand golden pounds offered for his capture. The Chief got clean away to the United States.

We have heard, though I do not know if it is true, that he travelled much of the time openly in daylight and was recognized by many, but that none gave him up to his enemies. Indeed, many must have aided him with shelter and food.

Dr. Rolph also escaped across the border, as did Mr. Montgomery after having been tried and sentenced to hang for treason. He told his judges that they would not hang him, that some day he would return and open a new inn on Yonge Street. Only the future can tell us if he is a good prophet.

Of Pat Rafferty we have heard nothing. I am sure that no news is good news in his case. He was not taken prisoner. Father checked that when I asked him. My guess is that he is with Mr. Mackenzie.

The saddest news of all is that Mr. Samuel Lount was hanged for his part in the rebellion. There were many who signed petitions — Father was one — begging the Governor to pardon him. All in vain. It is whispered that if Mr. Lount had given the names of all those connected with the revolt, he could have saved himself. People say that he refused to be such a lickspittle. The truth is that Mr. Lount and Mr. Mackenzie frightened the Tories too badly. The rebellion, as you should know, was so nearly successful. The Tories cannot forgive anyone who frightened them so much. Mr. Lount leaves a wife and eight children. God pity them, the poor things.

Many persons connected with the rebellion have been sent in prison ships away around the world to Van Diemen's Land. Father says that we have lost some of our best and noblest minds. It is very sad.

I must tell you, too, though I am reluctant to hurt you with the news, that Mr. Mackenzie has lost the sympathy of many who believed in him. He returned to Navy Island, which you will remember is a British island in the Niagara River. He declared himself head of a Canadian Republic and ran up on a pole a new flag — a red, white and blue one, with two stars that represent Upper and Lower Canada. Many feel that he is encouraging the Americans to attack us.

Mrs. Mackenzie joined him at Navy Island, I have heard, leaving the girls with their aunt here in Toronto. Mrs. Mackenzie Senior stayed behind with the girls. Before New Year's Day a Canadian force crossed the Niagara and burned Mr. Mackenzie's supply ship on American soil. People here feared that the Americans would invade us in revenge, but it has not happened. Father says that it will not, for the Americans are in no position to wage war at this time. The upshot of the whole affair was that Mr. Mackenzie was forced to abandon Navy Island for lack of a supply ship.

Father (I seem to be always quoting him!) says that in spite of Mr. Mackenzie's republican ideas, we in Upper Canada will see many changes for the better because of him — many reforms that the Chief tried to bring about. Father also says that the Rebellion may be dead, but so, also, is the Family Compact. So Mr. Mackenzie will still be our Great Reformer, yours and mine.

Write again and tell me all your news of Red River. I really want to know.

Ever your friend,
Laurence